"Complex layers...fast-paced...a novel of grief, love, and truth."
—**Kirkus Reviews**

"This is a strong and memorable work of fiction."
—**Foreword Reviews**, Winter Edition

"Spanning decades and continents, Secrets of Worry Dolls is a heartbreaking story about the ripple effect of our choices and the sometimes tragic consequence of survival. Mari and Lu will capture your imagination and your heart, and with Impellizzeri's signature magical touch, keep you flipping pages well into the night."

—**Kate Moretti**, New York Times best-selling author of
The Vanishing Year

"A truly original book—told with grace and style. Lu and Mari are vivid characters whose intertwining stories will move and surprise you."

—**Sarah Pekkanen**, Internationally best-selling
author of The Opposite of Me

"With heart, humor and her signature touch of magic, Amy brings to life the tale of a mother and daughter each facing all together extraordinary circumstances. Secrets of Worry Dolls will make you laugh, cry, and, in the end, leave you completely spellbound. It is easily one of my favorite books of the year!"

—**Kristy Woodson Harvey**, best-selling author of
Dear Carolina and Lies and Other Acts of Love

"Amy Impellizzeri's Secrets of Worry Dolls is a vivid and powerful story, infused with a lot of heart and pluck. Told in alternating perspectives—mother Mari and daughter Lu—we're swept away by this tale of self-discovery, which explores the role of fate, the power of secrets, and ultimately, the importance of forgiveness. It's a story that won't let you go, even after that last page is turned. I loved this book."

—**Karma Brown**, bestselling author of Come Away With Me
and The Choices We Make

"Tender, touching, and engagingly layered, *Secrets of Worry Dolls* paints a nuanced portrait of one family's struggle to deal with loss. Amy Impellizzeri clearly knows her way around the human heart."

> —**Camille Pagan**, bestselling author of *Life and Other Near-Death Experiences*

"In *Secrets of Worry Dolls*, Mari and Lu, mother and daughter, are separated by an abyss created by misgivings, long-held secrets and tragedies almost too great to bear. Every daughter will recognize the pull of self-discovery and every mother will feel the tension between who she must be as a parent and who she is destined to be as an autonomous person. Stirring, intricate and full of surprises, this story will propel readers forward through the twists of fortune in the lives of these two women, torn apart yet forever linked, not simply by fate and blood, but by true compassion—and a sprinkling of magic."

> —**Sonja Yoerg,** author of *House Broken* and *Middle of Somewhere*

"Exquisite and heartrending…Be warned: *Secrets of Worry Dolls* will sweep you into an irresistible current of heartbreak that stretches from the Semuc Champey pools of Guatemala to the fictional town of Rock Harbor, New York; a current in which those who don't drown learn that being a survivor is the cruelest chance of all."

> —**Scott Wilbanks**, award-winning author of *The Lemoncholy Life of Annie Aster*

"Masterful storyteller Amy interweaves the tales of Mari and Lu to create an unforgettable, tender portrayal of mother-daughter relationships, love, and hope."

> —**Cynthia Swanson**, *New York Times* and *USA Today* bestselling author of *The Bookseller: A Novel*

"*Secrets of Worry Dolls*, much like the mother-daughter relationship at the heart of the novel, explores themes of past and present, home and away, hope and loss, in a masterful way that kept me thinking about and rooting for Mari and Lu long after I'd read the last page."

> —**Susan Gloss**, author of *Vintage*

SECRETS

OF

WORRY DOLLS

Some Secrets are
meant to be
Shared!
XO

SECRETS

OF

WORRY DOLLS

From the award-winning author of *Lemongrass Hope*

A M Y   I M P E L L I Z Z E R I

Wyatt-MacKenzie Publishing
DEADWOOD, OREGON

ALSO BY AMY IMPELLIZZERI

Lemongrass Hope (Wyatt-MacKenzie)
Lawyer Interrupted (American Bar Association)

Secrets of Worry Dolls
Amy Impellizzeri

ISBN: 978-1-942545-65-1
Library of Congress Control Number: 2016951989

The characters and events in this book are fictitious. Any similarity to real
persons, living or dead, is coincidental and not intended by the author.

Wyatt-MacKenzie Publishing
DEADWOOD, OREGON

Wyatt-MacKenzie Publishing, Inc.
www.WyattMacKenzie.com
Contact us: info@wyattmackenzie.com

To my Grandmother, Lois, In Memoriam.

Because her legacy both haunts and inspires me daily.

And because she would have gotten a really big kick out of having a book of mine dedicated to her ...

AUTHOR'S NOTE

On November 12, 2001, American Airlines Flight 587 crashed on my residential corner in Belle Harbor, New York. All the passengers and crew and five of my neighbors on the ground died that morning. All reports of that day say there were no survivors.

But that is not true.

Belle Harbor, a beautiful, scrappy, and resilient seaside town with a large population of New York City firefighters and rescue personnel, was left to pick up the pieces of this devastating event just two months after 9/11, the date on which the small town had lost over 70 of its own residents to the terrorist attacks.

I was not supposed to be home on November 12, 2001, but as fate would have it, I had taken the day off from my Manhattan law office, and awakened just in time to see the plane breaking apart over Belle Harbor before it crashed outside my front door. The emergency response team arrived moments later (many having just left a shift at Manhattan's Ground Zero) and commandeered my home for the recovery operation. They had no choice really. My house was the only one of the four homes on the corner where the crash occurred that was not leveled or engulfed in burning jet fuel.

All these years later, I am still horrified, grateful, guilty, and relieved to relay this fact.

Secrets of Worry Dolls is entirely fictional, of course, including the plane crash it depicts, but it is still a deeply personal story for me—its tale of resiliency and hope is the phoenix that arose from the ashes of that day's tragedy, and I would be remiss in not remembering publicly the victims of that day.

And the survivors.

"At any given moment,
you have the power to say
that this is NOT how
the story is going to END."

—ANONYMOUS

When my sister, Rae, and I were about six years old, Mama gave us two packages wrapped in shiny paper that she said came from her home country of Guatemala—a place she rarely talked about at all.

Inside the paper were some decidedly un-shiny presents. Small wooden boxes filled with tiny creatures woven in bits of red and green and blue thread. One box was painted entirely red and one was still the natural color of the wood that shaped its box, save for a single blue stripe. Mama told us that the woven creatures were called "worry dolls" and that we should whisper our troubles to them each night before bed. The worry dolls would do all the worrying for us and allow us "peaceful sleep." I remember how she practically sang those words to us in her high lilting voice wrapped with her native accent.

My sister and I took one look at each other and burst out laughing.

"Dolls to worry *for* you?"

"That's ridiculous!"

And then we fought over who would get the red box.

My sister won, of course.

Up until the day Mama gave us those dolls, neither of us had given any thought about the need to place our worries somewhere. Indeed, neither of us had even thought to worry much at all at that point. But that was all about to change. Mama must have known that.

Every time I look back on that day, those dolls, her gift to us, I can't help but think, as crazy as it sounds—and believe me, I do know how crazy our story sounds—that Mama must have known everything that was about to happen.

PART I

OCTOBER 11, 2012
71 DAYS BEFORE THE END OF THE WORLD

"Here's to missed chances, untold secrets, and regrets."

The dark-haired woman next to me at the airport bar was holding up her glass at an alarming angle so dangerously close to me, it seemed my only two choices were to clink my glass on hers and continue the conversation, or invite a rather large splash from her drink into my lap.

"If you say so," I conceded.

She put her drink down after our toast and I thought maybe we were done. No such luck. "Well, you look too young to have any real secrets just yet, young lady. But you have time." My bar neighbor smiled broadly, and locked in on me with dark eyes that were outlined in thick makeup caking into deep creases. She smelled faintly of rose oil and olives and was dressed in a tweed skirt and jacket suited for professional travel like most of the patrons in the bar that morning. I looked down self-consciously at my linen pants and light-weight sweater that gave me away as a misfit among the crowd.

"You live in New York?" I nodded in response and offered, "Yes, in Rock Harbor," before clamming up again.

"Where ya headed?" she continued, undaunted by my silence. I thought I detected a slight slur. Maybe I was just being sensitive.

I glanced over my shoulder back down the hallway at Gate G12. My plane had departed without me about a half hour ago, and so her question wasn't an easy one. I glanced up at the television screen above the bar hoping for a distraction, and found one.

"Would you look at that?" I pointed up at the screen and felt relief when her thickly made-up eyes directed themselves away from me finally. "The world *is* ending."

The Mayan so-called long-count calendar—which spans roughly 5,125 years starting in 3114 B.C.—reaches the end of a cycle on December 21, 2012.

A bland-looking gentleman on a cable news channel was discussing a topic I had only heard about recently myself: the end of the Mayan calendar on December 21, 2012. Some were calling it the end of the world. I had dismissed it the first time I heard about it. But that was probably because my mother had brought it up. I pretended to pay more attention to it now.

Some say December 21 could mark the end of the world. Others say it's just a resetting back to start. Like an odometer on an old car that flips back to 0 after 99,999.99 miles.

The rose-and-olive-scented woman looked back at me and smiled. "See? Missed chances, secrets and regrets. When the end of the world *does* arrive, that's all that will be left. And cockroaches, of course."

She laughed heartily at her own joke, and I took the opportunity to jump up from my seat and start gathering my things. "So nice talking with you. I have to run now to catch my plane," I lied. Twice.

When I came out of the dimly lit airport bar, I blinked hard to adjust my eyes back to the light-filled terminal. I felt dizzy from the early morning drink and jumping up too fast from the airport bar stool, so I stood still for a few minutes trying to reacclimate and catch my ragged breath while the row of television screens all flipped over in unison to announce "Breaking News" and "Special Alerts." I stood frozen in front of them blinking and breathing.

At first all I could see on the screens were people crying. The tears seemed endless and oppressive. Standing nearest the first of a dozen screens that traveled down the airport corridor gave a Droste effect to the images and I felt my eyes crossing as I glanced down the corridor toward the gate— G12. For those first moments, I was removed from the event I was watching—like it was a faraway wave that could not reach me.

And then.

The wave changed course. It reached me after all. It crashed over me and took me with it, spinning me, taking my breath away, submerging me and releasing me, leaving me gasping in its wake.

Flight 555.

I was supposed to be on that plane.

The thought rang through my brain, competing with static and nausea as I stared at the television images outside the airport bar I had just exited.

I was tempted to look away—or to run away—but something kept my feet in place. Something kept me right where I was.

A momentum of activity overtook the airport terminal I was still standing in. A low hum quickly escalated to a collective high pitched shriek. I tuned it out. I tuned out everything but the corridor of televisions. The camera on the nearest screen panned on bits of twisted metal—familiar, strangely. I stared at the blurry white words in the black bar across the bottom of the television screen waiting for them to come back into focus. To confirm that what I had seen was correct. Eventually my knees buckled underneath me and my vision faded slowly to black. I remember that the fall seemed long, and I even thought briefly about putting my hands out to brace myself to stop the fall, but I couldn't because my limbs were paralyzed.

Just like that, my body was no longer my own.

And as I fell, all I could see were the words scrolling across the bottom of the screen coming back into focus finally: "Plane Bound for Guatemala Crashes On Residential Corner in Rock Harbor Moments After Take-Off."

MARI

My arms and legs and even my back are all numb and yet I can tell the sheets are soft.

Strange.

I am so tired that I just cannot wake up. Maybe it was the sleeping pills and wine cocktail I gave into finally last night, of all nights, I muse guiltily. But maybe—just maybe—it was something else.

Didn't Lu and I just have a conversation a few weeks ago about the world ending? Perhaps it's happening, after all.

There's an odd beeping noise that taps out a rhythm that is quiet enough to start out as soothing but quickly becomes annoying. I think about calling out to Lu to stop that racket, but I hear voices and none of them are Lu's. That worries me. Is something wrong with Lu? I start to feel really nervous and the beeping gets louder and faster and I hear more voices—louder voices this time—and then—I feel myself sink back into those so-soft sheets.

A calm feeling wraps around my brain and crowds out the other thoughts that are trying to step into my mind. So many people are fighting for priority in my memory reel now.

Joe.

Nery.

Tomas.

Mama.

Rae.

I keep them all out and I think only about Lu. That night we talked about the end of the Mayan calendar, I had asked her what *she* would do if the world as we know it was truly ending, and she surprised me with her answer. Perhaps that was the reason I failed to tell her what *I* would do.

What I *did*.

The voices become dimmer and I strain to listen for Lu's voice but it still isn't among them. The rhythm of the voices blends together to make a combined sound, making it impossible to pick out any single words. Save one.

Coma.

LU

I came to outside an airport bathroom with a very concerned and official-looking man waving something under my nose while continuing to look over his shoulder like there was somewhere else he needed to be.

I gagged a little and sat up. I felt some drool ooze out of the corner of my mouth and I wiped it with my fingers and then wiped my fingers in turn on my new linen pants. I imagined what my sister, Rae, would have said about this whole scene, if she were still alive.

How. Very. Glamorous.

I read the official-looking man's nametag and said, "I'm ok. I'm ok, Eric, thank you." I started to stand up.

"Miss, you need to wait here. I need to—there is a lot going on here this morning—and we are waiting for backup emergency personnel. Just wait here, until we can get more help."

I stayed sitting and reached for my purse that had splayed open next to me, dumping a few items on the floor. When I found my phone inside my purse, I tapped some numbers and listened to a strange clicking noise on the other end.

I started to stand again, while Eric the paramedic tried pushing me down again, his brow furrowed and his eyes distracted. I nodded at him, knowing full well that I would *not* be staying here at the airport. I needed to get home to Rock Harbor, and check on my mother. I needed to know that Mari was all right.

"Here, let me help you. Are you here with anyone?" Eric had given up pushing me back down to a sitting position and was now helping me stand, and also picking up some items that had fallen out of my purse. I shook my head slowly, testing how dizzy the movement made me feel.

As Eric handed me my lip gloss and wallet, he held onto a slip of flimsy paper, his eyes darting from me to the paper and back again.

"Miss?"

I nodded my head at him, trying to answer the imminent question without words, as I had none right now.

"Miss? Is this your boarding pass? Were you supposed to be on—"

I left the rest of his sentence hanging in the air as I turned abruptly, thinking I saw Mari coming out of the airport bar just then. It took only a half second to realize it wasn't Mari, of course, but the tweed-suited woman who had toasted to secrets and regrets and the end of the world with me just a few moments (*was it longer, now?*) ago.

"Is she all right?" The woman who was not Mari ignored me and asked the paramedic directly as he nodded and shooed her away with the free hand that was not holding me up but that was still holding onto my unused boarding pass. I turned away from the woman and Gate G12, and I let Eric guide me back down to a sitting position on the airport floor as my legs were suddenly feeling quite weak.

One month ago, Mari had invited me over for dinner. Not unheard of, but not a common event either in those last few months. Only a yard separated our dwelling spaces on Rock Harbor, but still we each kept to our own corners absent invitations. Mari said I didn't need to bring anything, but I brought a bottle of wine because I thought there was nothing I could bring that she would appreciate more.

Ungrateful probably. Also true.

Mari had made steaks on the grill with a killer marinade. Between her invitations, I had this habit of forgetting what a great cook my mother was. We took our plates into the living room, walking past the kitchen and dining room, and I marveled as I did every time we did this, how we would never have been allowed to eat like this when we were kids. How Rae had missed out on this version of Mari.

Barefoot, with loose jeans and her favorite bright red oversized knit sweater, Mari had settled into her favorite chair in the living room, with her feet tucked under her. Her still-thick, still-jet-black hair was up in a messy bun, the lines of her dark olive skin fading in the soft light of the living room. In that light, her bloated, puffy face was only a slight distraction from her otherwise bohemian beauty. I could still imagine Mari as beautiful even though I knew that a stranger on the street would not be able to look past the puffiness, bloat, red-blotched face and lines and dark circles—that aged Mari well past her 44 years—to see what I saw. While I could still make out some version of the younger Mari, I wished I didn't have all those barriers as well.

"They say the world is ending," Mari had said as she cut into her steak. And I in turn had rolled my eyes at my mother's dramatic flair.

"No really. Just a little more than three months from today. December 21, 2012. The end of the Mayan calendar. It's right around the corner, Niña." My mother almost never called me by my given name or my nickname. Her name for me always was little girl—*Niña*—and I hated it.

"Superstitious now, Mari?" I had taken to calling *her* by her first name out loud—and not just in my head—over the last few years to her grave dismay. I ignored her flinching as she always did when I called her Mari aloud.

"I don't remember you ever being afraid of black cats or broken mirrors, Mari."

"What are you talking about, Niña?"

Sometimes I forgot that for all her command of the English language, American sayings and shorthands still were sometimes lost on my mother despite the fact that she had lived here for all of my life—over 23 years now.

"Nothing. Tell me about the Mayan calendar. I have no idea what you are talking about." I settled into my steak and wine.

"Oh, it's silly, really," Mari conceded now. My mother's voice had a melodic ring I remembered from my childhood. Sometimes I wished I could close my eyes and only hear her.

"Hadn't thought about it since I was a child actually. But I saw a documentary on the news recently, and I thought: Well, wouldn't that make sense? Wouldn't all the things that happened to me—to us—make more sense if the end of the old world was actually upon us? Like the early Mayans had predicted."

I sipped my wine and shook my head morbidly. Same song, different tune with my mother. With a dead husband, dead daughter, insatiable homesickness and thirst for sleeping pills and pinot grigio, it was hard for her not to believe the world was ending every day. Now the world was ending because of a Mayan calendar.

"What would you do, Niña?" My mother leaned forward and asked conspiratorially. "What would you do if the world as we know it really was ending?"

I sipped my goblet of wine and said the first thing that came to my mind, incredible as it was. "Hmm. I'd travel, I guess. Go somewhere I've never been. Actually, that doesn't rule out very many places, does it?"

I had laughed then and Mari hadn't.

Rae was the one who had always talked about leaving Rock Harbor, not me. I had always wanted to stay behind. Which is exactly what happened. Only now it felt all wrong.

Mari stared at me long and hard as if she was just noticing something for the first time. Strangely, she did not show any surprise in my odd answer. "Well, why don't you then?" she replied.

"Take a trip?"

"Yes. What about finally going to see Guatemala? Your other homeland. Besides Rock Harbor, of course. You could even meet Sister Magdalena. I would write to her and tell her you are coming. She'd be overjoyed to meet you and—talk to you."

"Ah, Sister Magdalena." Somewhat of an urban legend in our home growing up, Sister Magdalena was head of the House of Mercies orphanage outside Lake Atitlan in Guatemala and the reason my mother had originally come to America some 24 years earlier. Apparently, Sister Magdalena had arranged for an American family to sponsor Mari and sent Mari here to New York to join the convent—to escape some trouble she had apparently gotten into in Guatemala. Trouble that had always been hinted at, but that Rae and I had never really been privy to.

In my mind's eye, Sister Magdalena had always been the reason a motherless and wayward child (well, a 20-year-old is practically still a child, no?) became my mother. It was Sister Magdalena who set the pieces in motion for Mari to meet the dashing blue-eyed New York City firefighter from Rock Harbor named Joe Roselli who became my father.

It was all *because* of Sister Magdalena—it was *all her fault really*—depending upon how you looked at it.

But all that happened before the world had ended. Our world that is.

And now, everyone's world was ending? I was intrigued, but not fearful. And I *had* actually been rolling over the idea of taking a trip. I was still working out a plan to put my new social work degree to good use but in the meantime I remained paralyzed on Rock Harbor Island, the place I had hardly ever left in my entire lifetime. And never really intended to. Until recently. Now that I had started to accept that Seamus wasn't worth sitting around pining away for.

Seamus.

God, that's a whole other story.

And so, perhaps a bit to spite my mother, and perhaps because in that moment I truly believed the world *was* ending, I had pulled up Expedia on my iPad and researched flights and hotel deals in Guatemala. What was the harm? I'd at least meet with the famous (*infamous?*) Sister Magdalena.

"You know what?" I said to Mari as I shut down my tablet. "That's a great idea. I'll tie up a few things and I'll fly to Guatemala in a few weeks." I sipped my wine dramatically while Mari continued staring at me, leaving her wine glass strangely untouched. "I'll finally see for myself the place we come from."

As I stood up to leave after dinner that night, before I even had a chance to say goodbye, Mari got up and walked over to the old ornately carved secretary in the hallway foyer. She wrote down Sister Magdalena's contact information, and handed it to me solemnly, sadly actually—now I realize it was deep sadness in her voice—as she said: "I think this is such a great idea, Niña. You go to Sister Magdalena first when you arrive in Guatemala. She will tell you everything you need to know."

⑤

After I finally escaped Eric the zealous paramedic and the commotion that was quickly overtaking the airport, it took me several hours to get home to Rock Harbor. There were police checkpoints and questions at every stop as I neared the island.

Yes, I live there. I repeated again and again, as I showed dubious officials my license through the taxi window. At the last checkpoint over the Rock Harbor bridge, I showed a police officer my license yet again, and he shook his head and whistled long and low through his teeth. "Luna Roselli? You live there?" He pointed incredulously at the address on my license as if it was some kind of famous address. I nodded but still corrected him. I hated that I had been named for my dead maternal grandmother. Rae got the name that basically means sunshine, and I got dead grandma. Don't think she didn't constantly remind me of that fact. You know, back when she was alive.

"Actually, it's Lu. Everyone calls me Lu." *Except Mari, who calls me 'Niña.'* I left that part out.

"You live alone?" I was startled by the question as it wasn't as easy to answer as he probably believed.

"No, I live with Mari—my mother—I stumbled over how best to identify Mari, and then continued: "Well, I live in the garage apartment behind her house."

He paused a beat, and I felt a little uncomfortable then. Because clearly the garage apartment was neither legal nor to code, and here I was admitting this all to a police officer—which I would never have done under ordinary circumstances. And so my mind started to wander: *Did I just get Mari and me in trouble?* The officer broke the uncomfortable silence, saying: "Come on, I'll take you home."

I wasn't sure why I needed to be taken home. Did he need to see for himself the illegal apartment so that he could write a citation?

As it did so often, my mind flashed through a thousand worst-case scenarios including me locked up in zoning jail which I immediately assumed was a real thing without questioning my imagination for a moment.

"Why do you always assume the worst is going to happen?" Seamus had asked me that incredible question recently. We had been sitting at a red light, and I told him he should have left more room between us and the car in front of us. "What if another car comes careening down the road behind you, Seamus? You hardly have enough room to move out of the way." Seamus had looked at me with genuine frustration as he asked me why I always think this way. I had kept all the possible and more specific responses locked behind gritted teeth, and instead had managed to spit out only: "Don't you think after all that's happened to me, I'm entitled to at least that much?"

MARI

I smell coffee, now. Soft sheets, quiet voices, and the smell of coffee. This is my life now. Simple and sensory. I like it.

I don't drink much coffee anymore, but I still enjoy the smell of fresh roasted coffee. I remember how much I hated bitter-tasting American coffee when I first came here—sent by Sister Magdalena after—well, after everything happened back home.

I found one coffee shop near the convent where I was living in Manhattan that had strong Guatemalan coffee and I started frequenting it.

Of course, I wasn't only there for the coffee. And one day after I'd been going to the coffee shop for weeks, I was greeted particularly warmly: "Oh. The gentleman who left before you actually paid for your coffee, Miss. So there you go." The clerk (back then we called them clerks and not baristas, and my daughter, Lu, was always trying to break me of the "clerk" habit later on) handed me my now-free coffee. I tried to smooth down the discomfort of having accepted a gift from a stranger. I looked over my shoulder, and saw that the gentleman was actually waiting outside the coffee shop where I'd trip over him on my way out.

So much for an anonymous show of chivalry. This gentleman clearly wanted to be thanked. I nodded at my coffee cup and at him on my way out, not slowing my stride one bit for fear I'd become locked in place. After all, I had noticed him almost daily. He always wore a dark blue shirt with a New York City fire house company number on the left front pocket. He had blue eyes under a dark black crew cut that were more than a bit intoxicating. But I hadn't come to this country looking for intoxicating blue eyes. I hadn't come to this country looking *for* anything. I had instead come to this country to run *from* everything.

I kept my pace as I rushed out the door past the fireman.

"Thank you, that was very kind of you," I said, without slowing down.

"You're welcome," he replied breathlessly as he hurried now to keep up with me down the sidewalk.

We walked like that for half a block when suddenly the skies opened up and it started to rain, and I was left holding only a soggy to-go coffee cup—no umbrella in sight.

Just then, the breathless man popped an oversized umbrella over my head and continued walking with long strides trying to keep pace with me—a feat made easier by the fact that I was now slowing down to stay under the umbrella's dry embrace. I glanced at him sideways, smiling and nodding again at him and the coffee cup repeatedly before stopping abruptly, and looking into his eyes. They were so blue they were almost clear, and I got lost in them immediately.

Oh no. Now I've done it.

He held out his one free hand, but I couldn't take it because I was holding the coffee cup in my right hand and I couldn't for the life of me figure out how to switch hands.

No matter. He kept his orphaned hand outstretched and said simply, "Hi. I'm Joe."

Later Joe told the story differently. He would say that I introduced myself in return under the umbrella and over the soggy cup.

But that part wasn't true. I know for certain that I didn't introduce myself to Joe that first day. Because I didn't want him to know who I was.

⑤

Joe and I met weekly after that rainy day outside the coffee shop. I always arrived early and found a seat outside, facing the very corner that he would round each morning. I had a routine, and after a while, if the same waitress found me, she'd fill my order without me even placing one. I'd get a chocolate chip muffin, and an unsweetened iced tea. Had to be unsweetened. If it was already sweetened, I would send it back and feel brazen as I did so. When the unsweetened tea arrived, I would fill it with three sugars—ripping off the corners of all three sugars at once and dumping them unceremoniously into the tea that I requested not be sweetened by anyone but me. I would devour the muffin and most of the iced tea before Joe would arrive, without guilt. I'd hide the muffin wrapper in a napkin only to keep it a secret how long I'd been waiting. I didn't want Joe to know I came early every time. I didn't want him to start coming earlier than he already did. I needed those few moments alone before he arrived.

Those few alone, sugared, and chocolate-fueled guilt-free moments.

That would evaporate dramatically when he arrived.

Guilt would wash over me every time I saw him turn the corner. Not because I was cheating on my now imminent vows, but because his eyes looked so hopeful, so tender, even at a distance.

I had my secret muffin, voluntarily sweetened tea, and early arrival time, and he had his routine as well. He would walk quickly on his way to me and I would stay in my seat. He'd arrive and swoop me out of my chair gracefully—folding me up in his long arms and kissing the top of my head hungrily.

"You're here," he'd whisper with relief every time, as if he had feared that maybe I wouldn't be.

"You're here," I'd mimic. But I wasn't relieved. Though he never seemed to sense that. Or if he did, he never let on.

About a month or two in, after he asked me out for dinner, and after I politely declined, I told him why. The first of so many confessions between Joe and me. "Joe, here is the truth. I'm not ... free."

"What do you mean? Are you married?"

"Well, in a way, yes. Or almost, at least. I'm supposed to take my vows next year."

"Your ... what?"

"My ... oh, Joe. I'm in the convent. The Sisters of Charity. I'm still a novice, and I'm supposed to take my vows next year."

Joe looked a little stricken. He did. There was nothing sexy for a third-generation Italian Catholic firefighter about wooing a young woman away from the convent, I promise you that. I had figured that out about Joe, just from our weekly meetings. I knew exactly how he'd respond when I got around to confessing to him, and I hated that look on his face. But worse than that—I hated the thought of never seeing his face again—stricken look or no. I had made up my mind that first day. The day he'd bought me coffee and stopped me in my tracks with clear blue eyes to tell me his name. The day he saved me from the sudden rain.

"But I'm leaving the convent, Joe."

"For me?" His expression was equal parts horrified and grateful.

"No. Don't worry. I'm leaving for me. I'm meeting with my Mother Superior this afternoon. I expect to be out on my ear as you Americans say by first thing tomorrow morning."

I forced a smile and reached over the café table for Joe's hand. "But I hope ... next week ... you'll ask me to dinner again. I'll say yes, then. I promise, Joe. I'll say yes."

We sat in silence for a few moments until I broke it. "So ask me to dinner next week, ok?"

He closed his eyes and rubbed his eyebrows with one hand for what felt like a very long time, before he responded, simply: "No."

I felt my shoulders slump, but I straightened up and replied, "I understand—"

"No. Not dinner. Let me take you surfing."

"Surfing?"

"Would you like to learn how to surf?"

I tilted my head up to look him directly in the eyes. My downfall, yet again. He had only asked me to surf but his eyes were pleading and my resolve was ebbing out of my body. I could almost hear his breathing quicken. My own pulse was loud in my ears and I thought for a moment of putting my hands over my ears to quell the noise—but I knew that wouldn't work. I looked up at the sky outside the coffee shop as if willing him to do the same, but when I looked back, he was still staring at me. He held my gaze, his hands clasped in front of him.

No nervousness. No doubt.

I wanted to ask him the question. I wanted to say "Are we going to do this? Are we really going to do this?" But I didn't ask because I already knew the answer.

The next week, we never even took the surfboard into the water. We left it on the sand on the beautiful Rock Harbor beach a few miles south of our Manhattan coffee shop, and Joe led me by the hand into the early morning ocean which was cold and stung my legs. I wrapped my arms around myself and bobbed with the current in front of Joe.

I studied Joe and his fierce eyes.

"You are so serious, Mari."

I sighed and wrapped my arms tighter around myself.

"You make me want to protect you, Mari. You make me feel like I was born to protect you."

And with those words, it was easy. I let my arms drop into a loose fold—no longer a tight hug around my belly. My shoulders dropped, my legs weakened. *He's the one. He can pull me out of this darkness.*

In that moment I felt it. I believed it.

I let Joe peel my arms apart and turn me into him where I stood in the water with my back against his chest. I let him kiss my shoulder blades, my neck, my arms, and then I let him turn me towards him and kiss my lips. He whispered again and again, "We were meant to find each other"—and each time I let him kiss me to show I agreed. The ocean bobbed around us carrying us further and further from shore as we wrapped around each other tighter. It carried Joe and me away and it whispered to us as we nearly drowned—*You were born for each other. You were born for this.*

Where was the point of no return? Where was the moment that all of our fates were sealed?

It was then.

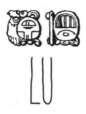

LU

I walked alongside the officer in silence for five Rock Harbor blocks while we travelled parallel to the ocean and toward my home. The smell of burning jet fuel made me cough as we got closer and closer—making illegal and not-to-code garage apartments a distant memory, as I felt the smoky, greasy pollution covering me as we walked.

I could see the houses where Mari and I lived in the distance as we got as close as two blocks away. Emergency vehicles lined the streets, their red soundless and blinking lights punctuating the foggy air that had settled over our homes. I had tried to call Mari several times from the taxi, but the phone had rung and rung with that strange clicking noise that didn't sound quite right. The answering machine didn't pick up and neither did Mari. I imagined many scenarios that had Mari pinned under plane wings and debris, scenarios that I had talked myself out of, but that seemed more and more plausible as I walked toward our corner.

"Here we are." The strangely jovial police officer announced when we arrived at my house, as if we had actually arrived at *his* home instead. And I began to wonder if maybe it was, since it didn't resemble any house I ever remembered seeing previously. The siding was charred black and brown on all visible sides. The front door was completely torn off its hinges—the wood along the side splintered and chopped, but the door itself had been leaned neatly against the blackened front siding. "Emergency crew had to let themselves in," he explained. I nodded quickly as if it was a common occurrence for people to break their way into my home.

"This—your home—is the command center for the entire

recovery operation. Our apologies for any inconvenience, but, there was no other—well, it's the only one standing, as you can see."

I turned my head to follow his hand that gestured around the block as he spoke. And I saw for the first time that the homes I had been seeing in the distance were all mangled and burned, and mostly missing fronts or backs or roofs or walls.

And then, suddenly, I heard it.

The silence.

Despite the buzzing of emergency generators and machines, and the crackling of once burning trees and wood, the block was eerily silent.

I put my hand on the officer's arm: "Where is everyone? My neighbors? Is anyone—"

I couldn't finish the sentence and I dropped my hand.

He reached up and put his hand on my shoulder kindly. "We're still working to gather all the facts—to account for everyone. Most were at work or school, and are perfectly safe, Thank God. We've identified five victims on the ground for now—in addition to—you know, the victims on the plane." His eyes went down to the ground solemnly.

"Who? Who died on the ground?" I clutched at my chest and picked and squeezed the buttons on my cardigan sweater. One popped off into my hand. I let it fall to the ground and started working on the next one.

"We can't—until we know all the details—contact the victims' families, et cetera—we can't really share any information just yet." He straightened up a bit as if shifting back into official duties.

"My mother, though—do you know anything about her? Mari Guarez Roselli? Maybe she's inside the house and perfectly fine?"

I started to turn toward the house, but the officer stopped me with only his words, "I've been in and out of the command center for the last few hours. The owner hasn't been here; I know that much."

I stood frozen for a few seconds.

His voice softened. "Listen, I'm sure I'm not supposed to say this, but her name doesn't sound familiar to me. I don't think she's on the list of victims. How about if you stay here and we'll try to find out what we can for you."

I agreed. What else could I do? Where else could I go? I needed to wait here for Mari. Certainly, if she had left the house for some reason, she'd be back, right?

The officer started to turn away, but then turned back. "Is there someone we can call for you? Someone, you know, who doesn't live on the island? Somewhere you could go for a short time?"

I wondered fleetingly why he kept saying "we." I even craned my neck around to look behind him and then over my shoulder to see if there was another officer following behind us that I seemed to have missed. But no, it was just he and I. I admitted soberly: "No. There's no one to call."

The once jovial officer now looked very concerned. I glanced for the first time at his badge. "Merry." Officer Merry. It made me chuckle to myself unwittingly. Officer Merry's brow furrowed aggressively at my apparent onset of hysteria, and I had that vague feeling I get when I am talking with someone who suddenly starts to realize that they have gotten more than they signed on for with me and so I straightened up.

"I'll just walk through and assess the damage here at my mother's house and mine. My apartment is out back." My self-consciousness was gone. Clearly there would be no citations for illegal garage apartments today. I gestured toward the building behind the house I had grown up in, a building that was really a garage that had been insulated into a makeshift apartment about a year ago so that Mari and I could live near each other—but still in separate quarters.

"I'll just see if I can get anything for the officers and rescue personnel. Maybe some dinner," I said, fraudulently, knowing there was not likely to be anything substantial in Mari's refrigerator other than pinot grigio, and there was certainly nothing in my own refrigerator but some leftover Coronas in case Seamus stopped by. And mustard. Expired mustard, no doubt.

I stopped picking at my buttons. I put my hands at my sides in an ongoing effort to convince Officer Merry that I was perfectly competent to be left alone. The gesture was awkward, but it worked. Officer Merry looked relieved that I was acting like a normal person and said, "That would be wonderful," and so I headed alone into Mari's house.

Rescue personnel lined up at the bathrooms inside the small bungalow. When I closed my eyes, the house—in marked contrast from the silence outside—had the buzzy din of a cocktail party from the long ago days when my mother and father used to throw such things. Conversation—even some light laughter—bounced off the walls. It had been so long since this house had been filled with anything like those sounds. I kept my eyes closed a few moments longer and breathed it all in to my jet fuel-stained lungs.

MARI

Joe loved to dance.

And oh! The lightness of my limbs on these so soft sheets is making me *feel* graceful.

Isn't that funny how some good soft sheets and peace and quiet has allowed me to remember those few quiet and good years when Lu and Rae were about four or five years old? When Joe and I would dance almost every night.

The years of babies and toddlerhood have blended into a hazy foggy wisp of memory that I associate more with exhaustion than anything else. And later, of course, the heaviness of everything I lost nearly crushed me.

But in those days after the twins were no longer toddlers, I used to *feel* better. The manual labor of caring for two helpless babies subsided. I was putting more and more years between the memories I had escaped in Guatemala. I wasn't drinking or taking pills to help me sleep.

I loved to cook, and Joe would keep the twins busy and occupied so I could make weekly dinners for our neighbors. I'd cook Mama's recipes from back home. Pork with sautéed peppers and tomatoes and perfect flans. Joe would sneak into the kitchen and taste the food and fuss over my cooking.

There was a neighbor couple—Rebecca and John—they were so lovely. "High school sweethearts," Rebecca told me when I asked how they had met. Eventually John started working more and more at his big accounting office in Manhattan, but back then they had more time for friends. And each other, I think. They had the most adorable son named Seamus with red brown hair that stuck straight up all over and who became such a big part of our lives. But that was later. Back then, Rebecca and John would get a babysitter for Seamus on Friday nights and I'd put the twins to bed early and we'd all sit in the living room and play cards, and eat, and laugh and ... dance.

I was happy then.

For *years*, I was happy.

I can't say for sure whether Lu remembers those years as happy or not, or even whether Rebecca does, but *I* remember them that way—I really do.

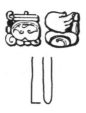

When we were around four or five, Rae and I used sneak out of our room to spy on my parents when they had company. Neighbors, firefighters who worked with Dad and their wives, Seamus' parents—all sitting together in our living room, laughing and whispering. My mother would cluck around them as the beautiful hostess that she was, and then Dad would inevitably click on his old record player, and pull my mother away from her hostessing duties and dance with her.

Later on, Rae and I would remember and rehash those years like crazy. Certain we'd get back to them. Certain *they* would get back to them. The memory and the possibility lived in our home like an extra family member, until that possibility became, of course, impossible.

And now, hours after a plane had crashed outside of this very home, I was standing with my eyes closed, pretending that the sound of emergency personnel was the sound of happiness reentering a place I had long given up hope would ever be filled with happy sounds again.

The memories of those long ago cocktail parties came to me vaguely and then left before they could really come sharply into focus as I opened my eyes inside Mari's charred and smoke-filled house. I walked down the hall and peeked inside Mari's room briefly to see a mess—some paintings had been shaken straight off the walls, but there was no sign of her so I headed down to the end of the hall to my old bedroom to lie down.

Five victims on the ground.

I tried not to think about that cruel sentence as I walked to my room. I meant to lie on my old bed, cover myself with my old down comforter that Mari still kept folded neatly at the base of the bed, and luxuriate in the foreign noise of the house for a few more minutes while Officer Merry gathered some information on Mari's whereabouts.

I stopped short, however, at my bedroom door. My down comforter was missing. Actually the bed had been stripped—hastily it seemed—as the mattress cover was still half on and half off the bed and the mattress leaned precariously and perpendicular against the box frame. The door to the linen closet just past my old bedroom door was open and rammed into the wall next to it. The linen closet was empty save for a handful of wash cloths and hand towels dropped haphazardly at the bottom of the closet and landing on top of cleaning supplies stuffed into an old blue bucket on the floor of the linen closet.

What the—?

Has someone looted us?

And why would they be stealing our linens?

I walked back out to the bathroom line down the hall and tapped on the shoulder of a sturdy-looking woman who was wearing a jacket with the letters F. B. I. emblazoned on the back, and was talking into a walkie-talkie. "Why are all the linens gone?"

The Agent clicked off her walkie-talkie. "Sweetheart, is this your home?"

I nodded wordlessly. She stepped out of the line, with her arm around me and I had the random thought that I should tell her not to give up her coveted spot in line for the bathroom. The thought made me giggle awkwardly, and my ill-timed giggle made her pull her arm around me more tightly. I realized that now she *and* Officer Merry thought I was hysterical.

The list was growing.

bravest." But beneath her evident worry and concern, she had a self-assuredness that I admired, but that also put me off a bit as I talked with her.

"So what is law school like?" I asked her. I was not really sure what else I *could* ask her.

"It's brutal. It's not something to do when you don't know what else to do. You know what I mean?"

I nodded falsely, because I actually had no idea what she meant.

"The problem is that too many people still go to law school for all the wrong reasons. They become disgruntled lawyers. They ruin the experience for the rest of us who actually are dying to *be* lawyers." I nodded some more while understanding even less.

While I was still trying to figure out what more I could talk to this confident young woman about, she rescued me by asking how Joe and I met, and I told her about the coffee shop. I left out the part about me leaving the convent, and left *in* the part about the oversized umbrella.

I concluded dramatically: "He saved me." And while I only meant for Tricia to understand that he had saved me from the sudden rain, she looked me in the eye for a few moments, seeming to hear more than I was saying out loud.

"And you have children?" she asked.

I began rattling off the kind of details mothers of six-year-olds typically rattle off.

"Two daughters—Lu and Rae."

"They are so funny. Well Lu is loudly funny. Rae is quietly funny."

"They fight all the time. But they love each other so much, too."

"They love school. They are best at math."

But Tricia interrupted me with one question: "Do you worry?"

I nodded hard. "Of course. All the time."

She shook her head. "No, I mean, do you worry about

being left alone with them? Because of—you know, what the boys do for a living? I'm terrified of having children. I don't think I'll be able to do it, and I've told that to Matthew only recently."

I was stunned a bit, but I nodded and shook my head in rapid and alternating succession. "Yes. It's wonderful. And terrifying. All at once." I thought about telling her about the small worry dolls I kept in my pockets and folded under my pillow each night. The ones who were kept busier and busier these days as Joe's schedule grew more hectic, and the girls grew older and more demanding. In fact, I had just given the girls each a set of their own around that time—with the hope that they would find solace in these same dolls that brought me so much comfort. But I felt silly telling this practical and accomplished young woman about my Mayan dolls. So I kept silent and looked to Joe to step in to save me as he so often did.

Joe seemed impervious to the discussion I was having with Tricia, simply holding out the deck to Tricia fanning his cards like a gypsy ... "pick a card ... any card." Tricia picked the four of clubs, showing it only to Matthew and me, not to Joe.

Joe shuffled the cards and dramatically revealed Tricia's card a few moments later. The ten of hearts, rather than a four of clubs. "I found your card," he yelled triumphantly. "And I turned it into a ten of hearts."

Everyone smiled and laughed at the trick. It *was* funny. But still, something happened that night. When I trace things back along a timeline of good years and bad years, that night was a turning point for me. And not a good one.

As we left Tricia and Matthew and as I thought about her decision not to have children, I had the sinking feeling that I had been turning too many fours of clubs into tens of hearts. That I had been pretending everything was ok, when in fact it was not. That I had been putting too much stock in my woven worry dolls, and forgetting to do the worrying myself.

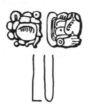

The sturdy F. B. I. Agent asked me my name and some other identification questions, and I stared at her badge as I always do when meeting a new person in uniform. "Love." Was that really her name? The cast of officers and agents in this terrible day was starting to feel oddly dreamlike and I became distracted by the fear that I had conjured this whole thing up.

Maybe I was still unconscious outside the airport bathroom?

Or worse—maybe I was—"Am I on the plane, after all?"

Agent Love looked very concerned and began biting on her pen. I noticed her nails were bitten too far down, and I crossed my hands over my chest and hugged my shoulders. I tried not to cry. "I mean. I was supposed to be on that plane. That very plane to Guatemala at 9:50 this morning. I was at the airport. I missed it. I missed the plane."

I got nervous about my responses. I wasn't exactly being honest, and here she was with an F. B. I. jacket on and everything. I backpedaled. "Ok. That's not true. I deliberately missed it. I didn't want to get on the plane after all, and ... now ... this is all starting to feel a bit surreal. I'm sorry."

Agent Love's expression softened and she let out a small gasp. "Oh, honey. I'm so sorry. Thank God. Thank God you were not on that plane."

I thought of asking her again about the missing linens but something stopped me, as I started to piece together an answer that I really did not want to hear.

October 11. I suddenly remembered the date that was stamped on my boarding pass that I never used that morning.

*Today is October 11. I will remember this date in the same way I re-
member September 11 each year.*

"Did you know my father?" I asked Agent Love suddenly.
She looked at me with a confused expression. Most people
around here knew who my father was. But she wasn't really
from around here, was she?

"My father—he died on 9/11. Most people here in town
know who he is. He died trying to save—" I stopped short
there. I wasn't about to tell her the whole story. After all, I
hadn't told *anyone* the true story of how my father died. Not
even Mari. That was a secret I intended to die with me. So I
just filled in with the usual one. "My sister. He died trying to
save my sister."

Agent Love continued writing, still looking down at her
notepad, while she asked: "Where is your sister? Does she
live here, too?"

"No."

Sigh.

"I said he *tried* to save her. He didn't though. Rae died on
9/11, too."

MARI

I was all alone when I first realized I was pregnant with the twins. It was dark outside when I heard Joe getting ready to leave the Rock Harbor bungalow he had inherited from a childless relative, and where we had been spending more and more time together. I left the convent, and got a job as a secretary for one of Joe's friends who was starting his own business on Rock Harbor. I wasn't very good, and I knew that Joe's friend was giving me a chance while I tried to find something better suited for me. Or got myself deported back to Guatemala.

We had given up coffee shop rendezvous and surfing lessons for sunrise walks on the beach and quiet nights in the bungalow. I was unsure if Joe understood exactly what he was getting with me. I was letting him see pieces of my life before him slowly. And rather than pushing him away, it seemed to be drawing him closer. "You're here now, Mari. You're *here* now," he'd say over and over again.

That morning as I woke, a wave of nausea settled over me like an ocean wave. I thought about pretending that I was still sleeping as I heard Joe dress, but we felt beyond all that—even then. I stayed on my belly and turned my head only to watch Joe drowsily as he dressed for the city firehouse. I pulled the covers up to my neck but one of my legs slid further out of the covers.

"Bye, Mari." He leaned down to kiss me on the top of my head and I murmured a sleepy "Bye Joe," in response. Just before I closed my eyes again, I saw him double back to the bedside. He stroked my leg softly and then tucked it back under the covers.

A few hours later I woke nauseated yet again. I barely made it to the bathroom in time to retch violently over and over again before retreating defeated to the lonely bed we had shared just a few hours earlier.

As I covered myself, my leg slid back out of the cover. I thought about the warmth of Joe's hand stroking my leg and re-covering it, and I thought: *I wish he hadn't done that.*

9

A week later, I was sitting on the side of the bed next to Joe, rubbing my arms. I couldn't get comfortable. I couldn't get warm. I had been cold all week, and maybe longer. As I rubbed my arms faster and faster, I tried to remember the last time I had been warm. Was it last week? Last month? Maybe I hadn't been warm ever in America? Maybe I hadn't been warm in Guatemala either. Maybe my memory was playing tricks on me.

Joe repeated his reassuring words.

"Mari, what's wrong? You can't tell me anything that's going to make me change my mind. I'm crazy about you—you know that—right?"

The TV was on in the bedroom. The morning news channel was creating a static of background noise that suddenly came into focus.

The weather was going to be warm and unseasonable for October. Traffic was backed up on the Long Island Expressway through exit 24. One of the local schools was holding a bakeoff to raise money for funds to send its marching band to Florida the following Spring.

More noise. I shook off the noise, and came back to the cold and Joe and—

"How long have we been meeting, Joe?"

"Meeting?" His smile dissolved into a laugh. "Is that what we're doing, Mari? Meeting?" He reached over and pulled me to him, and I let him in the hope that he could make me warm.

It didn't work.

"Let's see, I met you 154 days ago."

"You just made that up."

"Maybe."

He laughed and laid back down on the bed, his head crushing the too-soft pillow that was usually mine. "I have no idea, Mari. It's been months—over five months—I know that much for sure. It was spring when we met, wasn't it? I remember pulling you out of the spring rain that day. I remember what you were wearing. How you smelled under my umbrella. I wanted to kiss you right then and there. I can't tell you how hard it was not to. You've ruined me, Mari. Tell me I've ruined you, too."

"Oh, Joe." I sighed with resolution and frustration and awareness. Joe had never even known me before I was indeed ruined. He knew the American version of me. The me who was careless and went out in the cold wet rain without proper boots or an umbrella, and needed to be rescued. Where was the girl who had spirit and courage? Long gone. And Joe even knew why. I had told him as a test. To see if it made him leave. But it didn't. He stayed to rescue me, and now—"Joe, I have to confess something." I still used the church's English words. Perhaps I always would.

"I'm pregnant."

Joe sat up quickly and wrapped me in one of his folding hugs. "Oh Mari—thank God. I thought you were going to tell me you were leaving me." He rocked me back and forth on the bed. "I'll take care of you, Mari. We'll get married. Right away. Don't worry. Oh Mari, thank God."

He continued rocking me and his tears spilled over onto the top of my head. I made a noise and shook my shoulders and pretended to cry, too. I couldn't muster any tears, even though I was so sad. So very sad. "You'll never leave me now. You never have to leave again," he said.

When I realized he was right, I started to cry real tears. No more pretending. And no more leaving.

◎

The day the doctor confirmed the news about the twins, I was also alone.

Two babies. I would have laughed if it wasn't happening to me. If it wasn't happening all the way to me.

I was lying on a very cold bed in a doctor's office whose address I had found in the book with yellow pages stored in a drawer in Joe's Rock Harbor bungalow. I never understood why he called that drawer a "junk drawer" when it housed many important things—including this list of every important phone number and address that existed.

The doctor who was pressing the wand—which was even colder than the bed—all around my belly was a woman and that intrigued me. I kept asking her questions about her medical training, and while in hindsight, it must have seemed to her like I was questioning her qualifications to talk to me about my condition, in truth I was very impressed by her.

But still, I kept asking her over and over, what she had just said. As if I couldn't believe her. As if I didn't trust her.

"It's true, Miss Guarez. There are two babies. I very clearly hear two heartbeats, here and ... here."

I had barely gotten myself used to the idea of taking care of one baby, let alone two. Joe was so good, and I knew in my heart that I should be grateful—but I resented the care I knew was about to evaporate when the babies arrived. How would he have time to take care of me anymore, to protect me, when he was most certainly going to have to take care of new babies?

I knew what that care would entail. Milk and diapers and fussing, and crying, and love. Someone would have to love those babies. I felt certain I wouldn't be able to muster nearly enough love for one baby, let along two.

When I came home and told Joe, "There are two babies, Joe. Not one, but two," he lifted me high in the air and squealed and cheered.

When he put me down, he said: "I got us an appointment

at City Hall in the morning. Starting tomorrow you will be Mrs. Mari Roselli. Mother of my children. Love of my life." I smiled back at him, summoning as much hope as I could find in my core. Joe put his hand on my belly and I closed my eyes, remembering the heartbeats I'd heard a few hours earlier.

Ba-bum. Ba-bum. Ba-bum. Ba-bum.

So much life in a body that had felt dead for so long.

Maybe it would be enough. Between Joe and me, maybe there'd be enough love for these two babies.

After I mentioned my dead sister, Agent Love stopped scribbling notes furiously and looked at me long and hard. "Oh dear. And you were supposed to be on this plane." Agent Love started to point outside at the fuselage but caught herself in the gruesome act, and quickly pointed down at her paper instead.

I started babbling with nervous energy. "Yes. It's true. I was on my way to Guatemala—to my mother's birthplace and to meet someone there that my mother has always wanted me to meet—Sister Magdalena—oh I'm not making much sense here, I know—"

"It's ok," she reassured, without basis.

"I had second thoughts at the airport. I couldn't actually get on the plane. For years, I've had a fear of leaving the island, and while I have ... left the island, still, it seemed very overwhelming in that moment to leave like that. My God, I hadn't even been on a plane in years—not since we used to go visit my Grandmother Roselli in Florida when my dad was still alive. I just kind of freaked out at the gate and left. I guess those second thoughts were right, weren't they?"

Agent Love continued with her note-taking through my flustered gabbing, not bothering to look up, and because I didn't have to meet her gaze, I kept on talking. And she kept on writing.

"My mother. She is from Guatemala. Mari Guarez Roselli. We've had a very difficult decade—since you know, 9/11, as you can imagine. I just recently graduated with a social work degree, and I was feeling ready to move on to a new chapter in my life."

I started picking nervously at my cardigan buttons again. "Please. Can you find out if Mari is all right? I'm sure she is. I'm sure she walked down to have coffee with a neighbor to keep out of the way."

Wine, more likely.

"I just—I'd just really like to know that she's ok. Maybe I should walk around the neighborhood and knock on doors or something—" I started to stand up. Agent Love looked up at me deliberately. I shrunk under her gaze, and sat back down.

"Your mother. She lives here? In this house?"

"Yes. We both do. Well, technically we both do. We always have until recently. And now, I actually live in the apartment out back."

Agent Love made her first sour face and said, "All I can tell you is that we have five confirmed victims on the ground—maybe more—there's a lot of confusion about people's whereabouts right now. I really can't say more than that at this time. But you can't walk around the neighborhood right now. This whole block is cordoned off. There have been small fires all morning, and it's not universally safe all over. You're safe here, for now, though. Stay here. If your mother has walked away, she's likely to return *here*—no?"

I agreed without saying out loud the words that were fighting their way into my worried brain: *Not. Necessarily.*

I looked out the window again behind Agent Love and saw that gloved strangers were tapping down my mother's grass and beloved garden, picking up items and bagging them. They reminded me of the suited government workers from *E.T.*, the movie.

The spring after my father and Rae died, Mari took me to the movies, a rare event in those days, to watch the re-release of *E.T.*, which was apparently celebrating its 20th anniversary. It was my 13th birthday, and Mari—at a loss as to whether or how to celebrate the event—apparently thought a movie about an alien in a California town far away seemed innocuous and festive enough for her newly minted teenage daughter.

I was feeling ambivalent about celebrating at all. After all, it was my first birthday without Rae. For all of our other birthdays, Rae and I would moan and complain about having to share our day. I remember waking that morning, thinking I'd give anything not to celebrate this and future birthdays without my twin.

But I was as happy as I could be about the *E. T.* movie decision. Mari said I could invite Seamus if I'd like—but I was annoyed with him that week for something or other, so I invited him and then un-invited him again and again within a few days of the re-release date. By the time the night arrived, it was just me and Mari, and I was happy about that. Happy to be spending time with Mari outside of the house—thinking about something other than death, and plane crashes, and terrorists. So happy that I did not insist upon leaving when my throat felt like it would close up midway through the movie. So happy that I did not grab Mari's arm for comfort like I wanted to when I realized that the movie wasn't about aliens or California or Drew Barrymore.

It was about being left behind.

Agent Love seemed finished with me as I hadn't seen anything and had no more information about the crash scene than she had. She left me sitting there and got back in line for the bathroom. I marveled vaguely at the strength of her bladder. As she walked away, Agent Love dropped a piece of paper and I snatched it up sheepishly. It was a post-it with a few numbers on it, and I pocketed it, knowing that Rae would be rolling her eyes if she saw me now, and sneering that I was becoming: *Just.Like.Mama.* Because Mari had this weird habit of collecting post-it notes.

Who could say why?

MARI

It started by accident one day. I was walking through the produce section of the grocery store. The name of the store was King Kullen. I had always wondered at the strange names for the Rock Harbor shops, and the grocery store in particular. A funny name for a country that abhorred tyranny, I always joked with the girls when we all walked through its doors—as if it was the first time I had thought of it.

On this particular morning, it was just me, no girls. Rae was … gone by then. I can't remember where Lu was. Sleeping in, maybe? All I know is that I had walked to the King Kullen alone, and I had cut off a Saturday-Morning Dad to get the cart I was pushing, which was very uncharacteristic of me. Usually I would let the Saturday Dads go in front of me so I could follow them. Stalk them, some might say. Well, Lu would say that. After she explained to me what that meant—"stalking"—I tried not to see it that way, but I could see how others might.

The Saturday Dads came out on Saturday or Sunday but somewhere along the line I had just lumped them all together under the umbrella of Saturday. They came in their blue jeans and wrinkled tees and American ball caps and they had one or two kids along for the ride. They spent the morning shopping for wives who had worked hard all week and were perhaps getting Saturday morning manicures (I had been to the salon where all the Saturday Moms could be found, but only once; then I started avoiding the salon altogether).

From what I overheard while eavesdropping on the Saturday Dads, some of the Saturday Moms stayed in bed sleeping, or medicating, or hiding. The Saturday Dads would dote on their charges for the morning, lifting them high to pick grapefruits from the back of the pile, showing off for the other moms who were stuck in the King Kullen alone (or worse, with a few children in tow) unfortunate not to have such a generous mate, or a mate at all. The Saturday Dads looked like they knew what they were doing as they followed along lists with feminine script on them—lists made by their everyday wives.

Going to the market on Saturday mornings after 9/11 was like pouring salt in old wounds. I would wander the aisles studying the Saturday Dads like a student, wiping tears and ignoring glances in my direction that were full of pity and never endearing. A few times I abandoned my cart no matter how full it was because the tears would be streaming down my face with such volume I couldn't possibly hide them any longer.

But that day as I mentioned, I had already cut off a Saturday Dad in a blatant show of disregard for how this dance was usually carried out. I didn't follow behind anyone. I just pushed my cart into the store and placed my purse dramatically in the front compartment reserved for children, and ignored the Saturday Dads as I shopped for my own. Damn. Fruit.

I reached for grapefruits, apples, singularly examining each piece. I decided finally after painstakingly checking every single grapefruit that there was only one I would buy. I turned around to pull one of those ridiculous plastic bags off the scroll to house my one and only grapefruit, and I noticed it then. A post-it note stuck haphazardly to the scroll. Like someone had planted a note there for me. I gasped and jumped a bit, and looked all around me to see if anyone else had seen me jump—also to see if anyone had seen the note someone had clearly left just for me. I tried to read it secretly, but it was upside down. I looked around again and again, and then plucked the post-it off the scroll.

It read:

Post office (postcard stamps?)
    stamps / mail tax installment
Pick up vitamins at pharmacy
Grocery store:
    Bananas
    Raisin Bran
    Coffee (decaf and regular)
    Bread (whole wheat organic)
    Milk (2%, organic)
    Frozen vegetables (any except lima beans)
    Cream of mushroom soup
    Chicken (boneless breasts—about 2 pounds)
    Cold cuts (any except salami—provolone cheese please!)
    Gift for R
    Cupcakes (nut-free please!)

FLOWERS

I read it over and over again. It was a list. Someone's to-do list. And every single item was crossed out except the "Gift for R"—which—if you must know, troubled me more than I can admit.

But what affected me even more, was the fact that all the items on the post-it were written in feminine script with half connected and half printed words, except for the last entry—the note about "flowers" was in hard printed letters, masculine print.

He had added a note to the end of *her* list. This Saturday Dad was planning on surprising his wife with flowers.

It could have been Joe, I remember thinking.

It could have been Joe if he hadn't died.

That was one of the times I abandoned my cart right there in the vestibule of the King Kullen. But I took the purple post-it with me.

LU

Left on my own after my interview with Agent Love finished, I thought about heading to my garage apartment to hide from all the recovery personnel. But I wanted to stick around as I was still hoping Officer Merry would make good on his promise to get some information about Mari. While I waited hopefully, I wandered outside to watch the F. B. I. agents bag their treasures. I followed them surreptitiously around the house until we arrived together at the front of the house.

When they saw me, some agents shuffled me quickly away from the front of Mari's house—from an area that was taped off and surrounded by official-looking men and women and electrical buzzing equipment. "Is that the crash scene?" I asked one such official-looking gentleman with hard gray eyes and a ruddy complexion blocking my view.

He nodded silently, not looking at me, as if he were part of the queen's guard, and not allowed to drop character for even a moment. "I'm sorry Miss—you need to go back around to the other side—this area is restricted."

But I was already recoiling from the area of my own free will. I had gotten a glimpse of my old down comforter laid out behind him—covering who knows what. And I didn't want to accidentally see what lay beneath. I knew now that the linens had been taken to cover up the crash scene from eyes that shouldn't see it—including mine.

It was like 9/11 all over again. Restricted sites. Missing people.

It was history repeating itself all over again, I feared.

MARI

Limbo.

As I float gracefully through my thoughts and senses, the word comes to me like an old memory.

It's a word I learned after 9/11. Lu would use it all the time when people came to the house.

We are in limbo.

I asked her what it meant one day. "What is this limbo, Niña?"

"Limbo is the place between heaven and hell," she said, repeating a lesson from the parochial school she had attended with Rae on Rock Harbor. "The Sisters taught us at school. It fits us now. We are in between," she said.

So wise, my Niña. Even then. At the sweet young age of 12. But I suppose she had to be very grown up by then.

So yes, for a long time after 9/11—we were in limbo. From the beginning, we had Rae's body, but not Joe's. We thought we knew basically what had happened, and after about a day or so, we held little hope of finding Joe alive—and even less hope of finding his remains, but still we put off a burial or a memorial service until we could regroup. Until Lu and I could actually leave the house without vomiting or passing out or both.

The number of times I was asked for a DNA sample felt excessive. The number of times I thought about leaving—about walking out, about deserting Lu and Rock Harbor, about heading home to Guatemala—was more than I care to admit. Those were dark days. Really, really dark days.

Lu slept in my bed every night and while she slept fitfully,

I twisted my worry dolls around and around under my pillow in a useless exercise. Everything was overflowing then. The dolls could no longer keep everything to themselves. The worries spilled out under my pillow and threatened to devour me in my sleep.

One night I told her we needed to switch sides. She had taken to sleeping on my side of the bed, but it was closest to the nightstand. The place where I kept my sleeping pills. I had been trying to sleep without them while she lay in the bed with me, night after night, but it was useless. After too many sleepless nights, I was exhausted and depleted.

"Would you rather I sleep in my own bed, Mama?" Lu whispered as she readjusted onto Joe's old side of the bed.

"Soon enough, Niña. You can stay here for now, but soon, you'll have to go back to sleeping in your own room."

I saw her disappointed face disappear slowly as she pulled the covers high up over her head but I didn't reach over to stop her. As I felt the cold sleeping pill slide back over my tongue, I could not stop thinking that death and sadness would be following me all the rest of my days. That I had not left the darkness when I fled Guatemala like I had come to hope. Like Joe had allowed me to hope for all those years.

The truth was, while we stayed in between, Lu and I, I drifted closer to hell than heaven.

Starting from the time Rae and I were about six or seven, I remember that Mari got the flu. A lot.

Maybe she had the flu before that and we were too young and self-involved to notice, but around the time she gave us those worry dolls, we started to notice that she was sick, more and more often. Later, and especially after my father and Rae died, I learned that too much wine and sleeping pills also looked like the flu; but when we were kids, Mari's "flu" episodes were more mysterious and exotic, albeit frightening until something else happened to make us forget about them.

Like the time we were about nine. Mari was having one of her famous stomach aches and Rae and I were trying to keep quiet while she napped. We hadn't seen her in four days. Dad was the only one allowed in her room. He'd get home each day around the same time we finished school, and he'd take Mari some soup or food or tea, and when he came out of her room each day, he'd just tell us to stay as quiet as we could until bedtime. We'd usually do our home-work, or read books, or take a walk down the beach with Dad and look for night crabs, but on the fifth day it was a Satur-day, and rainy, and the day loomed long and tedious before us, as we set out on a plan not to make any noise. Rae asked Dad what we were having for lunch, and then I said that we were both bored with spaghetti and sauce from the jar. Rae looked at me like I had said something very stupid, and Dad looked like he might snap at us, and I was instantly sorry I said it. But then Dad ran his fingers though his jet black hair. "Ok—let's go to Serendipity. We'll have ice cream. For lunch," he announced ceremoniously.

Rae and I heard the words *ice cream* and the funny name of the ice cream place, and thought he said he was getting "Seven Dips for Me" and we each squealed, "Seven Dips? Can I get seven dips, too?"

We took the train into the city from nearby Sheepshead Bay, changing several times until we were just blocks from the promised ice cream lunch. The rain let up as we arrived in the City, which was a good thing, since we had to stand in line for what seemed like forever just to make it inside. We listened for funny accents, and tried to figure out where people were from. A boy and a girl stood in back of us who sounded like they were from England. She was very pretty with golden brown hair and rosy cheeks, and he had a face like a mouse, and he kept saying things like:

"I've always wanted to come here."

"I'm so happy you're here."

And she kept saying:

"Me, too."

"Me, too."

And we weren't sure at all that she could even understand English and then he leaned down to kiss her and we shrieked: "Ewwww. That's so gross!" The girl turned around then and looked at us so meanly that we figured out maybe she could understand a little English after all.

Dad let them go in front of us to make up for our embarrassing him—which was even better for Rae and me, because then we could keep a good eye on them without having to keep slyly looking backward. We could easily see if they were still trying to kiss each other and know whether or not she was still repeating, "Me, too."

The whole time in line, we kept repeating it over and over again, "Seven Dips, we want Seven Dips."

We were finally seated and my dad told us to hush and behave ourselves. This pretty red-headed waitress came over to take our order, and said we must be very grown up for our dad to bring us to such a fancy restaurant.

Fancy?

We put our hands over our mouths to keep from giggling. The tables and chairs were all mismatched and big lamps hung from the ceiling with all sorts of painted colors. It wasn't fancy like our Grandmother Roselli's dining room in Boynton Beach where we made a one-week pilgrimage every winter. Where everything matched and everything was white or blue and you were not allowed to touch anything or "please do not even look at the room before you have washed your hands, Rae and Lu, this means you, thank you very much." If this place was the real definition of "fancy" as opposed to what our Grandmother had been selling us for years, then we liked it.

The waitress called us each Princess (Princess Red and Princess Blue after the jacket colors we were wearing) and helped us learn how to say the name of the restaurant (Seren dippity Seren dippity Seren dippity). She told us that even though everyone always orders the frozen hot chocolate at Serendipity, her own favorite was the Humble Pie dessert. Rae and I argued over what we should order. I wanted frozen hot chocolates. Rae ordered Humble Pie desserts for both of us. I humphed a bit, but the pretty waitress smoothed things over by saying we could come back and next time order the frozen drinks, and also that maybe someday we'd come back and order the golden sundae that cost $1000. We looked at her wide-eyed, assuming she was joking again—like the "fancy" thing—and she just smiled at our dad and said: "Ok, Prince Charming, and what will you have?" We didn't even bother covering our mouths this time. We just put our heads down on the table and laughed and laughed at both the idea of Dad as someone's Prince Charming, and the funny look Dad had on his face when she called him that.

Of course, in hindsight, the funny look Dad had on his face? It might just have been genuine happiness.

MARI

Every winter that Joe was alive, we spent a week in Boynton Beach, Florida, visiting his mother, Carla Roselli.

Joe's firefighter father had died of lung cancer a few years before I met Joe, and Carla had sold her own home in Rock Harbor and headed South. The house Carla sold was the one Joe had grown up in, which was located a few blocks from the bungalow Joe inherited from his father's only sister. I never asked Joe aloud why—as an adult—he wanted to live in the inherited bungalow and let go of the home he had grown up in. Joe used to invite his mother to come visit us and the girls in Rock Harbor, but she always had an excuse for why she could not come North. The excuses usually involved tennis, bridge club, and the fact that her son had married a dark-skinned woman from Guatemala.

This last part was never said out loud of course. But it could be felt by all of us.

Joe stopped inviting Carla, and instead we took the girls down to Florida every winter for a week so that they could know their only living grandparent on neutral soil.

The visits were generally tense, and filled with awkward moments, where Carla would address only Joe—as if I had left the room.

"Joe, why didn't you tell me the girls were so big now? I'd have gotten their gifts in larger sizes."

"Joe, how is our old house? Are the new owners taking good care of it?"

"Joe, what does everyone eat these days? Shall I cook, or would everyone rather order some sort of take-out?"

And one time: "I hope the girls like the clothes I bought them. It's just so hard to know what color will look good on the twins, you know with their skin tone, and all."

I would suffer silently through the week, twist my worry dolls in my pocket with extra vigilance during the cool Florida nights, speak only when spoken to, and be respectful at all times. I would generally return to Rock Harbor with a sickness in my stomach. As much as I tried not to let it, Carla's disapproval weighed heavily on me. She was my husband's mother, knew him better than anyone alive, and she clearly did not approve of me.

Joe would apologize after each trip. "I know she's tough. Please try not to let it get to you. Please don't be angry with me. I will talk to her again."

But I wasn't angry at Joe. I wasn't even angry or resentful of Carla. After all, she simply seemed to sense the fact that I was unworthy of her son, and probably these girls. How could I argue with that?

On one trip south, when the girls were about seven or eight, Carla was more sullen than usual. Her Boynton Beach neighbor and dear friend, Ana, had cancer. An ugly English word. An even more ugly illness.

Carla moped about during that particular visit, and one morning I found myself alone with her in the kitchen, while I was trying to work the coffee maker and also find a shallow pan to make us all some eggs. "Ana's been in remission for years. That's the shocking part." I looked over my shoulder and saw that it was only Carla and me in the kitchen. I realized with a start that Carla was actually starting a conversation with me, something she very rarely did.

"Remission?" I wanted so much to have a conversation with Carla but her casual use of language often defeated me. "What is remission of cancer?" I asked.

"It was gone. Her cancer was just—gone. We had a party to celebrate last year and everything. She's been doing everything right. Everything her doctors told her to do. Eating no meat. Drinking those terrible tasting shakes made with kale and wheat grass and who knows what else? She's been exercising every day. Hell, she looks like she's about 45 again. "But this year, it came back. Remission over. Just like that."

"Just like that," I repeated, shaking my head, with an occasional crossing of myself. I continued stumbling around the kitchen, cracking eggs and whisking them into a breakfast food while Carla sat at her own kitchen table, staring emptily into her coffee mug. I stopped what I was doing to refill it, even though she didn't ask for more. And even though she didn't thank me for it.

We were quietly lost in our own thoughts as I stirred and scrambled eggs, and she stirred cream into her coffee, and I kept thinking these new words over and over again:

Cancer.

Remission.

I finally had some English words for my *own* experience. I had had a sort of cancer. Of the mind. And then Joe had saved me outside of a coffee shop and we had our girls and gradually, the cancer had gone away. But lately it seemed my worry dolls were having more and more trouble keeping their long-held secrets, and the remission of my mind was over.

Just like that.

I walked away from the restricted site as directed by the emergency personnel, and walked back through Mari's house to get to the back yard that separated her house from my illegal garage apartment. For some reason as I walked through the hallway to the kitchen that led out the back door—my eyes landed on a picture that I must have seen a million times coming in and out of this house but had never once touched with my hands. It was knocked on its side, so I picked it up and, as I did so, I stared long and hard at it.

A picture of me and Seamus and Rae. Arm in arm in arm—about 10 years old. Seamus—his now darker hair more auburn back then, his freckles so much more pronounced, sandwiched between two gangly dark-haired girls, who were still a hair taller than him then, identical but for the shape of their eyes and their smiles. My smile was more crooked and tentative. Rae's smile was full, confident, and easy. My mother's dark skin and round face had been reinterpreted on Rae and me by our father's Italian genes so that Rae and I shared the same olive skin and pointed chins. Our eyes reflected the dark cacao-colored irises that had been my mother's most beautiful feature always. It was the shape of our eyes that set Rae and me apart. Rae's were round—"the shape of the sun, Rae"—my mother would often point out. Mine were more oval—the "shape of a half moon, Luna"—my mother would say. And Rae would usually add then: "Half-moon? More like a squashed sun." And perhaps because the English was lost on her, or perhaps because it was true, Mari never corrected Rae when she said that.

If you missed the shape of our eyes, you could also tell

us apart because Rae had a heart-shaped splotch of a beauty mark covering her left cheek. I squinted to see Rae's eyes and the beauty mark in the picture as I held my finger over Seamus's lanky 10-year-old body in the middle of the frame. I forgot Mari even had this photograph. How had I never asked her to put it away? How had she kept it here under my nose all this time?

The photo—though not necessarily taken the same day—reminded me of a day we three were out back playing hide and seek.

⊚

"Lu! Seamus! Where are you? I'm giving up. I mean it. I'm not even playing anymore." Seamus and I were crouched behind an old piece of abandoned plywood leaning tenuously against the birch tree behind our house while Rae was supposed to be looking for us. We were no older than we were in the crashed picture in Mari's hallway. Seamus sat very still next to me—effortlessly so—and I tried to be similarly still even though I was crouching uncomfortably and my left leg was shaking a little with the awkward position. I didn't dare move. I was so close to Seamus; his hair was touching my cheek. I had to swallow the strangest sensation that was overcoming me to reach out and pluck a few strands of his auburn hair right out of his head.

After Rae yelled her give-up speech, I looked over at Seamus, to see his finger held up to his mouth in a "shush" sign. He needn't have. I wasn't going to give up our spot. I knew Rae was lying. Rae rarely gave up. It was one of the things I loved most about her. It was also one of the things Seamus loved most about her. I knew even then that Seamus would never love me the way he loved Rae.

After Rae died on 9/11, Seamus and I clung to each other. We started spending all of our free time together. And we'd pretend that there wasn't someone missing.

One night, when we were both 14, we were down in his basement watching a movie after finishing our homework.

I went upstairs at a commercial break to get Seamus and me two bottles of chocolate milk and saw that Mari had come over. She and Rebecca were drinking tea and eating Rebecca's famous homemade scones. "Oh. Do we have to leave?" I asked when I saw Mari, worried about why she might have come over to get me rather than letting me walk home as I usually did by 8 pm on school nights. "No, it's ok, Niña. You can stay for a little while longer. I just came over so you wouldn't have to walk home alone. It's getting dark earlier now." She took a bite of her scone and I watched some crumbs stick to the side of her mouth. I shook off an urge to walk over and wipe them away for her, and instead helped myself to two Yoo Hoo bottles from Rebecca's refrigerator door, inhaling deeply as I passed by her to see if I smelled wine on her that might explain her attentive behavior on that night. But no, just the sweet flowery scent of her perfume. I exhaled loudly with relief and headed down to the basement.

Downstairs Seamus gulped down a glass bottle of Yoo Hoo chocolate milk in two seconds. "That's disgusting," I said and threw a pillow at him from the opposite end of the couch. "I just did that so we can play spin the bottle." He looked at me out of the corner of his eye. My heart skipped a beat and I was glad the basement lighting was too dim for him to see me blushing.

"Don't you need more than two people to play that game?" I asked to cover up my nervousness.

"Not if you want to fix the game. Come on, Lu."

We sat on the floor across from each other and he spun the bottle between us. First it pointed to the futon, and then to the TV, but finally it pointed squarely at me, and Seamus leaned across the bottle to kiss me. I let him. The kiss was delicious and sweet and tender, but I couldn't ignore the fact that he reached up and brushed my cheek, the left one, in the exact place where Rae's faded, splotchy beauty mark was. Maybe it was just an unconscious thing on his part—but that's not really a great answer either.

☺

I shuddered at the memory of my long ago first kiss, opened my eyes and righted the picture of Seamus and me and Rae in Mari's hallway, and then walked around to the back of the house. I arrived in a fog to the area that lay between Mari's house and my garage apartment. There were no more F. B. I. agents bagging up evidence, but they seemed to have missed pieces of debris or deliberately left some behind. I wondered as I stared at it—what made a seat belt remnant hanging from the birch tree less valuable than whatever it was they had taken and bagged and marked in its place.

Bits of burned material and a piece of charred scrap metal in various colors were in the garden. I wasn't sure whether to touch them or not but I had an irrational rage that they had been left behind to contaminate Mari's gardening soil. I felt indignant on her behalf. She'd have to dig up all the soil and replace it. Or worse, move the garden to another side of the house altogether where neither the sun or the soil would be as perfect as the side she chose after years of trial and effort. Beach soil was fickle and Mari had spent many years discerning the perfect place for her garden. The garden had only just succeeded a year or so ago.

It was frustrating to listen to these nonsensical and trivial thoughts force themselves into my head at such a tragic time. And yet, it was comforting, too. The crowding of these thoughts and the active effort it took to push them out kept me from thinking about what had really happened.

That a plane had crashed right here on the corner where we lived.

That Mari had been home when it happened.

That I was supposed to be on that plane.

That Mari was missing—maybe even killed—and I was once again, the one who was left behind.

☺

A few minutes after I went inside my apartment, a reporter, who identified herself as being from *Time Magazine* came to my door asking questions.

Are you all right, Miss?

How are you coping?

This town is astounding in its ability to rebound from devastation and loss. I read somewhere that over 70 firefighters and first responders in the 9/11 tragedy were Rock Harbor residents ...

Do you agree that Rock Harbor will rise above the ashes after today's tragedy as well?

I was lonely enough that I welcomed her in. I made her a cup of tea—relieved in light of my lack of provisions when I found a solitary tea bag in the cupboard, and was informed by the reporter that she took her tea without milk or sugar. Over black tea, I told the reporter that I was supposed to be on the plane myself. She winced visibly when I said this, and I decided not to be angry at her for intruding on all of my sadness and grief, or even on my guilt. I let her stay for a little while and take pictures from my living room, while I exited the back door and headed to the beach.

I had no qualms about leaving the reporter alone unsupervised in my home. What could she take? What more could anyone take from me?

I walked on auto-pilot the two blocks from our house to the beach, and walked quietly along the waterline. Usually I didn't walk this close to the water after dusk, but the beach was backlit by the flood lights at Rock Harbor's own Ground Zero, and it seemed to give me some bravery to walk the water line. Or maybe I just didn't care anymore. With everyone gone—maybe it felt silly to care about something like walking too close to the ocean at dark, when crews of fire and rescue personnel were right now up the street locating the pilot and co-pilot in a smoky rubble, and identifying them as the last found victims of Flight 555.

MARI

One year for our anniversary, Joe bought me a new coffee maker. I knew that Joe thought the coffee machine was a romantic gesture in tribute to the very place that had brought us together, but it was a little too fancy and had all sorts of buttons, and a timer, and I found it very difficult to work, even when I read the part of the instructions that were written in someone's idea of translated Spanish.

The coffeemaker looked so awkward on our kitchen counter, taking up most of the white corian counter with its silver and black body. I would arrive in front of it each morning, not quite sure what to do with it, longing for the days when I got my coffee from a clerk in Manhattan.

Besides its fancy buttons and hard-to-work settings, the coffee machine drove me crazy because I couldn't figure out how to make a single cup of coffee. I would stand in front of it ready for a cup of coffee while it whirred and buzzed and brewed and finally started to spit out coffee. I would pull the carafe out and insert my mug anxious for a cup of coffee, but Joe would always correct me.

"Mari. It's not meant to be used like that. Let it finish brewing. Then you can pour it."

"I just want one." I always replied. It was excessive, this enormous pot.

Years after Joe died, Lu bought me my first single cup Keurig coffee maker, and looked up at me joyfully as I unwrapped it. "You've always wanted one of these. It will just make one cup, Mama!"

I could only nod sadly, at the irony of finally having a coffeemaker for one.

⑨

Lu.

Her face floats in front of me and I forget that I'm not actually seeing her. My eyes are closed, and while I tried to fix that at first, my heavy eyes keep resisting and I have simply accepted that they will be staying closed for now.

I hope Lu is all right.

Dios Mio—I am always leaving her on her own—my poor girl. I hope she knows I'm thinking about her.

Dios Mio—I hope she doesn't turn to Seamus for comfort. That boy. I love him. I do. Just not for Lu.

Oh! He reminds me of Nery. Far too much. I just realized that. For the first time, I just realized that *Seamus* reminds me of *Nery*. Always leaving. Or about to leave. Always with his heart in another place while it is pretending to be *here*.

I wish I had thought of that in time to say it out loud to Lu. Then again, I wish she had known about me and Nery. I think it might have helped Lu and me.

Funny that I'm only just now coming to that realization. Why did I never tell her about Nery?

Sigh.

I try to shake off the heaviness that is pinning me to this bed, its soft sheets, and all of my memories. But I just cannot do it. Nor do I want to.

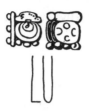

The first time Seamus and I made love, I felt mostly ... confused.

We were seniors in high school and he was headed off to college in a few short months. Afterward, we were lying in his bed with the house to ourselves for a few hours, while Rebecca was visiting her mother in a nursing home in Manhattan. "We'll still see each other after I leave for school," Seamus said off-handedly in response to no question I had asked, as if it was something *he* needed reassurance about rather than me.

"I know," I replied, thinking literally that he was my neighbor and Rebecca's son, so of *course* we'd be seeing each other.

"Do you ever think about 9/11, Seamus?" He flinched a bit like I'd hit him. I continued on nonetheless. "You never really talk about it. And ..." I stopped, in mid-sentence, wanting to ask the real questions, but not daring to.

Do you miss Rae, Seamus?

Are you only with me, Seamus, because I'm the one who's here while Rae is not?

I bit my tongue to keep from saying all I wanted to say, and instead said simply, "I'm sorry." To which, Seamus said nothing, but just nodded.

Which as I said, left me feeling mostly ... confused.

This past summer, just a few short months before the plane crash, Seamus announced that he would be moving to Los Angeles after graduation, which was, after some delays, apparently happening this December. "I'll believe it when I see it," I said when he told me. The graduating part, not the moving to LA.

I knew he was leaving—I'd known that much for a while now. I wasn't tying him here to Rock Harbor. No one was. He had his own plan—he was going to hook up with some connections he had out West—to try his hand as an intern at an up and coming sports agency. I had to admit, that seemed like something Seamus could in fact be good at, if he could just get his foot in the door.

He told me over dinner one night. As if I had no say in the matter whatsoever.

And so I didn't.

I just pushed my food around my plate until Seamus asked for the check, and I said, "Well, I guess that's it, then."

And he said, "What? Did you want dessert?"

And I laughed—became borderline hysterical actually—at the ridiculousness of the question. I marveled at the disconnect between Seamus and myself that had always been there and would likely always be there. But still my heart hurt with a pain I hadn't known in many, many years. "Why are you laughing?" Seamus asked. "Are you laughing *at* me? At this decision?"

"I'm sorry." I stopped laughing and wiped my face on my napkin.

"Well, ok then."

"No. I'm not apologizing to you. I'm apologizing to *me*. How could I have wasted this on you?" It had been ten years since our first kiss over the glass bottle in Seamus's basement. The memory caught up to me as it often did, and propelled me to keep scolding Seamus. "Memories and moments for an entire decade. On you? These are the only ones I'll have of this time. And they're full of *you*. And that was a mistake. On my part."

Seamus nodded but his expression told me he still didn't really understand, and for the first time, I didn't feel like the only confused one in this relationship.

MARI

There's a new smell in the room. Faintly antiseptic with a cool wave of vanilla ... and also raw steaks.

Steaks?

I wonder if I'm imagining that part.

Ok, if you must know, I had a crush on the Rock Harbor butcher. I did. Even before Joe died, I had a crush on that butcher. Lu used that word once when she went with me to buy steaks and I blushed as the white-haired butcher handed me my steaks wrapped in brown paper and called me beautiful with his customary greeting. "Here you go, Beautiful Mari. Enjoy your steaks. Think of me when you cook them tonight!" And as the butcher called after me, I ushered Lu out while she rolled her eyes: "Mama! That's gross. You have a crush on the butcher."

"What's this crush?" I had asked her.

"You like him. He makes you smile. You know, you *like* him."

It's true, he made me smile. He was one of the few who could do that. On Rock Harbor everyone smiled, and I always *tried* to smile back—but I could never muster the same genuine enthusiasm they all seemed to be able to summon without much effort.

From the day I came to live in that bungalow Joe had inherited from his childless aunt, I acknowledged that Rock Harbor was a beautiful town on a beautiful island. That much I couldn't deny. No one could. An island handwrought by primarily two immigrant populations—Irish Catholic and Italian Catholic—and now inhabited by the subsequent generations of those same immigrant families, handing down beach bungalows and beachfront property in a small oasis that was just 10 miles south of New York City. Never more than five blocks between the bay and the ocean throughout the entire length of the island, the water and warm sand seemingly wrapped all of its hard-working residents in a warm hug. All of its residents except me.

And to tell you the truth, I was never sure if the the problem was *only* the color of the ocean, but certainly one of the most wrong things on Rock Harbor—in my opinon—*was* the color of the ocean. It was not crystal blue like I had heard the water would be here in America nor was it the green/blue color of the forest bordered seas I was used to seeing in Guatemala. It was instead a brownish-blue, presumably from eons of washing up against the dark rocks all along its inlet that gave the island its proud name.

It was the color of the ocean I told myself when my sadness overwhelmed me. It was frequent in those early years, just after the twins were born. I missed … home.

The loneliness and fear and worry overtook me almost daily. I'd reach my hand into the pocket of my dress, searching for one of the worry dolls that I kept in there every day, and I'd twist it around and around in my hand, with a sort of a prayer. *Please. Let it be only the color of the ocean that is wrong. Let it be nothing else. Let me start over truly.* But the dolls didn't answer and they didn't change things. They simply worried along with me as I never really handed over my worries to them, but rather shared my worries with them, like old friends.

Every morning after I would go to the market or the butcher or the bank or some other of my dozens of errands each week, I would paint in the garage outside the Rock Harbor home I shared with Joe and the babies. I'd pay one of several neighbors $10 to sit with the babies and rock them for hours—a task I knew in my heart that *I* should be doing and should not be delegating to strangers—and I'd head instead to the garage that I shared with no one. Joe agreed to keep his beloved car parked on the street. Even though Joe was unapologetic about his devotion for the orange painted car, still he relented to allow my own space after the babies arrived. The car—with its shiny metal adornments and "JOESVETTE" license plate was whipped mercilessly by wind that carried sand and salt from the nearby beach—debris that had to be eliminated carefully in Joe's hand waxing sessions that occurred weekly—and not coincidentally—before church every Sunday like they were simply an extension of religious fervor. Even though all of these things were true, still Joe allowed me my space in the garage. To paint.

And I was grateful in my own way even though I hated the space and cursed it every time I entered it. Because of its uninsulated walls, the drafts and extreme heat—depending on the season—would attack me the minute I'd enter. The cement floor seemed always cold—despite the season—and I'd sink into it when I arrived in the garage on days when the sadness attacked me more viciously than others. Even though I hated the space—hated that Joe had to sacrifice a place for his car to give it to me—and hated that I needed it— I did. I needed it. Daily. I'd retreat there and paint for hours— lost in my world of canvas and paints. I swirled my knife on the palate and the canvas and back again—in a violent dance to try to rid myself of the worries. I'd paint and paint, blue and green oceans—never brown.

It's just the color of the ocean that's bothering me, I told myself as I painted miles and miles of canvases filled with blue and green forest oceans from memory and from dreams. There were years I painted nothing else besides ocean scenes, because the other things that came to mind seemed much too personal. And true.

The painting helped. As the twins emerged from toddlerhood, I continued to paint. Boats on the horizon, running children on the beach, even Joe's orange car. Scenes from our life found their way onto the canvas, and the painting helped in a way even my worry dolls could not. We were happy for years until the darkness started to creep its way back in. In the years just before 9/11, I started painting the ocean again. My paintings were dark and light depending upon my moods, which I could never quite get control of.

And then one day—a few months after 9/11—I painted a huge platter of steaks. I took it to the butcher to hang in his shop. But he wasn't there. He had closed the shop. I found out later that his wife had also died on 9/11. And I mourned that he was gone, too, along with so much else that I had lost.

So yes, I loved Joe Roselli, but I had a crush on the butcher. He was a man on the island who called me beautiful and made me smile occasionally. So be it. I never felt badly about that. Because it had always been hard for me to smile on that island, but after September 11th, it became nearly impossible.

Our sixth-grade Social Studies teacher, Miss Bouther, was very innovative. Very creative. Rae and I both loved her. When we got to the lesson about the Great Depression, we didn't just talk about the stock market crash, we relived it. We learned about the market, and investing, and the value of money. We learned about how the American economy has always done better when it relies on its people, and the value of making things, rather than on the pretend value of currency.

"Very progressive," my dad used to call her.

In 2001, we ended the school year with a final semester-long project. It counted as half of our grade. We each invested $20,000 of play money in the market at the beginning of the semester, and wrote essays on why we chose the stocks we did, and what we anticipated happening at the end of June at the close of the quarter, and most companies' fiscal years. Miss Bouther had taught us things like fiscal years and dividends, and we really enjoyed the project.

I lost most of my money but still got an A in Miss Bouther's class. Rae got an A, too. But she made $1,800. Go figure.

In July, Miss Bouther, wrote our whole class individual notes, letting us know that every last one of us had gotten a 100% on the semester-long stock assignment. She was so impressed with our efforts that she had arranged a very special field trip at the beginning of the following school year to celebrate our accomplishments. We were headed to an investment firm at the World Trade Center in New York City where we'd eat in their fancy company cafeteria and get out of school for the entire day. Our parents had to sign the permission form that was enclosed with the handwritten note from Miss Bouther.

I wish I had kept that note.

⑨

On September 11, 2001, I was up early the day of the field trip, not able to sleep. My dad had signed the permission slip for both Rae and me, but I was petrified of going into the city for the class trip. Rae didn't seem nervous at all.

"Aren't you worried, Rae? That we won't know where to go or what to do when we get there? I'm worried I'll lose you. We can't separate even for a minute today. Promise me."

"Geez, Lu, you suffocate people, you know that? Some-times, I really can't wait to get away from you. You and Rock Harbor. Far, far away."

I wanted to hurt her back so I said: "Why are you even going? You complained about the assignment from Day 1. You practically cheated off mine."

"I did not. I just looked at what you invested in, and I in-vested in the opposites." Rae looked almost scornful.

"The opposites?"

"Yes, when you invested in Staples, I invested in Office Depot. When you invested in Starbucks, I invested in Dunkin Donuts." She was triumphant with her logic until I pointed out that Dunkin Donuts was not even a public company. I knew because I had checked before investing in Starbucks.

Rae dismissed me. "Well, anyway—if you're just going to spend the whole day worrying yourself silly, I really don't want you there. It will just be a black cloud on my day—and I literally cannot wait. It's going to be the best day of my entire life. And Seamus is going, too. And it will be the first time he's ever even been to Manhattan—can you imagine? And so I'm probably going to be hanging out with him more than you—and then you'll whine and tell Mama and Dad on me, so ..."

"Rae, I get it. I don't want to go on this stupid trip any-way. I want to go into the city when Dad can take me and it can be something fun—like Serendipity or something."

"Serendipity?"

I remember just the word got her a little. And I felt so vindicated by her reaction. She still remembered Serendipity and the promise of a golden sundae, and the way we had laughed sodas out our noses over the red-haired waitress who called Dad "Prince Charming." We had a moment then, a moment of connection over ice cream and memories and Dad and what that whole day all those years before was meant to make us forget.

I looked over my shoulder down the hall toward Mari's room. Dad had left for work already, and Mari was still in bed. Rae and I would be walking ourselves to school early to meet Miss Bouther and the rest of our group for the field trip. *If* I decided to go.

I vowed right there on the spot to bring up the good memories more. To bring up Serendipity more. To make Dad take us there again. To ask Dad to pull us out of school on one sunny Tuesday and take the train and stand in line for an hour debating which of the tourists would buy only frozen hot chocolates and which would stay for lunch, too. We would do that and more from now on. We wouldn't wait for Mari to get better. We wouldn't wait for tomorrow. We'd do it all now.

"I'm skipping the field trip," I said, as I pulled my school uniform on. "I'll just stay in the classroom with the other losers who couldn't convince their parents to sign the permission slips."

"Good," Rae said. "I'm glad you're not going. Now I can wear this."

And with that, she snatched up my favorite navy linen pants and tan cardigan twinset that I had laid out the night before to wear for the field trip.

MARI

It was a miracle that Lu did not go into New York City that September day. No other explanation in my eyes.

When Rebecca came pounding on my door that morning asking if I'd heard the news, I felt the floor disappear under me. Rebecca had Seamus with her. He had apparently missed the field trip bus and she was just about to drive him into the city to catch up with the class at the World Trade Center when they heard the news on the car radio.

We three drove together to the school to see what news they had about the kids, and Lu came running out of her classroom in tears when she saw me. "Lu! Thank God! You girls didn't go after all." I hugged and hugged her, weeping into her hair. "Where's Rae?" She just kept shaking her head, and I continued asking "Lu. Tell me. Where is Rae?" I asked and asked until Rebecca stopped me. I held Lu out at the end of my arms and her eyes looked haunted. I stared at her trying to figure out why, until I realized it was my own reflection that I was seeing there.

"Mari, let's just take the kids back to my house and wait for everyone to come back." Rebecca said, and as I remember it, I followed her soundlessly. I remember little else from the rest of that day.

The next day, as I awoke, I looked at Lu curled up in my bed wearing her school uniform from the day before, and I thought: *God is punishing me for everything I have done.*

Not by taking Joe and Rae away from me, but by leaving Lu here. Lying there on September 12, I thought: *When you fail at loving someone properly, fail at taking care of them the way you are supposed to, God doesn't take them away.*

He leaves them in your path as a constant reminder of your failure.

Later the same night, surrounded still by emergency generators, rescue personnel, and heavy machinery thuds, a wrinkled fire fighter showed up at my door while I was still awaiting news about Mari. He asked if I was Joe Roselli's daughter. He had known my father and his family, he said.

I just nodded wearily. I didn't even invite him in. We stared at each other for a while as if we were trying in vain for some point of mutual recognition.

He spoke finally.

"I'm so glad you are all right. When I realized where this was, how close Joe's house was to the crash scene, well, I just had to come make sure his family was all right."

"It's just me," I said, sounding like an apology to my ears. I didn't add—*and I'm far from all right.*

He seemed to understand anyway, though. He nodded wearily in return and turned in silence and headed back to the crash scene. Back to work.

As I stood at the door watching him walk away, I saw Officer Merry step out of a police car that had pulled up in front of my home. I saw him emerge out of the fog and smoke on the street corner and walk toward me.

"Lu?"

I was touched he remembered to use my preferred nickname.

"I found out about your mother."

I reached up and starting picking at my cardigan buttons again in response.

"She was transported to New York City Hospital in Manhattan shortly after the crash. She's alive—but—she was hit in the head by debris in the house during the crash and—she's not doing very well, I'm afraid. I'll take you there."

I didn't have the audacity to be cheerful that she was still alive. I just got in the police car solemnly and headed to the hospital to see Mari.

MARI

Carla Roselli died of a sudden heart attack in the spring of 2001. Well, I guess it wasn't exactly *sudden*. She had been a heavy smoker, refusing to quit even after lung cancer struck her husband down in his 50s, or after Ana died of cancer as well. Smoke rings used to fill that Florida house on our winter trips south and I would try to shuffle the girls outside away from Carla's puffs of smoke even as my own eyes would water and sting from the heavy air in the condo.

"I moved here for the clean air." Carla would exhale between drags on her cigarettes. No one corrected her or pointed out the strangeness of her words. I didn't want to be the first.

Outside of earshot, Joe would say that his mother had become such a "cliché."

"What is this cliché?" I asked.

"It's something that is just so ordinary—so common—that it's ridiculous."

"Like what, Joe? What things are so ordinary in America that they are ridiculous?"

"Not you, Mari," he laughed and kissed the top of my head. "Nothing ordinary about you."

When Carla Roselli died that spring, Joe went down to clean out the house and get it ready to sell, and when he returned home, he brought a will that Carla's lawyer had given to him. Tricia was now Matthew's wife with a high-powered law firm job in the city. She came over one night as a favor to Joe and me to help us sort through the paperwork. Carla had left most of her estate to Joe directly. I tried not to notice that it was left only to Joe and alternately to the local humane society in Florida—no mention of either me or the girls. Tricia tried not to notice either, instead focusing on the fact that Joe was an only child, and that there would be no one contesting the estate. "So this will all wrap up fairly quickly," Tricia had said before adding, "I see some estates get mired down in family fighting for years when there are multiple children involved." I remembered Tricia's resolution not to have any children, and indeed she still hadn't. I couldn't help but think that her experience with grown children fighting over their parents' money had only strengthened the resolve she had revealed to me all those years before.

In the end, Carla did leave a small piece of costume jewelry each to all three of us—the girls and me—which surprised no one more than me. The girls twirled their necklaces around on each of their necks watching them glitter and shine and it made me happy to see them so joyful. "Thanks, Gram!" They had both said with eyes up to the sky like they could just about see her.

Later that year, when I prepared for the joint memorial service for both Rae and Joe, I found myself thinking kind thoughts about Carla Roselli—namely that it was a blessing she had passed away that spring. She wouldn't have to come to the memorial of her own son.

It was frustrating to plan the memorial even though we had nothing to bury of Joe other than a picture of him in his firefighter gear taken shortly after we had been married. And while I wanted to have but one memorial service, it was a difficult decision for me to have a funeral for Joe without proof. It felt far too familiar—like he was one of the "disappeared" from Guatemala. I tried to explain that to the officials who would contact me periodically. In my country, during the war, hundreds of thousands of men and women had disappeared without a trace.

"Please," I found myself begging one woman from the medical examiner's office whom I spoke with frequently. "Please give me some news."

I was actually grateful when—almost a year later—we received word that some of Joe's remains had been identified in the North Tower rubble. I exhaled that day. For the first time in a long time, I felt some pressure in my chest lift, and I felt relief. Some short-lived relief.

Of course, even without proof, I knew from the earliest hours of September 11, that Joe was gone. I felt his absence in my soul as surely as I felt Rae's, so I went ahead with the service—one service to honor both Joe and Rae. I put the inherited costume jewelry on as I prepared for the memorial, so that Carla would be present in some small way at her son's funeral. *No mother should have to bury her child*, I repeated the chorus over and over even as I prepared to bury my husband and daughter.

I wondered, too, where the costume piece had even come from since I had never seen Carla wear any jewelry when she was alive. And in fact, the day I opened the box of Carla's jewelry was the first time it occurred to me that there may have been a Carla that neither I nor Joe had known. A woman with pains and heartaches and decorations that she had not shown to her children or grandchildren. I have wondered about that woman—*that* Carla—on many occasions since then—and have even regretted not talking to Carla more in life.

I regret having not asked more questions about her life before all of us.

I regret having not shown Lu and Rae more of my life before all of *them*.

I had often talked about being homesick to Joe, and he usually responded by asking whether I wanted to take the girls back there and show them my birthplace. But that's not what I wanted.

I loved my home and missed it, but there were far too many complications to going home again. My father and stepmother died a few years after I left, so eventually there wasn't even any family to introduce my daughters to. Other than Sister Magdalena, of course.

But recently, I wanted Lu to go to Guatemala. I wanted her to finally hear my story from Sister Magdalena.

And I know that sounds cowardly, but honestly it wasn't that I was afraid to tell her what had happened. I wanted her to know why I had left my home. Why I had done what I did. But I wanted her to *believe* it.

I figured that after all those years of hiding it, she would hear it all as an excuse or an ill-fitting apology coming from me. And that's not what I wanted. I wanted her to hear it as the *truth*.

LU

"So essentially Mari is in a coma?"

"Yes, she is."

The room was filled with white coats. I kept looking around for a badge, expecting more comic names in this tragic theatre to go along with Officer Merry and Agent Love. But none of the doctors or nurses had visible nametags. They all wore various-colored medical scrubs embroidered with City Hospital on the chest and lanyards which presumably contained their names and photos but were all twisted around on their necks. All of these twisted, dangling lanyards with hidden names were distracting me from completely understanding what the scrubs-wearing people were saying for quite a while.

Mari was alive, yes.

But she had suffered a severe head injury. Apparently, she had been lying in bed when the plane crashed and a heavy painting of the ocean—one of her own actually—in a gilded gold frame came crashing down on her because of the vibrations caused by the plane crash.

She hadn't been killed by the plane crashing—but she had been gravely injured at the moment of impact nonetheless. It seemed like one of those odd things that could only happen to us. To Mari.

"So when will she wake from her coma?" I asked the doctor in the middle—choosing to address him for no reason other than that the lobbing of my head back and forth among the people in the room was starting to hurt my neck.

The doctor in the middle sighed and rubbed his eyebrows, something I irrationally took as a good sign. I can't explain why. I just did. Which is why I was surprised when he followed up the eyebrow rubbing with: "She might not."

"What do you mean by that?"

"Your mother is in a vegetative state. You need to understand what her prognosis is. The likelihood that she will ever wake is quite low."

Quite low.

His words crashed into me violently, and I sat far back in my chair. "Can she hear me? Can I talk to her?"

"The correct physician response here is no. She's not responsive and she's not aware, and I need to tell you that."

"Is there a 'but' there?"

"Yes. She's exhibiting some strange eye flutters and erratic hand squeezing that defies the dysfunction we are reading of her cerebral hemispheres on MRI. It's not uncommon for a patient in a persistent vegetative state to have some complex reflexes—eye movements, yawning for example—but this is a bit different."

"Oh." I leaned forward to pat his hand reflexively, seeming to startle the doctor in the middle. "You need to know that this is Mari. She does everything a bit differently. Good to know that up front if you are going to be taking care of her for the long haul." I thought I detected a smile cross the good doctor's eyes and lips, before he turned very somber again—apparently hell bent on making me understand that this was bad. That Mari was in bad shape and that things were, you know, very, very bad.

"There's more."

I was still looking at the doctor in the middle, but I realized his lips were not moving. Someone else to the left of him was talking. Repeating the words: "There's more."

A woman's voice. I turned to find its owner.

A woman sitting off to the side was watching me carefully. A woman I suddenly remembered as having introduced herself as a social worker. "I just graduated with my degree in social work, too," I had replied buoyantly when she introduced herself—as if this were a job interview or a networking event.

"More?" I asked her.

"In running your mother's blood work at admission, the physicians have discovered that she is pregnant. We estimate about 23 weeks pregnant actually."

I choked a bit. This news was more shocking than the head injury, the persistent vegetative state, and the "quite low" likelihood that she would ever wake.

How on earth?

I tried to count backwards—replaying the last 23 weeks on fast rewind. Were there any signs?

My 44-year-old mother was pregnant. I kept repeating the words in my head. It took a while for those words to change shape. Eventually they became: *My mother is having a baby.*

"What will happen? To the baby, I mean?" I asked aloud finally.

"Well, there is some precedent for this. Women have been able to give birth while in comas in a few cases. In fact, in 2001, a Kentucky woman, named Chastity Cooper, carried her baby for months while in a coma following a car crash."

"2001?" I seized on that year always when mentioned in conversation, as if it had some unique connection to me.

The social worked looked at me confused, but continued nonetheless. "Even if your mother never—even if her condition remains as it is currently, she can still carry the baby to term, we believe. Given her age, the doctors have run the requisite tests and both she and the baby are actually in good health, you know, considering."

Considering her steady diet of white wine, Ambien, and neglect? I bit my tongue before the words slid past it.

One of the doctors in the middle began talking again, demanding my attention in the middle of the room. "Yes, all signs currently point to a high likelihood of success of allowing her to carry the baby to term. Her natural due date is probably early February."

"And then what? What will happen to the baby, if Mari doesn't—if she can't—"

"Well, that's why I have been assigned to this case." The social worker was talking again now. "There will be decisions that need to be made. Guardianship. Custody. Adoption."

The weight of decisions I didn't want to make began to press down on my chest. "You mean we need to find a family to adopt the baby?"

"Is that—what you think she would want?" The social worker was asking me this question and all of the other faces in the room were looking at me deliberately.

I laughed a short abrupt laugh—another of many moments of misplaced hysteria throughout this long day. "What my mother would want? How the hell would I know what she would want? I don't know who the father is. I don't even know if she knew she was pregnant. What I do know is that my mother had twin daughters, and she never really seemed to want *them*. So how would I know what she wants to do with this one?"

The social worker leaned over and wrote something down on her pad of paper and I thought: *Guess I won't be getting any letters of recommendation from her down the road.* I stood up and walked to the back of the room of white coats where there remained one kindly face left in my opinion. This was officially too much. I turned to Officer Merry. "Please take me home. I just need a little sleep. I can deal with all of this tomorrow. Please."

Officer Merry drove me home in silence, and I headed straight to my garage apartment, where there was surprisingly very little evidence of a plane crash, a nearly-dead mother, or a new baby on the way. The rescue personnel had not come inside, and everything seemed relatively untouched. The minimal décor of my apartment was undisturbed. The few paintings—all of which had been painted by Mari—were still on the wall, and nothing looked like it had been disturbed by the crash.

As I looked around, everything looked relatively un-scathed in fact. Until I caught a glimpse of myself in a mirror. My bloodshot eyes, sooty black hair, and tear-streaked face in the reflection made me look every bit the lone survivor that I was.

Again.

MARI

I love sunrise on the beach at Rock Harbor. I love the majesty and the colors. I love that every day is different—a little bit different, no matter how reliable sunrise is.

And in those early days after Joe and Rae died, I convinced myself that I was living—that I was being adventurous because here I was on the beach with a different sunrise every day, feeding Lu and doing her laundry and sending her off to school and caring for someone other than myself. I was making appearances at King Kullen and trying not to cut off the Saturday-Morning Dads.

I was stepping outside of myself. Even though my brain always felt like it was clamping shut. I tried to describe that feeling to Lu every now and then when I'd have to take to my room for the rest of the day, but she didn't understand. I didn't have Joe as my buffer anymore. I had to show more and more of my pain to Lu. I knew that she was starting to resent me and so I kept trying to put on a brave face.

I kept waking every morning. Every. Single. Morning.

I told myself all of this showed incredible bravery. I actually said that out loud as I went about my day and counted my steps on the beach each morning and at afternoon and even at dusk, counting down the minutes until each day was over.

For many years, I spent most of my days counting, counting, counting, and waiting for the darkness to arrive and swallow me back up.

PART II

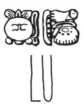

The next day after sleeping fitfully with the weight of Mari's condition and the baby news settling deep into my consciousness, I woke early to pack for a day at the hospital. I stockpiled water bottles and Mari's favorite hand cream from her bathroom medicine cabinet: Clinique Happy. I grabbed a notepad to take notes. I scribbled a list of questions to ask the doctors. I would not be someone's daughter today. I had just finished my degree in social work the spring before the plane crash, and I would be the social worker for a 44-year-old pregnant and comatose woman today, I resolved. I would make hard decisions and stick by them.

The problem was—I wasn't exactly known for sticking to things.

After taking a year off after high school to sulk around the island, I enrolled in Rock Harbor's Community College. Seamus had already been studying at a university in Pennsylvania for a year by then, and I started college with few aspirations besides leaving Mari alone for a few hours each day. A small trust fund that had been set up for me after 9/11 was more than enough to fund my new venture, and Mari, as executor, authorized checks with more glee than I had seen her muster in years. I wasn't sure if she was happy to be doing something for me, or happy to help me leave.

I switched my major eight times in college. When I finally settled on social work with barely two years left to finish four years' worth of prerequisites, my college advisor said that I had "broken the record for indecisiveness among co-eds." I thanked him before I realized he wasn't actually proud of me.

While it might have seemed natural that I would gravitate toward a field focused on vulnerable populations, the truth is I never really considered social work as a field of study, let alone a career, until I sat in on Dr. Vell's talk during my third year of college.

Dr. Vell was visiting from England and she had written some pretty interesting articles. I was trying to impress my new sociology professor who had handed out the flyer for Dr. Vell's talk in class.

First memories.

All of Dr. Vell's research was on first memories. Everyone's first memory, she hypothesized, affected everything that came next. The thing, the people, the event, the connection you make at the time you are first forming your memories becomes the thing that affects everything after.

"It's not nature. It's nurture," she said definitively. Controversially. "No one is born as they will be. It's those first memories that shape you as you grow. That nurture you."

I remember she was looking right at me when she said that. And for a moment, I thought she could see.

Could actually *see* my first memory.

I shuddered in my seat visibly, causing the gentleman next to me to offer his coat. His malodorous tweed coat that smelled like it had been offered to far too many people. I shook my head rudely and kept my eyes on Dr. Vell.

When Dr. Vell entertained questions at the end of her talk, I raised my hand. "Yes," she said. "You in the orange sweater. By the way," she interrupted my permission to speak by turning to the crowd at large. "There is always one person at each talk I give that catches my eye. I end up delivering my speech to that one person as a representative of the whole. An old orator's trick I was taught in high school debate. Tonight it was this lovely lady. She represents all of you tonight. So, lovely lady in orange—what have you to ask me?" She looked amused.

I waved off the thought that I could represent anyone, let alone an auditorium of sociology students, asking my question before I lost my nerve. "Couldn't it be instead that the reason your *first* memory *becomes* your first memory is because your very nature—formed at birth—makes you susceptible to this particular moment? In other words, isn't it, Doctor—a bit of a chicken and egg argument?"

Dr. Vell looked amused still.

"Interesting. Well, what is your first memory, dear?" Dr. Vell put me on the spot, and I sat frozen and silent in my highly visible orange sweater in the middle of the auditorium. "Do you care to share?" Dr. Vell seemingly punished me for challenging her in front of a room full of participants. But I decided to play along nonetheless. I racked my brain for my first memory.

It wasn't truly my first memory. I had plenty of other memories I could have called upon—happy memories, memories of my mother and father dancing, memories of my mother smiling and cooking before all the chaos settled over our lives. Instead, I told Dr. Vell that my first memory was when my sister and I were fighting over worry doll boxes, convinced that we had no need for the worry dolls themselves. Two girls for whom—until that very moment standing with their mother and the woven bits of thread fashioned into dolls—had never given a thought to the fact that maybe they should worry. And that from that moment on, those girls did nothing *but* worry.

Until one of them died, leaving the other to worry in her place.

I admitted all of this to Dr. Vell, the man next to me with the smelly tweed coat, and the rest of my class.

Dr. Vell nodded as if I had just proven her right, and while I wasn't quite sure how, in that moment ... I believed her. It had nothing to do with birth. It was what we were born into.

Nurture was the answer.

It was then that I decided to officially major in social work, catching up on my prerequisites in record time. But bystanders who misinterpreted my path as ambitious would be proven wrong by the fact that five months after graduation, I was still just a 23-year-old woman trying to figure out a better use for my degree than analyzing Mari's and my relationship, and pouring coffee as a waitress at a café in town. Even that waitressing job was on hold as I had taken a leave to head off to Guatemala for a few weeks.

My boss, Mr. Sheehan, at the café had greeted the news that I was leaving with enthusiasm. "Of course, Lu, I always knew the time would come when you would head out into the world and make your way, becoming my favorite customer instead of my favorite waitress. Slainte!"

"Oh no, Mr. Sheehan, it's just a few weeks' vacation. I want to come back here at the end of October."

Mr. Sheehan looked disappointed as he said, "Well, sure, Lu. You can come back anytime you need to."

Looks like I'll be needing to, Mr. Sheehan.

Just before I left the house for the hospital, I walked by a picture of my father in his firefighter gear on Mari's bedroom nightstand—a copy of the picture we buried in lieu of remains. The same photo I had found my mother holding in her bed crying to on so many nights following the funeral. One such night, I had looked at my mother's wet and wrinkled face and asked her the question I was afraid to hear the answer to.

"Mama, do wish he was still here? Do you wish things were different and that he was still here?"

"Of course, Niña. I wish everything was different. What I wouldn't give to have him back."

Years later, I remembered those words like a punch in the gut because I was the only one who knew. Knew why he wasn't here. That was a secret I'd take to *my* grave, I always swore.

I took my father's photo from the nightstand and packed it in the bag I was taking to the hospital, and as I turned the lights out in Mari's room, I had a strange thought that would have made Dr. Vell proud:

I wonder what Mari's first memories were.

MARI

I have been thinking of my mother a lot lately. For so long it hurt to think about her and so I kept her from every thought. But lately, she is with me all the time.

When I was a child, my father owned a hotel on the banks of Semuc Champey near Lanquin in Guatemala. There were lush springs and waterfalls within walking distance of the hotel. The English brochure declared it the "most beautiful spot in the world." Few disagreed when they arrived.

We were a tourist hotel. Guatemalans never stayed with us. But Americans and Europeans—young men and women from far away—they did. They came in erratically, as Semuc Champey was hard to get to—a whole day's trip from the more popular Lake Atitlan area. But when the tourists did come, they had money to spend, and spend they did. My mother and I did all of the cooking and cleaning at the hotel. We spent all our time together and my first memories of childhood are largely about cleaning alongside my mother as she told me stories of her own childhood.

We would cook all sorts of meals together, but the one that stands out the most these days was the *fiambre* we would make every year on November 1, *Dia de los Muertos*, (*the Day of the Dead*). The *fiambre* was typical in Guatemala and not unlike the enormous salads Joe used to get on Italian holidays from the Rock Harbor deli that he called *antipasti*. The *fiambre*, too, was a salad, and was supposed to be mixed from many different ingredients. Mama said that usually many family members were meant to bring ingredients to mix together. But since we had no other family, we would mix the ingredients ourselves. Sausages and meats, pickled baby corn, beets, onions, chicken, pacaya flower. It was as lovely as it was delicious, and I would help my mother clean and slice and chop until we had created something almost too beautiful to eat. My mother would pray over the *fiambre* for lost and gone family members. I would watch her reverently as she shed some tears, and my father would exhale with impatience and interrupt her prayer by slicing into the salad with a large wooden serving spoon.

We were wealthy for Guatemalan standards, which were not very high standards at that time. Guatemala was in the midst of a civil war, but we did not talk about that much to the Americans and Europeans who came to stay with us. My father was not at all political—deliberately, as he was a businessman—but my mother had many opinions. She would share them with me as we made beds and cooked dinner side by side. My father would tell her to "hush, Luna!" He would protest that her words would get us all killed one day.

She gradually became quieter around my father. My mother, however, never hushed around me. While we worked, my mother told me that she had seen terrible things. She had seen her own brothers set on fire for protesting the inhumane conditions imposed by the Guatemalan government. She told me, too, of the "disappeared." The people who had gone missing—killed or maybe worse—for aligning themselves with the insurgency. My two older brothers were among them. They had disappeared or died when I was only a toddler. I had no memory of them at all.

Despite all the horrors she had witnessed, my mother told me that she *rooted* for the insurgency. She hoped America would help Guatemala. She had what I considered an odd love for a far-away country that she had never been to—like a godfather who would come save us. She treated the Americans who came to visit us as if they were special, and I began to do the same.

Often, I asked her how she could have so much hope in spite of everything she had seen. And she smiled and sang to me. She told me it was all about perspective. "You can see it all as the end or just the beginning," she said. "It's up to you."

When I was 15, my father came into my room one morning to tell me very simply that my mother was gone—that she had died. There was no funeral. There was no goodbye. There was simply, as he put it, "work to do."

I couldn't get out of my bed for three days—I was so paralyzed with grief. I was certain that my mother had been "disappeared" by the government. For nights on end, I woke in my bed sheets drenched with sweat after having dreams of my mother surrounded by flames and darkness.

I would call out to her, "Mama, Mama." But no one came. Not even my father.

I tried to explain to my father that my mother was not dead, but rather had been taken away from us. "We have to find her, Papa. We have to go look for her."

In response, he called me stupid and told me to stop saying such things or I would be sorry. But, I couldn't stop, and my father lost patience with me. One day, my father hired a woman from nearby Lanquin to live with him and cook and clean for the tourists, and sent me to an orphanage called "House of Mercies" hours away, outside Lake Atitlan where I would live and work for a small wage that was sent directly home to him.

"House of Mercies" was run by nuns who had traveled to Guatemala from around the world, but there was one nun—Sister Magdalena—originally from America. She was the one who changed my life.

Well, she and Nery, really. It's hard to know which of the two had the bigger impact, frankly.

LU

At the hospital, I rubbed Mari's "Happy" lotion on her hands and forearms, amazed at how serene she looked. She appeared less bloated somehow, which I attributed to the hospital care. The right side of her head was bandaged due to a head wound caused by a crashing picture frame. The bandaged portion was not the problem, the attending doctors had informed me when I questioned them. It was the injury inside her brain that had caused all of this. The injury no one could actually see.

As I rubbed the sweet-smelling lotion into Mari's hands, I admired—as I often did—her slender fingers and the unlined backs of her hands. Mari had beautiful hands that could often be seen crossing herself throughout the day when things were going well. And when things weren't going well. And just because.

As I massaged her hands, I smiled in spite of myself, thinking about how sometimes I said things to aggravate Mari on purpose just to watch the motions of her hands moving up and down her face, her eyes closing and opening in rhythm with her beautiful olive-colored hands.

I continued massaging the "Happy" lotion into her forearm, tracing letters as I did so.

M
A
R
I.

I smiled as the old muscle memory came to me. And then I frowned again, remembering.

When we were little girls, late at night when we were supposed to be sleeping, Rae and I would trace letters on each other's back. Spelling out secret words and stifling giggles so our parents wouldn't come in and yell at us.

S
E
A
M
U
S.

"Seamus? You love Seamus?" Rae whispered one night as I traced his name on her back.

"No! You do." I treaded carefully. I wanted Rae to say I could have him. I knew she didn't really love him, and I wanted her to say it so we could stop pretending and then I could have Seamus.

"Oh Lu, I can't love Seamus. He's a momma's boy and he is a coward."

"He is not!" I yelled defensively, and Rae shushed me even louder.

"SHHHH!! Don't wake up Mama ... or she'll send Dad in here to yell at us. Can you WHISPER??"

I lowered my voice to a strained whisper. It was hard to be indignant and quiet at the same time. "He is not a coward, Rae. How can you even say that about him? You're horrible."

"Oh good lord, don't tell me you love Seamus?"

"No, I don't. We're friends. We're all friends. Aren't we?"

"Well, it's hard to all be friends when someone loves someone else."

"I don't love him, Rae. Stop saying that." The physical effort of keeping my voice down was hurting my throat. I massaged it and cleared my throat quietly.

"You're *loco*. I'm talking about Seamus." Rae said.

"You think Seamus loves me?" I said in a too-loud voice and braced myself for Rae's loud and mean shush.

But instead came Rae's loud and mean, "No silly, Seamus. Loves. Me."

MARI

As a 15-year-old girl helping out at the House of Mercies orphanage, I made few friends.

Nery and I however became fast friends. Nery was a local Mayan orphan a few years older than me who was living and working at the House of Mercies. Nery helped clean and do repairs around the aging and sagging building. He was not much taller than me, but he was so much stronger. He had thick black curls, broad hands and a square jaw that was usually covered in the beginnings of a beard that he never really had time or resources to shave away. I was always amazed that his broad hands could go from siding the orphanage to more delicate work around the building that was needed. And in fact, he even made small wooden boxes of worry dolls that the orphanage used to send out to far away benefactors as gratitude gifts.

Sister Magdalena would often assign me a list of chores that would end with: "And then check with Nery to see what else he needs help with." We worked together like that for nearly two years—time that flew by when I think back on it now.

Working closely with the only person even close to my age day in and day out made me talkative. I told Nery about my father's hotel and about the beautiful area that was Semuc Champey. I described the waterfalls and the lush beauty of the area.

"Do you miss it?" he asked.

"Not exactly. I miss being there with my mother."

I told Nery about my mother, and confessed that I was worried she had been disappeared. Or murdered. He wasn't shocked by this news, and instead set aside a few worry doll boxes for me, and told me to use them to sleep, as the war was not over yet. He had so many strong views on politics and the insurgency.

When he wasn't working around the orphanage, Nery painted all the time. He said it was so terrible to paint stripes and dots on the worry doll boxes all day, and that he looked forward each night to painting something for himself.

After I had been at the House of Mercies for about a year, Nery told me he would be leaving in a year or two for a camp. He was going to join the insurgency. In fact, he had been meeting with a few of the older men who helped out around the orphanage from town. They were on their way to a training camp as soon as they saved up enough money. Nery revealed to me for the first time since I had met him that his entire family had been "disappeared" one day while he was outside on the farm, and since then he had only one goal. Redemption. And freedom for Guatemala.

When I look back on that time, I realize that Nery was a wonderful replacement for my mother. He made me miss her less. And I grew so close to him in a short time.

One night we decided to walk into town after spending all day sanding wooden floor planks in the new storage shed at the House of Mercies. Sister Magdalena routinely paid Nery his week's wages directly, but mine were usually sent into town and mailed directly to the hotel as per my father's directions.

But this particular night, as Sister Magdalena handed Nery his payment, I looked expectantly at her, and tried: "Sister, do you think I could send the wages from town myself this week? Just this one time?"

Sister Magdalena had looked at me for a few moments before answering. "Yes, dear. Just this one time."

Nery and I headed into San Marcos and walked around hand in hand. There was a market with chicken and eggs and we paid the farmer a few dollars from each of our wages for a basketful of food that we took to the lake for a picnic.

Later, we sat on the lake bank with our bellies full and our bodies tired. "So, tell me Mari, will you be married off when you return home?" It seemed like a faraway thought— home. And marriage. I thought about my mother, with her passions and beliefs, being shushed by my father. Shushed until the day she died. Or disappeared. Or both. "I hope not. I don't believe in marriage."

"Me neither." Nery agreed. "And I'm glad you don't believe in marriage either, Mari. Your spirit. It should never be contained by one man."

I threw a piece of bread at him. "You talk like an old man."

He laughed and jumped into the lake, suddenly revitalized by the full meal, and I joined him to swim for hours until we realized the sun was nearly down, and it was time to head back to the House of Mercies before Sister Magdalena started to worry about us.

When I got home from the hospital later that day, I saw her in Mari's yard, standing frozen.

Catt.

She heard me or smelled me and turned to face me. I remained frozen, afraid she'd bolt. I was horrified, realizing that I hadn't thought about her in the last 24 hours with all that had happened. Hadn't remembered at all that Mari had a crazy dog named Catt with separation anxiety who was certain to be wandering the streets of Rock Harbor looking for her missing master. Or worse.

I approached her slowly. She was still wearing her collar so I knew if I could get close enough to her, she'd let me grab her. I wasn't sure how skittish she'd be given all that happened. I wasn't sure what she'd seen in the last 24 hours. What she knew.

Catt.

I whispered softly as I walked closer. Turned out all of my slow gingerly approach toward Catt wasn't necessary. She had neither the inclination nor the energy to bolt. She let me take her collar and lead her back into Mari's house, where I looked through the cabinets, the pantry, and eventually down in the basement where I found the bags of kibble lined up like wooden soldiers.

I poured Catt's food in a cereal bowl and placed it down on the kitchen floor. She sat patiently, staring at me and staring at the bowl, waiting for something. I remembered vaguely that Mari had trained this dog to do a few tricks. Waiting for her food seemed to be one of them. I couldn't remember the command to eat so I yelled: "Eat!"

But Catt continued staring at me.

"Go!"

More staring.

"Ok, Catt, I give up."

She trotted to her bowl and ate.

The code word was either "ok" or "I-give-up."

Figures.

MARI

The dog cannot be left. Literally cannot be left.

If I leave, she spins in circles, and scratches her nose on the crate until it bleeds. The very first time I left her to run errands, I came home to a bloodbath, and I let her out in the yard to relieve herself and give me some time to clean out her crate. She wouldn't go to the bathroom outside but as soon I came inside the house to clean the cage, she followed me in and covered the last corner of my world in shit.

I decided I needed a dog the day my laughter started to scare me. About a week after 9/11, it took on a fairly hysterical ring, that I was afraid Lu would pick up on. And so, with Joe and Rae gone less than a week, all I could think about was getting a dog.

Not for Lu. Not for myself. Just as a distraction from the overwhelming grief. I wanted to come home from burying Joe and Rae and have something so consuming to think about that I could not let myself think about grief. Lu would not fit the bill. Her own grief and guilt were almost impossible for me to watch. I kept myself at arm's length from her almost immediately after the planes crashed into the Towers. No, we needed a dog, I decided.

I had researched breeders through local animal associations. Names and contact information filled a legal pad of paper that I pulled from a desk drawer in the old secretary in the hallway. It was half used. Its pages, if searched long enough, were dotted with impressions of grocery lists and TO DO lists from over the years.

The first breeder I contacted had a long list of questions.

Do you have a fence?

Would you say you have an active or sedentary lifestyle?

Do you have hobbies? What are they?

"*Dios Mio.* No one asked me this many questions when I brought my human children home," I laughed inappropriately into the phone to one breeder.

The breeder did not laugh in response.

"It's important that we make sure you are the right fit for this dog, and that she is the right fit for you. We breed all of our dogs for quality and temperament."

"Breed for temperament? What does that mean?"

"It means we choose the mother and father carefully. We make sure they have the proper personalities, the proper dispositions and traits to create offspring of like quality."

And then, I remember, that I had laughed so hard just before the laughter turned into choking sobs, and the breeder across the telephone line had said "Ma'am? Ma'am" into the phone repeatedly and I simply hung up on her, crossed her name off the list, and moved on.

After the breeder avenue started to look too daunting, I looked for rescue dogs. Instead of funeral arrangements, I spent hours on the phone to local rescue shelters. The shelters, too, asked me more questions than I was prepared to answer.

Do you have a fence? Small children? Other pets?

Finally, to one kind-sounding woman at a local no-kill shelter, I blurted out: "My husband and daughter just died in the World Trade Center. Can you please find a dog for me?"

The phone line filled with silence, and then, "Can you come in today at 3 pm with a photo ID and a utility bill?"

"Do you need DNA?" I was only asking since everyone had needed DNA samples lately.

"No, ma'am. We just need you to come today at 3 pm. We have a weimaraner puppy who was left homeless after her owner died in the World Trade Center, too. I think you'd be perfect together."

The shelter was about an hour away on Long Island, and I asked Rebecca to stay with Lu while I made the drive alone. Both Lu and Rebecca seemed shocked that I would want to spend half a day driving to pick up a new puppy, but Lu didn't ask to go with me, and I didn't offer to take her.

When I brought the puppy home, Lu didn't jump up and down or get excited over the puppy. She simply asked, "What will we call her?"

I hadn't thought of that—so at first I suggested, Luna.

"Why Luna? Are you really naming another creature in this house after your dead mother?"

I winced with actual pain at the mention of my mother. I never really thought of her as dead. Even then.

"Lu—I'd be naming her after *you*."

"No," Lu said simply. "She needs her own name. Something that is her own."

I thought about the only thing that felt like *my* own—the waterfalls at Semuc Champey. "How about Semuc?" Lots more violent head shaking. "No way. Too weird."

I couldn't stop thinking about Semuc Champey, though. Instead of the town and the waterfall, I remembered the beautiful orchids that used to grow wild there.

"How about Cattleya?"

"What is that?"

"It's a flower I remember from Guatemala. It used to grow on the banks of the waterfalls where I loved to swim."

"How do you spell that?"

"C-A-T-T-L-E-Y-A"

Lu shook her head and made a face before compromising. "Ok—but we'll call her Catt. With two Ts. A dog named Catt. Rae would think that was a riot."

Since I couldn't argue that fact with her, it was settled.

Another week later, when I came home from the funeral, where my husband and daughter had been lauded for bravery and patriotism, I stood outside the front door with

Lu. I kept my key poised at the keyhole, listening, my heart in my throat. Because I knew by then that this dog could not be left, and we had been gone for hours. If I would have heard crying, at least I'd know Catt was still alive. The silence should have made me want to run in immediately to check on her. It was so deafening. Through my head ran all the various scenarios in a flip screen fashion, bloody, half dead, completely dead, choked on the elaborate configuration of baby gates I left for her, impaled on a pencil—a pencil?— where did that one come from? I closed my eyes, and let the images rush at me one by one. I felt my pulse quicken and then relax as all the possible scenarios ran through my head.

Yes, I've thought of them all. Now nothing can surprise me— nothing that I see on the other side of this door will throw me. Prepare for blood. Be ready for it all.

I turned the key slowly in the lock, listening to the silence, wondering vaguely if it would turn to excited yelping, but suspecting that it wouldn't. The door opened and Catt and I met each other with wild eyes. She was standing at the ready by the door, tail wagging furiously, a fresh puddle of pee pooling underneath her as she saw me—and I told myself I was crazy to assign that expression on her face to relief. But that's what it looked like. Like she, too, had thought of many scenarios and none of them involved seeing me and Lu come through the door, but that she was glad that's what she was seeing. I leaned down with one knee in the puppy pee and caressed her behind her velvet ears. The tears streaming down my face were desperate and relieved.

"I won't leave anymore, Catt. I won't leave," I told her. *And I meant it.*

LU

I relied on Seamus a lot in the years after Dad and Rae died. When he went off to college, I wasn't surprised, but still it was hard to say goodbye to him. He stayed away a year. For a whole year I was left behind yet again. Unfortunately, it was a familiar feeling.

A year can go by very quickly or very slowly. For me it was both. I read somewhere—the days are long but the years go fast. Which is sort of what happened to me. Each day felt like an eternity. I would wake in the morning and try to think of ways to fill the day. There was still a comfortable settlement waiting for me in the bank since September 11. Mari said I could use it on college, but I couldn't imagine actually spending that money on anything.

And at that time, I certainly couldn't imagine leaving Mari and heading out into the world. I had no idea what would happen to Mari if I wasn't around. I was paralyzed by that fear, among others.

It seems to me that everyone is always waiting and wishing and hoping for a day when they can do nothing all day. I was doing the opposite. Waiting and hoping for the day when I could do *something*. When I would wake up without the pressure on my chest that I'd spend all day trying to will away—and would only go away at night when I took an Ambien.

With Seamus—my one actual friend (if you could even call him that)—away at college, I chose to be a recluse. Turns out Rock Harbor was an easy town in which to be a recluse. I'd do all my shopping in town, sometimes alone, sometimes accompanied by Catt, who always was more of Mari's dog than mine, but who I would take out for walks occasionally anyway. Most of the shop owners let her come inside— whether out of pity for me or Mari, or for the dog, who was stuck with the both of us. I'd shop for Mari and me and Catt only for each day because who knew what the next day would bring. I'd head to town on foot and purchase one day's worth of food and supplies—except in the case of pet food. I bought dog food in bulk because I had a fear of Mari and me dying suddenly in the house, while the dog was forced to start eating us ... I'd read stories about that.

Each day, I'd fill Catt's bowl with enough kibble to last two to three days and by days' end, she'd have eaten more than she should have, but I'd relax all day, knowing that just in case I did die that day—she'd probably last for at least 1-2 days before the shopkeeper thought to call the police.

I told Mr. O'Meare at the corner market that very thing. "If you ever don't see me one day, please call the police and have them check on me." He smiled and said, "Certainly Lu, is someone after you? Do you owe someone money? Who are you worried about Lu?"

He thought he was making a joke, and I knew that, so I felt a little badly about the very serious expression I kept on my face, while I said to him: "Mr. O'Meare, none of us knows if we are going to be alive or dead tomorrow. I like to be prepared. Unlike my dad. Or my sister."

His expression was so sad and remorseful, but I didn't care. *Better to be prepared than save people's feelings.*

MARI

I hear Lu a lot these days. Her voice sounds strong and yet I do worry that she is putting on a brave face for others. She has that tendency. Something she learned from growing up in a house with an odd mix of cowardice and bravery, I assume.

There were times after Joe and Rae died that I thought about sending Lu away. After all, I had been sent away after my mother died. The House of Mercies and Sister Magdalena had stepped in to care for me when my father could not. Perhaps I was doing a disservice to Lu by simply keeping her.

I thought about that a lot during those years. In a way, I suppose I did send her away, by not interfering in her relationship with Seamus even though I knew he was all wrong for my Lu. He was always talking about leaving Rock Harbor, while Lu wanted so much to stay. Rae was the one who would have grown up and left as soon as she could. Not Lu. I watched Lu try to hold on to Seamus, knowing of course, that he would never be held. But still, I didn't tell Lu to let go of Seamus. Even if he wasn't the one I wanted her to spend the rest of her days with, I needed to share her.

I hear Seamus's mother and my old friend, Rebecca, a lot these days, too. She has a beautiful voice but given my complicated history with her, it's hard to hear her and so I let my mind wander when she is here.

Not so when Lu is here. When Lu is here, I strain and strain to focus on what she is saying, even when it is not very much, to try to figure out what she is feeling. I wonder if she has already left and returned from Guatemala. Has she met Sister Magdalena?

I spend a lot of time when Lu is here wondering where my worry dolls are.

And I wonder how much Lu knows by now.

I went back to work at the Rock Harbor café not long after the October 11 plane crash—resuming my morning shift pouring coffee and delivering egg white omelets to morning commuters, senior citizens, and breakfast meeting attendees. The days blended into each other so I'm surprised I even noticed that it had been two weeks.

Two full weeks of heading into the city every day to rub lotion into Mari's hands and arms. To stare at her belly which was growing ever so slightly as it continued housing a new child. Two full weeks of answering questions and asking more. Two full weeks after the plane crash was the day I heard Seamus's car drive by my house as I changed from my café clothes into hospital clothes, and realized he was home for the weekend.

Fall break, most likely.

When I heard Seamus's car, generally recognizable by the loud music blaring as he headed down the street toward his own home, the sound sliced through me and made me shudder. Every time I see him—every single time—it's like we are saying goodbye all over again.

I know Seamus's routine by heart now. He'll be running with his dog soon. Past my house, conspicuously, waiting to be noticed, wanting to be noticed. I will notice him. I will ignore him. He will refuse to be ignored. He'll show up with the dog and kick off his sweaty running shoes at my front door, and I will actually press my nose to the dog who will smell better than Seamus, and yet less intoxicating. He will say something horrible to me like "I've missed you," or "you look beautiful," and I will struggle to let his words drown out the doubt ringing in my ears trying to remind me that he would not be here to see *me* if Rae were still alive. And it's not because he'd be with Rae. She wouldn't have him if she was still alive. But she wouldn't let me have him either.

I suddenly wanted to see him, even though Seamus hadn't even bothered to check on me since the crash, and wouldsurely protest that his mother, Rebecca, had been keeping him updated, that he wasn't sure at all what to say, or what to do. Even though he had made a thoughtless announcement about his leaving for LA in a few short months, and even though he is about as reliable as a Rorschach inkblot test, still I felt all these conflicting feelings about him when he drove by on his way home. I have always had trouble seeing him with clear vision.

The problem is that even though I still hear Rae's voice in my ear occasionally warning me off Seamus Brennan, Seamus did a really, really good thing for me once. And truth be told, while I always had filtered vision when it came to Seamus, it was even harder for me to see him clearly after he did that really, really good thing.

It was two summers ago. We had been lying on the beach together and Seamus asked me what was wrong. I was impressed that he realized anything was wrong at all. But I couldn't tell him. I had been missing Rae so much.

So I told him what I was feeling—in a different way. Without mentioning Rae exactly. "I feel very paralyzed. I can't leave the island ... I can head across town for class and for school but leaving? I just don't do it. Somehow I feel safe here but only here. I'm worried about what will happen after I finish my social work degree. How will I ever get a job if I can't leave?"

I didn't say: "And I wait around for you to return, Seamus. To want to live here only because I cannot venture out."

Instead I said: "I'm afraid all the time. But I hate being afraid. It's a constant struggle. I feel like I'll never leave. When I even think about leaving Rock Harbor, my throat starts to close. And my brain clamps shut."

The words made me laugh even though I didn't feel very funny as I said them. My mother's words. *My brain clamps shut.* She'd been using those words for years, always just before she'd retreat to her room with a goblet of wine and a bottle of sleeping pills, and now I'd borrowed them for me. Maybe I was starting to understand what she was feeling all those years. Maybe she was just as afraid as I was.

I tried explaining all of this to Seamus, and to my surprise and relief, he did not chide me like I was crazy. He rolled up on his elbow and I saw him out of the corner of my eye staring at me with his green eyes partially covered by his dark hair. He needed a haircut. He liked to think he resembled Colin Farrell, and I was always telling him he was nuts; but in fact, at this angle, he did look a little like the Irish heartthrob. I did not return the stare. I looked straight up and then he lay back down and stared up at the sky next to me, and for that I was relieved again.

And so lying on the beach together under a starless cloudy night, Seamus asked me without turning toward me, "What is one place you think you could leave here for?"

"Any place at all?"

"One place. I'll take you anywhere you want to go. Up North or to Nashville to hear that silly music you like so much played live. I'll take you to Sedona or Alaska. I'll take you to the Grand Canyon. You name it. How can we help you get over this? How can I help you get over this?"

"Serendipity." I said softly, and then again, with more conviction. "Serendipity."

"The ice cream place." Seamus laughed and shook his

head at me like I was crazy. Which I was probably.

"Yes, the ice cream place," I confirmed.

"Ok. Then that's where we'll go."

☉

Seamus held my hand on the train and told me to close my eyes. "You're not going to blindfold me, are you?" I asked.

"No—nothing like that. They'd arrest me for blindfolding a woman and dragging her along with me on the Q train."

"Actually they probably wouldn't. This is New York after all."

"Yeah, but people would gawk. It would be weird. Just close your eyes, would you?" Seamus seemed uncharacteristically nervous, which comforted me. I liked that his usual confidence had melted away—I always knew it was all a façade anyway; how much more lovely it was to deal with my Seamus—stripped away of all that bluster and bravado.

My Seamus.

I closed my eyes, and thought the words over and over again in my head, until he leaned in and put his lips on my ear: "Come on sleepyhead—let's go." He pulled my arm roughly and I jumped up out of my daydream, or real dream, or whatever it was and in the nanosecond it took for me to skip over the gap between the train and the platform while instinctively holding my breath—my mind flew in a hundred directions, imagining my foot stuck, imagining my purse stuck in the doors as the train flew out of the tunnel, and on and on.

There were a million ways I could come to a gruesome end right then and there. I flipped through the scenes involuntarily and noted peripherally that they didn't cause me any more grief than normal. I took that as a positive sign.

Seamus turned to me after we hopped the gap and stepped away from the crowd of people trying to rush past us to fill in the crevices of the train we had just exited. He looked me up and down. "Are you ok, Lu?" I took that as a positive sign, too.

Seamus and I were no longer holding hands as we exited the station, passing a drunk homeless man who was reeking of desperation and cheap beer, and was holding a carboard sign that said simply "Thank You." I wished I could close my eyes again. I wished Seamus had indeed blindfolded me. The sights and sounds of the city overwhelmed me and I felt my heart race and my breath quicken. I reached up discreetly and covered my heart with my hand in some weird kind of pledge of allegiance simulation. My heart was jumping so much I wanted to cover it. I was afraid passersby would see. I was afraid someone—perhaps even a small child—would see my chest thumping so visibly that they would point and stare and call attention to me. I was worried someone or something might make Seamus notice the thing he did not seem to be noticing: that I was in a state of panic, which I was talk ing my way through and out of and into, all at the same time.

Seamus looked over and whether he saw my weird pledge of allegiance motion or something else in my eyes that was primitive and harried, he took my hand again and squeezed it gently and put his lips to my ear and whispered something so much better than "are you ok?"...

"Lu, you *are* ok."

And those words, just that confidence they denoted, eased their way into my skull, wrapped around my panicked brain and squeezed it ever so gently, the pressure relieving my racing heart and my quickened breath. I replied "yes," honestly this time.

From outside the restaurant window, I looked in irrationally for the red-headed waitress from all those years ago. She wasn't there, of course, which was both a disappointment and a relief. The sight of her in living color would surely have sent me into a cascade of panic and sadness that no amount of Seamus whispering in my ear would have allowed me to recover from as quickly as I did the gap next to the train and the smelly homeless man.

We arrived at the door, and a short line had already

formed. I took my place in it, but Seamus nudged me to the front where a woman with a neat ponytail held a clipboard. "Brennan," he said to her, and to my surprise, she scrolled down her list, made a dramatic checkmark and waved us in.

"We have reservations," he said with obvious pride in himself.

"I didn't even know you could make reservations for this place. Isn't that kind of the point? You have to stand outside with the masses waiting to get in and eat their ice cream?"

"No. You can make a lunch reservation and if you do, you avoid the masses."

I was tempted to be annoyed at Seamus for circumventing the system yet again. So like him. But instead I decided to be incredibly grateful that he had rescued me from standing on the curb where my mind was already rehearsing ways that a taxi could jump onto the sidewalk, or that I might trip and fall over onto the muddy street, where I might catch lepto or diphtheria, or worse.

We were led to a small table in the back of Serendipity with mismatched chairs and a Tiffany lamp poised above us. The waitress we did have was young and aloof, clearly persuaded by her status as a server in one of the most famous restaurants in New York City. I pointed above us at the lamp and said out loud "Tiffany" just as I noticed both the lamp and that our waitress's name tag in fact said "Tiffanie"; so I followed with: "You too! But with an 'ie,'" and then clapped my hand over my mouth and laughed so hard that the waitress rolled her eyes visibly and said, "I'll give you two a moment."

Seamus reached over and grabbed my hand, and said "I'm so proud of you. Look at you. You're in the city. You're in the world. You're enjoying yourself, aren't you?"

"So much. You're the best. You really are. "

"I love you, Lu."

I wanted to spit the words right back at him. In gratitude for his saying it first. I wanted to say so many things like, "I can't live without you. I can't do things like this without you. I love you and I would walk through fire for you. And I am so glad you got me here Seamus. And I miss my father and Rae so much." All the words bubbled up inside me and I was afraid I'd say them all.

So I bit my tongue hard. And I squeezed Seamus's hand, and quieted my breathing, and replied simply. "Thank you."

One more squeeze and then he looked down at the menu. "So what's good here?"

I thought about the red-headed waitress, and my father and Rae one last time before I banished them all from this particular trip, and replied, "The frozen hot chocolate. I've always wanted to try that. Let's do it."

⑤

By the end of that same summer with the trip to Serendipity, Seamus had said "I love you" to me six times, and "we should really get married someday, Lu" another four times. But on the last day, as I saw him down the street through my window, packing up his car for yet another semester at school, he looked like he might be leaving without saying goodbye. So I headed over before dusk and asked the obvious.

"You leaving?"

He nodded and grunted a little.

"Tomorrow?"

More nodding. More grunting.

Another summer was over. Just like that. I could almost hear Rae whispering to me: *When are you going to learn, Lu Roselli?*

But while I know my hopeless infatuation with Seamus seems just that—what with the ghost of Rae between us, the fickle attitude and the erratic attention—it has always seemed to me that Seamus just isn't the stuff of fairy tales.

He's real.

And I've always kind of liked that about him.

⑤

Seamus didn't even bother stopping by or running by or coming by with the dog that day he arrived in town two weeks after the plane crash. So I headed down to his house myself after my shifts at the café and the hospital. He wasn't home either. He had apparently only come home for the afternoon on his way to or from somewhere else. That's what Rebecca said when she opened the door and wrapped me in a big hug.

"Hi, Lu."

I inhaled her shampoo and the scent of lemons her house always emanated and let her hold me in the doorway for a few extra minutes before she invited me inside.

"Have you eaten?"

I wasn't sure how long a time period the question was actually encompassing, so I shrugged, and followed Rebecca into the kitchen, planting myself on a stool at the kitchen island. Rebecca grabbed a ceramic bowl and ladled some homemade chicken soup and pushed it and a spoon across the island at me.

"Thank you," I said simply.

I settled into the soup realizing suddenly that I hadn't eaten much that wasn't takeout or fast food in the last few weeks. I ate as Rebecca watched on silently, before she said: "I was going to make some scones. Stay and help me."

I put my bowl in the sink and joined her at the island where she was starting to place gathered ingredients.

Whenever I feel weak for continuing to love Seamus despite all of his unreliability, I remind myself that I have known and loved Seamus since we were toddlers. That alone should be explanation, I often feel. But there's more. Of course there's more.

Seamus comes with his mother, Rebecca. Like a package deal. The mother I always wanted. The beautiful and regal Rebecca. With her shoulder-length auburn hair inevitably pulled back into a headband, revealing her freckled forehead and nose and green flecked eyes that dance in the light of every room and make her words seem light-hearted even when they are not.

Rebecca. Always present. Always engaged. Always mothering. Dispensing advice at every turn. It was worth keeping Seamus around just to have Rebecca in my life.

As we each cut pieces of butter and folded them into scone dough, I said: "I love him, Rebecca."

"I know you do."

"And he loves me."

"In his own way, yes."

I ignored the disclaimer.

"I cannot believe Seamus just left. Without even stopping by to say hello." Rebecca remained silent.

So I continued on. "What is it?" Because there was something. She was looking at me with the something in her eyes. I just couldn't put my finger on it.

"Here's the truth, Lu. And it's going to sound ugly to you, but here it is anyway. Life is not like the fairytales. There are lots of little heartbreaks along the way. And they don't always lead to one singular happily ever after. Every man you love is not going to complete you. Not the first one and not the last one. No single man, woman, child, or experience is going to fulfill you. The composite of all these experiences. At the end. That is what will complete you."

"How will you know you are completed?"

"Because you will be done. Do you feel done, Lu?"

I avoided answering her. "So you're telling me not to wait for Seamus?"

"I'm telling you—don't wait for Seamus because you think he is the first—and therefore the last man on this Earth you will love. Don't wait for Seamus because you feel that he fixes in you what you believe is broken. Don't wait for any man for that reason."

"You don't think Seamus can fix me?"

"I don't think you're broken, Lu."

"What am I then?"

Rebecca leaned toward me and whispered in my ear in that familiar Brennan way—as if secrets were about to be spilled, revealed and uncovered. Seamus did it, too. It was his secret weapon. Among others.

As Rebecca leaned in, she said, "Lu, you're human. And that's ok."

"He's so lucky to have you." I said it desperately—trying to appeal to her—trying to make her understand why I needed him so much.

"Lu, you don't need Seamus or anyone else in your life to tell you *you're* ok."

"Please don't, Rebecca. Please don't tell me something ridiculous like all I really need to know is in my heart. In my own soul. That I'm ok and I've known that all along. Click my ruby red heels or something like that."

Rebecca looked so confused that I kept talking as we rolled the dough sparsely, careful not to over-handle it and inadvertently toughen the kneaded dough.

"This isn't Wizard of Oz, Rebecca, or even Wicked."

"Ah." Rebecca closed her eyes and shook her head—I could almost believe she was going to lose her temper with me. I half wanted to see that and wondered what it would look like, having never seen Rebecca flustered or impatient in my entire life. My heart started to race, and I put my hand up to my chest to quiet my heartbeat.

"Lu, you don't need anyone to tell you you're ok. You just need to *be* ok."

I watched Rebecca cut the scone dough into perfect triangles, and I suddenly needed to know something. "How do you feel about Seamus going off to LA, Rebecca?"

Rebecca's knife came down crooked in the dough, and she re-kneaded it and started over. "I feel ... hopeful for him. But also nervous, if I'm being honest. I hope this is the right move for him, but I also hope it's what he wants to do, and not just what he feels his father and I want for him."

It occurred to me for the first time how difficult it would

be to have Rebecca as a mother instead of my own. Perfect Rebecca. How could anyone measure up to her? I felt some pity for Seamus for even trying.

I watched Rebecca continue to cut perfect triangles as my heart kept its pace under my hand. And then I put my hand down, because it was no use quieting my heart. It was beating uncontrollably and the vision of the hundred things that could go wrong were running through my brain. I could trip on a raised kitchen tile and fall over. I could knock over Rebecca's favorite vase perched on the end of the kitchen island and break it. I could step on the dog that kept winding his way around my feet while we made scones. I could kill the dog just by accidentally falling down on top of it.

A million things could go wrong, I thought as my heart raced and raced as Rebecca cut each mound of dough into eight pieces and slid it into the hot oven behind me.

I could make a mistake.

I could wait for Seamus.

MARI

I've always had mixed feelings about Rebecca. I love how warm and sweet she is to my daughter. How could I not? But, I also envy her ease with my daughter, and that envy eats at me. Even though I've always encouraged their relationship. Even though it brought me great relief, and continues to do so.

It is not just that I wish I had that relationship with my own daughter; I also miss having it with my own mother. I can't help but wonder if my mother had lived, had stayed in my life, whether our relationship would ever have eroded the way mine has with Lu. My mother—she too had experienced great atrocities, great sadnesses in her life. She had seen things, witnessed things, known things that no woman should see or know. But still, she was compassionate with me. She was able to rise above. We ran my father's business together—she and I. She poured her energy into something good.

I tried to emulate her. In those early years in America, when the girls were small, I would have coffee with Rebecca and we would load up the strollers and head to playgrounds, libraries, community parks, even the beach—with toddlers and preschoolers in tow. We'd complain about our husband's busy schedules and we'd share cooking tips. I went through the motions, and I watched Rebecca with Seamus and tried to follow along. I sought to impress her even. I told her about my worry dolls one day, and when she gasped at the beauty of the idea, I gave her a set of her own. Ten dolls in a wooden box, wrapped up in powdery blue paper for a birthday one year when the kids were all about three or four.

It worked for a long time. All that following and emulating and mothering. Probably up until the girls started school. When they left me every day and in turn stole the amount of time I could distract myself with their daily needs, things changed dramatically for me. When the hard manual labor required to be the girls' mother started to ease up—when I had more time to paint, to reflect, to think, to remember ...I did just that.

Around that same time, I met Matthew's Tricia who had told me she thought she'd never be able to make the decision that I had made to have children. Little did she know the decision had always been made *for* me. And around that time, I started to question whether Rebecca and I had less or more in common than I originally had thought.

I asked Rebecca one day when we picked up the kids from school on an early dismissal day and took them to the Rock Harbor ice cream parlor. The kids were about six or seven. I had to quiet and scold the girls even more than usual as they fought over napkins, their seat next to Seamus, and who was allowed to get black raspberry and who was "just copying me." It was a particularly exhausting day as I remember, but Rebecca looked unfazed and wide awake. It came to me then. I reached into my pocket to roll a doll around my fingertips as I asked: "Rebecca, do you ever use those dolls I gave you?"

The girls had looked up momentarily from their cones, "Dolls? Did you give some of those funny dolls to Seamus's mom, too?" But I shushed them and they went back to their sugar treats while laughing and fighting along with Seamus in the oversized fake leather booth at the ice cream parlor.

Rebecca looked at me quizzically, but asked gently, "What dolls, Mari? Oh! The worry dolls, do you mean?"

"Yes."

"I do! I use them all the time. I put one inside Get Well or Condolence cards when I need to send someone a little pick me up. They're so beautiful."

That's the day I stopped pretending to be like Rebecca. That day in the ice cream shop. When Rebecca admitted to not needing the very dolls that some days I believed were actually keeping me alive.

Whenever Mari got the flu, we'd spend days and weeks tiptoeing around the house and Mari herself as she'd emerge and cook and do laundry and shuffle around in dirty clothes, looking like she was a zombie in one of those shows Rae had made me watch as part of a late night game of truth or dare.

Mari would speak very little to us during these times, other than, "Please, girls, please be quiet. I just need a little rest."

And then as quickly as the flu came on, it would lift. Mari would emerge from her room, showered with blow-dried hair swept into a marbled hair clip. Almost every time, she'd whisk us into Sheepshead Bay for a shopping spree, complete with hugs and happy whispers: "How about new outfits, girls?" And even though the instructions about "being quiet" were not part of these trips ever, we *would* be—quiet that is—so glad to have our Mama back that we would not dream of doing or saying anything that might send her away again.

For weeks, and sometimes months, she'd stay out of her room. She'd volunteer at school and take us for library trips on Saturday morning. She'd help us clean our rooms, or scold us to clean them like any other normal mother would. She'd take us for ice cream and we'd help her make gazpacho and pork dinners together. She'd share her late mother, Grandmother Luna's, old recipes with us, including a funny looking salad we made every November called *fiambre*, that looked a heck of a lot like *antipasti*, and she'd laugh and sing while she cooked.

She'd be there for long periods of time, and then she

wouldn't be again. And that was the problem with Mari, of course.

It wasn't that she disappeared after September 11. Anyone could forgive her for that.

It was that she wasn't always there even before September 11.

⑨

Three weeks after the plane crash, Mari's social worker came into her room to announce it was time. "We need to discuss some difficult issues, Lu."

Each day I had been putting her off, saying only that I wanted to spend the day with Mari. Each day, I pretended that I was a dutiful daughter and she was a loving mother. I sat at her bedside day after day, week after week, and tried to imagine what all of this would look like if we were not us.

I knew the social worker wanted to ask me if I was taking this baby home. It's the question I would be asking if I were in her shoes. But that option felt as impossible as Mari waking up right now.

So I answered the unasked question: "Yes. I want to help start the process for adoption. How do I do that? Where do we start?"

The social worker handed me forms and took notes while Mari's machines beeped in the background. I tried to keep focused but she kept asking me one question that I couldn't answer. One question that she said could put a wrench in ensuring a seamless adoption. And I knew from my training that she was right. "If the father can be identified or comes forward, he will have the right to raise this baby by himself. This baby is someone else's child, too."

The baby's father. Who could it possibly be? I puzzled over this question on the legal forms. And it all felt a bit much for me. I looked at Mari close by in the bed, and yet so very far away, and found myself thinking: *Was all of this finally too much for Mari, too?*

⑨

The next day there appeared a new nurse at the tail end of the morning shift when I arrived. Her nametag read Anita, and I liked the way she puttered around the room, checking and measuring and patting my shoulder as she walked by. She told me she had been caring for my mother since they brought her here after the plane crash—but usually on the late night shift—after visiting hours ended. Her new shift would allow us to cross paths more. She was a sturdy woman who smelled a bit like vanilla and anti-bacterial soap, with kind eyes and a matron's figure—large breasts and an even larger lap when she sat in a chair in the room filling out paperwork. I had the oddest desire to crawl into her lap, which made me giggle and she smiled at me warmly when I did.

Giggle that is, not climb into her lap.

"My father died on September 11," I blurted out inexplicably to Anita the very day I met her. After weeks of sitting in the room relatively quietly, I found myself strangely talkative.

Anita didn't wince or gasp so I continued on. "And my sister. She died, too, that day. I was the only one left. Well, me and Mari, that is. Me and my mother." I gestured toward the bed as if Anita might have forgotten who I was talking about.

"What a tragedy." Anita exhaled the words.

"We buried them together. It was a beautiful funeral." I was instantly angry with myself for murmuring those meaningless words. I hated those words. Had hated hearing my mother say them in the days and weeks after the funeral, like a robot. She was fed that line by a mourner who was at a loss for words, and then my mother continued regurgitating the words day after day so she wouldn't have to reach inside herself for anything original to say.

"Well, that's a lot for one family," Anita said finally. "You might say, it is too much for one family."

"Yes," I was relieved. "It was certainly too much for my mother."

Anita reached over and took my hand while both of us continued staring straight ahead at the blinking lights and steadily beeping monitors.

"You see; I think that's why she's here. I think she did this to herself." I said aloud the thing I had been thinking for weeks. "I don't think a plane did this to her."

"She's beautiful, your mother." Anita said in response. "I can tell she has a beautiful spirit."

"You can tell that?" I asked, startled suddenly.

"I can," Anita replied.

"I believe she did. Once." I confessed. "There's a painting," I said to Anita, trusting her with something I'd never told anyone. I described to Anita the painting that hung at one time in her bedroom over the nightstand. It appeared one day after my father and Rae died. I stopped in the hallway the first time I saw it as I passed her room and stared at it.

A young girl in a white dress with a dark blue Van Gogh-like background. Without the young girl, you'd mistake it for an amateurish Starry Night. But the detail on the young girl that I saw as I entered my mother's room to get a closer look made it clear that this painting was no amateur effort. The girl was reaching up to a birdcage with a small yellow bird— her hand moving either toward or away from the open birdcage door. It was unclear whether the young girl was opening or closing the birdcage. Whether she was releasing or imprisoning the bird.

It was only clear that the girl in the painting was my mother.

MARI

Nery was the one who taught me to paint. Or he taught me that I already knew how to paint. I could never really tell which it was.

One hot night, after we finished our work around the grounds of the House of Mercies, we were lying in the cool grass. I was leaning against a tree with my sweater balled up in a makeshift pillow. I was wearing a dress that had once been white but that now was dirty and stained with two years of work since I had first arrived. I smoothed out my dress, suddenly self-conscious as I watched Nery.

"Where do you get your ideas for your paintings, Nery?" My words vibrated against the stillness of the night. Nery swatted a bug away from his paint.

"Lots of places."

More stillness. More swatting.

"My mind, mostly."

Nery handed me some paints. "Try it."

"But—how?"

"There." Nery gestured to the last side of the House of Mercies that remained unpainted. We had been painting the outside walls a deep blue gray to cover years of dirt and wear, but this side was a fresh canvas. I could paint anything I wanted.

I closed my eyes and looked inside my mind to see if there was anything to paint. I saw nothing but rivers of orange and red. I couldn't think of any way to convert the inside of my eyelids and their coursing life into a work of art. So I opened my eyes again and looked at my own inspiration—Nery.

I watched his arm and hand move for over an hour. I memorized the muscles in his arm and the veins in his hand. I memorized the way his arm changed and contracted and shifted with each paint stroke. It was dizzying. I painted colors and shapes on the side of the wall that did not resemble anything other than the emotion I was feeling.

All the while, Nery would glance up and down as if he were painting me. After a little while, I caught a glimpse of a white dress on his piece of wood. *My* white dress. I realized he was indeed painting me, and so I stopped painting and I sat very, very still. Watching and memorizing.

My mind wandered as I sat there. I thought about what Nery had been telling me for the last year. That he would be leaving for the camp. That he would be going soon.

"Nery, when the war is over, should we go to America, do you think?"

Nery continued painting silently, and then looked up and asked me: "Niña, what do you think America will be like? Why do you want to go there so badly?"

"I think it will be like this, only bigger." I jumped up then, yelling out an echoing "bigger" as I swung around and around in a circle before collapsing, nauseated, into the grass next to Nery—where he promptly turned so I could not yet see the painting he was working on.

"Nery?"

"Yes, Mari?"

"Can I see the painting?"

He smiled gently. "Soon. It's for you, Niña. It's to have when I leave. To remember me."

"But it's of me—no? How is a painting of me going to help me remember you? That doesn't make sense."

As he handed me the painting—and I saw what he had painted—my face—not dirty—not sad—my dress as pure white as the orchids that grew on the banks of Semuc Champey—and my arms reached up to a birdcage—setting the wild creature free—I saw that he was not painting me at all. But rather his dream for me.

And so yes, the painting became a reminder of him for all time, and not of me at all.

Later—much later—from the convent in New York a few months before I met Joe, I wrote Nery a letter that I never mailed.

Dear Nery,

It's cold here.

Which is bad enough.

But worse than that, everyone wants to talk about how cold it is all the time.

And nothing else.

"Isn't it cold outside?"

"Oh I know—have you heard it's supposed to be even colder?"

"Really? They are calling for snow all week."

And then everyone runs to the store. As if maybe it will close down after the snow. Even though this country never seems to close. Or quiet itself for even a moment.

It's so strange.

Everything looks dead now for the winter, and while I vaguely remember that when I arrived, it was beautiful and alive, that seems like a very long time ago, and I feel like nothing will ever be alive again.

I miss the forest. Even when it rains there, it is beautiful and comforting. I miss warm rain. I miss things being alive.

I miss what it feels like to be alive.

I wonder where you are now.

And I wonder do you miss it, too?

After the painting appeared on her wall, I stopped at Mari's bedroom door many mornings on my way to and from my own room to glance at the painting, but it took months for me to actually gather the words to ask Mari about it.

"Who painted it?"

"An artist I knew a long time ago. A man named Nery Santiago."

And then, because I already knew the answer from the expression on Mari's face, I said rather than asked the very obvious: "You loved him. And he loved you." I instantly regretted my words, because as they reached the air, Mari stood up on her toes and touched the painting reverently, before taking it down and placing it upside down in the nearest dresser drawer.

"I never saw that painting again." I shared all of this with Anita and then I stayed at Mari's side for a few more hours after Anita's shift ended. I grew restless, and I sorted through the guardianship papers from the day before. I stacked them in a neat pile and then shoved them carelessly into my bag. I left the hospital and started walking and found myself at the last place I expected to end up. Or maybe not.

Serendipity.

I walked right in and ordered myself a frozen hot chocolate.

MARI

I started having a peculiar recurring dream while at the House of Mercies.

The dream bothered me for many reasons, not the least of which was because it had nothing to do with my mother. Ever since she had disappeared I had been hoping and praying to see her in my dreams. But she never came.

In the dream, I was swimming in the springs at Semuc Champey—happy and content. I would pull myself up out of the springs, and always then I would see two small birds. I would study them intently, silently, and without moving, anxious to observe the birds without sending them flying away into the sky.

They were unusual birds—with yellow and white and black feathers and bright blue eyes the color of the water I had just been swimming in. In the dream, they always stared me right in the eye. Then one would fly away and the other would stay. But not of its own will. The bird's foot was trapped on a twisted twig. To my horror that lone bird would struggle against the twig, and I would always stare at it helplessly, thinking in my dream that there was absolutely nothing I could do to help.

Each time I had the dream, I would wake, sweating and gasping, and wondering aloud: "Why didn't I just free the bird's leg?"

My mother left when Rae and I were about 10 years old.

The night she left we were standing in our bedroom closet, my sister and I, as we had on so many nights to listen to our parents fighting. Or rather, to hear when it ended. It always did—and we waited for that part—for the moment when my father would say, "Come on Mari, don't do this. I love you."

It was like my mother had to hear it five or six times before she'd stop. Before she'd stop screaming or blaming or yelling or whatever she was doing that particular night. Five or six usually, sometimes a few more. We'd wait in the closet and count as a way to keep track, a way of distracting ourselves from the fighting and shouts.

We'd wait for her to surrender, which was always signaled with one word: "Joe." She'd say it softly over and over, and then she'd weep deep primal pained cries that sounded like gulps and that would relieve us strangely. They'd mean the fight was over for the night and we'd catch our breath. We would nod violently at one another and then crawl into the same bed and fight over the covers like we were normal sisters on a normal evening in a normal house. On those nights, Rae would usually confirm, "Someday, I can't *wait* to get out of here and have my own room and my own covers, and say *Adios*, Lu!"

Sometimes Mari would come in and kiss us goodnight— dripping her sorrow and apologies on our cheeks with her tears. "I'm sorry, girls. I'm sorry if you heard your father and me fighting. It's ok. Everything is ok. We just had a little disagreement and now it's over. Just go to sleep, angels. I love you. We love you."

We'd nod through sleepy half-closed eyes. We didn't even need the apology to us. We needed to hear our mother apologize to Joe. We only needed to hear the closet wall sobs, and then we could sleep.

But that night, the night she left, there were no dripping apologies or surrenders heard through the closet wall. We sat in the closet for what seemed hours, counting pleas from our father.

One.

Two.

"Mari, please don't do this. I can't take it anymore. I truly cannot take anymore."

Three.

Three.

We were stuck on three for a while. A long while.

There were sobs. From both our father and our mother— but no surrenders. No apologies. And then we heard our father say, "Then go. If you want to go so badly, just leave me with the girls and go."

We gasped out loud. My mother and father had to hear it. It was so loud and pained.

"She can't leave," I said to Rae. I didn't bother to whisper.

"She won't leave," Rae replied confidently. But I noticed she whispered.

We held on three. I wished silently for a number four. Maybe it would only take four tonight, instead of five or six.

We were still in the closet in the morning. We'd fallen asleep in there and our father came for us, peeking through an ajar door when it was time to wake us for school. His eyes were bloodshot and he smelled bad when he came for us. He didn't yell at us for sleeping on the floor of our closet. He didn't even yell at us for eavesdropping like he must have known we were doing. He just said, "Come on, girls, your mom had to go away for a few days, and I'm going to get you off to school this morning."

I remember how groggy I was as I stretched on the closet floor next to Rae and took in his words. As I heard my father say Mari was gone I realized we wouldn't have to sleep in the closet anymore.

Unless she came back.

MARI

When the girls were 10, I went back to Guatemala. For a week. An entire week. What was I looking for? What did I think I would find?

Nery, really. I thought I would find Nery.

I thought I would bring him back to America and he would help me see myself the way he once did—the way he had painted me. When we were children. Before everything else had happened.

I was so lost. I see that now. But how could I see that then? In the middle of so much sadness. So much grief. It consumed me. The girls were growing and blossoming while I was dying.

It was unfair to all of us. And every time I tried to explain to Joe he would look at me with an expression that said only "Please, Mari. Not again." And I know what he thought. *You have to forget all of that. You have to move forward.* He was of this place. Rock Harbor. Strong and resilient, third generation immigrant stock in America. He could pull himself out of anything, I believed.

But I was not of this place, and its potent power had not yet reached me. I wasn't resilient or strong. So I left, and after a visit to the House of Mercies, I stayed near Lake Atitlan where I stumbled around for a few days. I did not bother to go back to Semuc Champey. There was nothing left for me there and I did not want to see the graves and the ruins. At any rate, Lake Atitlan is called "*El ombligo*." The umbilical cord. All roads lead back to it, I suppose.

There was something anonymous and freeing about

wandering around San Marcos and the other towns neighboring Lake Atitlan with the volcanoes looming on all sides. I missed the girls and Joe only vaguely while I became distracted by the changes that had happened to my homeland in the more than 10 years that I'd been away.

San Marcos in 1999 was so different than that town I had walked hand in hand with Nery when we were teenagers, working all day at the House of Mercies. In fact, the town was what the Americans would call an "artisan town." Every time I walked by a shallow shop, the artist just inside its doors lifted his or her wares and came to the door to place it in my hands, forcing me to touch it and love it. Like children, they hoped once I held their creations I would never want to put them down.

Baskets and pieces of art and jewelry. As I walked the streets, my eyes scanned the rickety shelves and tabletop collections—ornate and eclectic and beautiful in their chaos. My eyes often settled on small wooden boxes of woven dolls. But I bought nothing. I especially couldn't imagine buying worry dolls. I couldn't own any dolls made by hands other than Nery's.

One beautiful woman with a face lined with a thousand experiences watched me eye her boxes of worry dolls without picking them up.

"You no like?"

I flinched at the fact that I apparently looked so American now that this woman actually greeted me in English rather than in my native tongue. I shook my head and kept walking.

There was an older man next door decorating a clay bowl. His hair was so dark over his weathered forehead; I did a double take wondering as I did so whether he dyed his hair with the paint he was using to press ornate patterns into the clay. I watched his thin brush move slyly under his gaze. He glanced up at me. "You like?"

I nodded. "How do you keep your hand so steady?" I

asked him in Spanish.

"It's a secret," he responded in English.

Another smaller gray-haired woman a few shops later asked me as I put her basket back on the shelf after she had placed it gently in my hands like a baby, "You no find what you want?"

I shook my head again, answering neither in English nor Spanish, as I continued feeling hopelessly between worlds.

At the end of the week, there was a landslide across the lake—a common occurrence in the area that I had all but forgotten about. As I heard the mud roaring down the volcano, which was dangerously close to me, I packed up my things and returned home immediately to Joe and the girls.

I remember the day I got home to Joe from Guatemala. What he said to me, when I came home to him—truly came home to him—was: "Let's stick this out, Mari. Let's fight and make up. Let's be messy in front of each other. But let's stick this out."

I said to him: "I want to forget everything about these last 10 years. I want to start over with you."

"No," he said quickly and violently. "Let's spend every day remembering those days—every moment of them. Let's never forget what it was to be apart. Let's never forget the pain. So that we don't go and do anything stupid enough to separate us again.

"Let's never take this for granted again. This togetherness. With you and the girls. *That's* what will sustain me and you all the rest of our days. I swear it." He held me and lifted me and my feet dangled a bit as he did and I buried my head in his neck and inhaled the salt air, the meaty iron scent from the nearby butcher shop, and the scent of the all-wrong-color ocean.

And I believed Joe when he said it was all going to be ok this time. I really did.

I stopped frozen about 50 yards away when I saw Catt wandering around the back yard on my way home from the café one day in late October. She had somehow gotten out of the house again and I realized I must have left at least one door ajar when I left. That's all it really took with Catt. She'd find an escape route if you left her one, although in the end, she didn't really want to escape from you. She wanted to escape *to* you.

I approached her gingerly the way I had when she first reappeared again after the plane crash, but it was unnecessary as it had been then. She let me approach her and even lay down when I arrived next to her. If she was human, I'd have sworn the expression on her face was relief. I led her back into the house but she walked slowly, tentatively, and refused to eat the kibble that I poured out for her. She curled up instead on the floor next to me in the kitchen with a small tremble in her hind legs that frightened me.

I was concerned enough to reschedule the next day's shift at the café and make an appointment with the vet. *I'm sure it's nothing,* I told myself. *How could it be anything? Haven't I got enough on my plate right now?*

The next morning, an expensive prescription and a few cleaned-up accidents in the veterinary office waiting room later, I was walking back into Mari's house with a tired dog and a heavy heart.

Cancer.

Catt had cancer, and no one was willing to tell me how much longer she had to live. A thought flitted through my mind—*At least Mari won't have to know. I won't have to tell her.*

She loves this damn dog so much.

⑨

Later that day, I called Anita in to show her. "Look! She's crying."

Tears were streaming down Mari's face and her features had shifted—her expression had changed.

"Lu, I'm going to get the doctor, and he's going to tell you the same thing I'm going to tell you—only not so gently. So allow me first. In the vegetative state that your mother is in, this is not uncommon. And it does not mean what you think it does. The eyes may water ... they may even produce tears. I have seen patients appear to frown just like this—and indeed I have seen them appear to smile. The families think it means they are about to wake up. They think it means they are coming out of the coma. It doesn't mean that, Lu. And I'll have the doctor explain it in more scientific terms, but for now, please, Lu, don't get your hopes up. Your mother is not improving."

"No," I resisted Anita's explanations. My mother was still here.

The social worker had just left moments ago, after informing me that she had a lead on a very good family for Mari's baby. She believed the family would be open to fostering Mari's baby with the intent to adopt down the road.

"And what do we do if the father shows up?" I had asked.

"We cross that bridge when we get there. Listen, Lu. This will be a wonderful home for the baby."

I wasn't feeling the same optimism the social worker exhibited, and when she left me alone in the room, and I looked down to see my mother's tears, I celebrated *them* instead of the social worker's news, strangely enough. Because it meant thought—didn't it? And improvement? A move toward the old status quo—no?

My mother's sad face and streaming tears were things I was very used to indeed.

⑨

The next morning while walking Catt along the beach just after sunrise, I thought about the long afternoon before spent in a room full of white coats explaining to me why Mari was crying without crying. They had handed me an excerpt from a medical journal to read and reread on my own.

"Signs of an intact reticular formation (*e.g.,* eye opening) may be present ... More complex brain stem reflexes, including yawning may be present ... Arousal and startle reflexes may be preserved ... loud sounds may elicit eye opening ... Eyes may water and produce tears ... should not be misinterpreted by observers as evidence of awareness."

I put my head in my hands and rubbed my temples. I was exhausted. I hadn't been sleeping very well. *This dog.* All the moments not spent worrying about my mother and her unborn baby and her unborn baby's unknown father were now spent worrying about this dog.

Sitting near the shoreline, I continued rubbing my temples with both hands for a few seconds before realizing why my hands were free to do so.

No leash!

The dog!

My mind sprung alert and pushed me up to my feet.

Where the hell are you, Catt? I thought rather than called. I was paralyzed with fear and embarrassment, as I turned and stared down the beach in both directions. I was embarrassed to call out her name, embarrassed for anyone to know that I had lost a dog—but it was still early, and there was no one on the beach to even see me.

As I stood in my tracks, feet frozen to the spot—my torso spinning this way and that—the sunrise sparked a bright light off a nearby home with floor-to-ceiling windows facing the ocean. A large home with an old white-haired man waving to me soundlessly with one hand. And in the other hand, the leash of a dog who was sitting and staying so patiently, she couldn't possibly be Catt, but of course she was.

Head bowed in shame (mine, not Catt's), I headed

quickly up the sand toward the house with the waving man. When I neared him, I realized that my earlier assessment of "old" was incorrect. His shock-white hair framed a thin face that was lined, yes, but was more tanned, than weathered. He had light blue eyes, the same color as the sweater he was wearing over jeans—another sign that he might not be as old as I had initially thought. *Not many old men wear jeans,* I thought. His age was difficult to judge—maybe 50s or 60s. But he certainly was not as old as he looked from far away.

Not unlike Mari, I thought in spite of myself.

The white-haired man was looking at me curiously. Not exactly smiling, not exactly frowning. Just ... looking at me. And then he said, "Lu, right?"

I nodded. I recognized him. He was the former butcher in town—his shop long closed ever since 9/11. I didn't know his name, but still he knew me. I didn't bother to ask why before launching into a long-winded apology. "I'm so sorry about my dog. Well, she's not really my dog. That's kind of the problem." I reached out for her leash, but he kept his hold on it. I stared at this obedient version of Catt sitting calmly, tongue out, tail wagging gaily.

"It's all right. I know her. I—"

He took a deep breath before continuing. "I know your mom. We're—friends. I've been over to the house a few times to check on her over the last weeks. But I haven't found any-one home yet. Is she ok?"

Tears rolled down my face. "No. She's not."

I saw the man's shoulders slump and I realized he knew my mother very well. His eyes started to well up, too. "Oh, Lu," he said familiarly.

He stepped back toward a nearby chair and sat down in it. I followed his lead and took a seat in a matching rattan patio chair. I reached my hand out for Catt's leash, but he kept a firm hold on her leash and Catt moved closer to him.

I studied his grief carefully, and then without warning, tried some news out on him. "You see, she's in a coma. And she's pregnant. And the doctors are not at all sure she will wake up."

I watched the butcher slump forward and openly cry, just after he finally handed me Catt's leash. Catt turned back and forth between us not sure what to do, until finally she got up, walked over to my chair and sat down close to me, obediently, and unfamiliarly, but nevertheless, a relief.

MARI

On my 17th birthday, my father summoned me back to the hotel at Semuc Champey. He was very busy now. He had married the woman from Lanquin but he needed more help.

Nery was long gone—headed off to the insurgency camp he had spoken of for years. I hugged him on his last day at the House of Mercies but he pulled away from my hug within moments. "You always pull away first," I said.

Nery only rushed off in response—anxious to leave. Anxious to get started with his plans of saving Guatemala.

Short letters from him reached me at the House of Mercies, which reassured me that he was alive—but assured me that he would never be back. Not the way I wanted him to be, at least.

At my father's hotel, there were more Americans and Europeans who came through the resort every week, and I was in charge of turning over the rooms each week—the job my mother and I had done together all those years, I now did alone. I was always alternately intrigued by and disgusted by the filth left behind by the tourists. Near-empty bottles of cerveza littering every surface, including the bathroom counter. *Who takes cerveza into the bathroom?* I'd often wonder as I cleared the counters and wiped down the smeared surfaces.

Sometimes I'd find small treasures—like unopened lipsticks or a pair of golden earrings. I'd put the items into a drawer and wait to see if their owners would contact my father to notify him that something had been left behind, but they hardly ever did. I marveled that these tourists had so many belongings that the lost items would take weeks, if not months or years to discover lost, and by that time, the tourists would forget where they even had them last. I sorted the items by date found, and after about three weeks, I'd move them from the "lost drawer" in my room to "my drawer." I'd paint my lips and cheeks with the wares—careful to wash my face in the springs before my father caught sight of me, and I'd decorate my ears and neck with the delicate and often ornate jewelry left behind.

I spoke very little to the tourists—pretending not to speak any English so I could eavesdrop and listen in on their conversations. I learned most of my English during that time.

I was startled one day to hear a handsome dark-haired American boy call after me as I walked down the hall with my garbage bag and cleaning bottle. "Señorita?" He said it in such an American voice—pronouncing every syllable as if he had practiced it on the plane ride here. He didn't actually speak Spanish; I was sure of it in an instant.

I turned to him anyway, and I replied in perfect English, "Yes, can I help you?" I liked the way he smiled at me then. His lip curved up as if we had shared a secret.

And he continued on in English. "Did you happen to find a watch in my room? A metal watch?" He spoke slowly and pointed to his wrist as he said the words—still clearly feeling out my command of his language. I eyed him slowly, this handsome American. His ridiculous flowered swim trunks meant to mirror his surroundings when instead they mocked them. His American tan that was blotchy with red and brown splattered across his chest. But his eyes—they looked so carefree. And unpredictable. And he held my gaze just as long as I held his. Without looking away.

You always pull away first. I shook off the memory.

I waited just another second, basking in the pivotal silence between us before I responded—again in perfect English. "I haven't. But come with me, I'll help you look for it."

I returned with him to his room, and started picking up

the dirty laundry around the room, folding and placing it intimately on the bed, while he stood at the door silent, shifting as if uncomfortable, until I found a large clunky watch on the floor peeking out from the bed.

"Is this it?" I handed it to the still silent, still assessing, American boy.

"Yes, thank you."

"You're very welcome. I'm Mari, by the way." I said even though he didn't ask.

"Nice to meet you, Mari"—he held out his hand stiffly as he said—"I'm Tomas."

And I laughed at his ill-fitting name—although he seemed to think that I was laughing at his extended hand—because he quickly dropped it, which required me to reach down to his side and draw his hand away from his thigh where I placed it between both of my hands and said: "Nice to meet you, Tomas."

Then I turned, picked up my garbage bag and cleaning solvent, and left the room before he had a chance to respond or reject or pull away before I did.

⑨

Tomas was registered to stay at the hotel for the next 10 days—I checked—and I started meeting him each night after I was done cleaning the rooms. He had arrived with a larger party but they returned home to America with whispers about going back to school and work while Tomas stayed behind. I wondered—without asking him—why he didn't seem to have anything to go back home to. But I was glad that he stayed.

On Tomas's last registered night at the hotel we "stole" the buggy that the tour guides used to take hotel guests to the waterfalls at Semuc Champey.

I say "stole" because that's the word Tomas used and it seemed to excite him to do something that he believed was forbidden even though my father would have probably allowed me to take the buggy out at night, while there were no tours scheduled, to appease one of his American guests. And even though we actually could have walked—a means of getting to the waterfalls that I much enjoyed and preferred. The buggy ride was less romantic. But Tomas didn't seem interested in romance—he seemed interested in forbidden.

We bumped along the rocky path to the waterfall and I held on for dear life. Tomas was a little drunk, but I tried to overlook his bloodshot eyes and garbled words. I tried to focus instead on the moment. The color of the sky—a shade of blue that was dark and foreboding and beautiful all at once. The whirring noises of the rainforest as we headed past the howler monkey tribes and the invisible macaws quietly staking out their spots in the trees above.

Even the sound of Tomas's distracted humming hypnotized me. What was he humming? I wanted to ask but I really didn't want to break the spell I was under. I was there alone—in the moment—without him, as he was paying very little attention to me, but no matter—I really didn't want it to end.

It was the American aspects of his personality that I found so mesmerizing. His Spanish name, and his love for my own country and its food and sights and sounds were endearing. But the American in him was what would be my downfall, I knew. Because I really wanted to go to America. Well, it was more than that really. Ever since I had heard my mother talk about a country she loved without meeting, I wanted to *be* American.

I stole glances at Tomas while we drove (truly stole, because he didn't talk to me or seem to acknowledge me at all on the trip), measuring the length of his jaw, the smooth lines of his hand on the buggy shift, the muscles in his leg that were exposed at this angle while his swim trunks rode up his thigh. When we arrived at the waterfall, he put the buggy in park and turned to me. "Now what?"

I sighed with disappointment. I wanted to believe that he had spent the whole trip planning a moonlight stroll around the waterfall, a nude swim in its waters, maybe even just kissing me fiercely in the buggy under the stars. I wanted to believe he had thought of any of these things—instead of just the wind, and the sounds, and the macaws and the monkeys and the blue-swirled shades of the sky. But, the truth was, he hadn't thought about or noticed those things either. He hadn't thought about anything, other than stealing the buggy and getting me into trouble. And while I thought about punishing him by telling him he'd done neither of those things—instead I just grabbed his hand, took control, and said: "Come on, I'll show you to a secret spot."

His eyes lit up as he said, "Sure!"

I took him somewhere that was neither secret nor a place: it was a time—*moonrise*—but that didn't seem to matter either. He just wanted to do something forbidden. And not necessarily with me. I think he had already figured out—there wasn't too much I was planning on forbidding him.

As the moon rose high in the sky, I climbed to the top of the waterfall, stripped away my clothes, and dove into the cool waters below. "Come in!" I yelled to Tomas, but he looked back and forth at me and the height I had dove from and looked frightened as he yelled, "You're nuts!"

He headed back to the buggy where he waited for me while I swam in the cool water for another half hour.

◎

We made love finally back at his hotel room after we returned the "stolen" buggy.

I wrapped my legs around his back and tried to lose myself in the moment, but I could not enjoy him. I could not think "He's here." I could think nothing but "He'll be gone soon."

Life will go back to the way it was around here.

That thought was not comforting. Tomas had distracted me from my loneliness—from missing my mother ... and Nery ... for the last 10 days or so.

I reached up and grabbed my feet, pulling them together in a vice grip in the middle of his back. And I tried to feel something other than his inevitable absence. I closed my eyes and inhaled him. He smelled like moss and grass and rain and not too faintly of tangy cerveza and perspiration. I released my vice-gripping legs, and ran my fingers up and down his back. I wove them into his hair—I even thought about pulling out a strand. For a moment I thought I had actually pulled. Because he cried out and his eyes flew open in alarm. But, no, he was just—

Done.

I lay next to him, holding my breath. Willing my eyes not to fill up with tears. Digging my nails into my palms because the physical pain was actually distracting and held the tears back. Tomas reached over and moved a hair out of my eyes. It wasn't exactly tender, but it was enough to make my vulnerable eyes pool over. And he just said: "Don't, Mari. Don't. Don't love me. You can't—you know—just love me and keep me here. That's not how it works."

"Jesus, Tomas. I *know* how this works. Don't be such a prick." I had learned much English from the tourists.

His words sucked the air out of my lungs, and the tears from my eyes. I turned on my side and listened to him dress clumsily behind me and pack up his room. And then he left.

He took with him the mossy smell, which I then realized for the first time was not all that pleasant, and he left the sweet smell of sex behind. The scent of me, I realized sadly. He left me utterly behind. And I cried into my pillow, wishing he had left some of the grass and moss and taken some of me with him to America instead.

I think of that night often. Mostly how it felt to swim naked in the waters of Semuc Champey where I could touch the soft mist with my outstretched hands while the water caressed me like an adoring lover. Swimming while Tomas headed back to the buggy alone. After that day, we never made love again.

Not even after we were married.

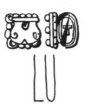

LU

Last year, as part of the work needed to finish up my degree in social work, I had to accompany a licensed social worker on almost weekly field visits.

I was assigned to a seasoned social worker named Lynn Cooper. Lynn was both beautiful and fierce as nails. The first day I met her at our designated meeting place—outside of a housing project on the opposite end of Rock Harbor—I had been standing across the street from her for about five minutes, watching her scroll through her Blackberry and bark orders into it ferociously. We had only talked by phone and she was not at all what I was expecting. For starters, she was about 10 years younger than her authoritative voice had sounded. I crossed over the street, and as I did, I heard her familiar voice: "That was not what I said at all. I'll be back in the office in about two hours, and we will discuss it then. Yes, I'll have my reports done by this weekend. I have Freda Cross on my calendar today and my other cases this week have been just as challenging. Be patient, would you?"

"Hi Lynn, I'm Lu." I put my hand out, and watched Lynn click her phone off and size me up in my long, patterned skirt, and oversized tunic; I knew I didn't look nearly as professional as she did in her black pantsuit. I shifted uncomfortably in my Toms shoes.

"Hunh. Lu. Well, hi. Are you ready? Let's head on in and I'll introduce you to Miss Freda Cross." She didn't give me a chance to answer as she held the lobby door open to the apartment building and I crossed over the threshold to enter. I stepped over some garbage in the lobby and avoided the looks that some older men were giving Lynn and me from a corner of the lobby where a tall ashtray was standing on a pedestal and receiving ashes from a single cigarette being passed around. I caught Lynn eying me up and down again as we climbed onto the elevator and she pressed "8."

I couldn't help but think that maybe I wasn't what she was expecting either.

⑨

Freda Cross opened her apartment door naked.

I gasped and put my hand over my mouth, and Lynn looked at me sharply, before turning to Freda. "Hello, Freda. Now I know you were expecting me today. So why didn't you bother dressing for me?"

Freda gave us a glassy-eyed shrug and waved us into the small apartment's kitchen. Dishes littered the sink and there was a smell of old garbage—long past sweet fermentation—and incense. A small table sat in the middle of the kitchen with a chipped, green Formica cover and scattered burn marks littering what was left of the Formica. The counter was covered with a similar pattern of burn holes. There was only one chair next to the table and Freda took it.

Lynn walked over to the table and slapped her bag down on top of the scorched and cracked table covering. "Ok, Freda. I have pictures of Roberto in here, but you don't get to see them until you go in the other room and get dressed."

Freda looked from me to Lynn to me to Lynn. "Who's this?" Her voice was hoarse and scratchy.

"She's my associate. I'll introduce you properly when you get dressed." I wasn't sure whether it was the promise of meeting me or seeing pictures of her son that ultimately convinced her to go get dressed, but after a few moments, Freda got up and vacated the chair and went to the only other apparent room in the apartment.

Lynn gave me a look with eyes turned up and face smirking that said "what can you do?"—looking more like we had happened upon a girlfriend who wasn't quite ready for a girls' night out, rather than a naked opiate addict.

My eyes scanned the room more carefully. The "dishes" that were in the sink were actually take-out containers and more garbage. Empty pasta boxes and juice bottles were piled up in a precarious tower mixed in with some plates and spoons that looked like they were all caked with layers of food that had never been washed off, but rather piled on top of the layer before like a child's art project. I did a double take when I thought I saw one of the pasta boxes moving, but then I remembered that pasta boxes don't move, and that it was probably just a bug. That thought vaguely comforted me, until I remembered: *Ugh. Not just a bug. Probably a roach. Probably lots of them.*

I kept scanning the room—trying to look at something other than the sink. There was no actual drug paraphernalia readily visible, and other than the smell of incense and scorched countertops, no real reason to order Freda to have a urine test. Of course, her nude greeting couldn't be discounted. I thought about jotting some notes down, but didn't even know where I would start.

After a few minutes, and Lynn's banging on the door repeatedly, Freda came out with what looked more like a long shirt than a dress or actual clothes. Her eyes still looked glassy to me, but I wondered if I was really even qualified to make such an assessment. I thought Lynn might make Freda go back and put more clothes on. But instead, Lynn accepted the concession and motioned for Freda to sit in the only chair.

Lynn opened up her bag and scattered some pictures of a brown-eyed boy in front of Freda. He had a tuft of black hair dropping into his eyes in every picture, but never covering them. As he looked up at us all from the burned table with those beautiful and sad eyes, I gasped again. I didn't look up at Lynn—I knew she'd be giving me another warning look—as she said: "Roberto misses you Freda. But he is being well taken care of."

"I was taking care of him. You didn't need to take him away and put him with my sister."

"Freda, you can't take care of Roberto until you stop using. How many times have we been through this?"

"I ain't using. And you are a liar." Freda made a loud choking sound and then spat at Lynn.

I flinched and took an involuntary step back in an effort to stay out of mucous range, but Lynn looked unruffled. She packed up the pictures, and bent down to look Freda in the eye. I admired her bravery—leaning in so close to Freda's mouth like that. "I want Roberto to live with his mama. I want you to be clean and sober for more than 24 hours. I know the you when you are sober, Freda, and I like that you very much. I don't like this you very much. And I know—sure as hell—you don't like her either. Do I need to order a urine test? Do you want to dry out in jail for a few weeks for breaking your parole?"

Freda's shoulders slumped visibly and she looked at me again. "You told me you were going to tell me who this was."

"This is Lu Roselli. She's in training. You might be seeing some more of her in the future, so be nice."

"You going to start stealing people's babies, too?" Freda challenged me.

"Just the ones whose mamas give up," I replied.

Freda's head jerked back like I had just slapped her. My eyes went to her mouth, wondering if she was loading up to spit at me, too. "What makes you think I gave up?"

"I don't know if you did or not, Freda." I kept my gaze locked on her, albeit primarily at her mouth. "My mama left us a long time ago. Me and my dad and my—my sister." I swallowed hard.

"What happened to your sister?"

"She's dead."

Freda stared at me for a minute, and then her red glassy eyes pooled over. "I ain't giving up."

While Lynn looked at me with a careful and guarded expression, I reached over and put my hand on Freda's wrinkled and bruised hand and pressed down firmly, as I said: "That's good, Freda. That's really good."

MARI

After 9/11, I was sorry for a great many things, including that Lu was left with no siblings. When my brothers died in the war, I was left alone with my father and mother, and later my father and stepmother, and I often wondered if just having siblings might have changed the course of everything. I had seen for myself at the House of Mercies that siblings can help when you are left behind.

What was that damn alien movie I took Lu to all those years ago? Oh yes, *E.T.*, it was called.

My heart hurt for Lu celebrating her first birthday without Rae. Even though I was already lost in sorrow, getting through Lu and Rae's first birthday after September 11 felt like a milestone that would drown me. When Lu mentioned some alien movie playing at the local theatre, it seemed like such a good idea, until we got in the dark, and suddenly the alien was all alone—left behind by his family and being probed like some kind of medical specimen, and suddenly our lives were being played out on the movie screen in front of us. I could hardly take it.

I looked at Lu soon after the movie revealed its plot to us, and wondered if we should just leave, but she looked fine. She gobbled up popcorn and chocolate raisins, and looked like she was enjoying the movie. She didn't look like she was wishing the little alien had some siblings left behind on earth with him, who would help him fight off those crazy medical people.

Sigh.

I'm not fighting the medical people. I realize that now. I'm simply being kept alive by machines that have one goal and one goal only—keeping me just alive enough until you are ready to be born. So I can die.

It's like the Mayan calendar. It's either the end of time or turning over a new page. It all depends upon your perspective. Isn't that what Mama always used to tell me as we'd clean those rooms together day after day, night after night?

Mama.

"Mama, Mama!" We bolted through the door on our way home from school one day in 5th grade.

We had been studying Central America, including Guatemala and the Civil War. We felt like celebrities that day—like we had something to add to the history lesson. So we rushed home for more information from Mari.

"Did you ever get lost?" we greeted Mari who was folding laundry in the living room with the television set in the background broadcasting Spanish soap operas.

"Lost? Where am I going?"

"Not now, Mama—then. When you were in Guatemala. Did you ever get lost?"

"I don't understand you girls."

She kept folding her laundry. Sleeve, sleeve, bend in half, meet the ends.

"Mrs. Roberts says that in Guatemala—there was a civil war ..."

"Um hmmm ..." Mari continued on. Sleeve, sleeve, bend in half, meet the ends.

"Civil war ... and people got lost."

Sleeve, sleeve, bend in half, meet the ends.

"People got lost for years. And some forever. Mama—did you ever know anyone who got lost? Did you?"

Sleeve, sleeve, drop—Mari sat down on the side of the sofa amidst the folded and now half folded and unfolded laundry.

"Mama, did you ever know anyone that got lost?"

She took another shirt and laid it against her belly. Sleeve, sleeve, bend in half, meet the ends.

I guess we never really got our answer.

MARI

Soon after our moonrise buggy ride, Tomas decided to stay in Guatemala. He lazed around the countryside for two weeks, and then showed back up at the hotel, and told me he had decided to stay. I wanted to believe he was staying for me, but even I am not that naïve.

He had missed several weeks of college by now, and had no job lined up in America after he graduated college. His parents had practically disowned him, he told me, and so he said there was no reason to even go back and finish school at all. There was no one and nothing to go back to.

With our one mossy night still stuck in my memory, I told him that I would talk to my father about giving him a job at the hotel. A good job. Not cleaning and cooking like I did. He seemed so happy about this idea that I shook off my certainty that it was a terrible idea. I shook off my mother's voice in my head that told me to run from this young man. I shook off Nery's voice in my head that told me I was better than this.

I asked my father if the American boy could join us for dinner one night. I told him I had been spending a lot of time with him, and that he would be a wonderful asset to the hotel. I told him about his watch and exaggerated what I had seen in his room. I made my father think Tomas had money and breeding in addition to American citizenship. My father looked at me skeptically at first, but went along with my request.

My father invited Tomas to dinner at the hotel, and Tomas showed up wearing long pants, abandoning his tropical shorts for more conservative attire. I smiled and fussed over him. I brought him extra meat, and refilled his beer while he laughed and talked with my father. Tomas smiled politely at me and looked at me as though he was seeing me for the first time every time I walked back into the room. Then he'd look to my father and they'd start back up with their animated discussion.

My father liked Tomas immediately and offered him a job, on one condition. He wanted us to marry. In just a couple of months. I had unwittingly convinced my father about Tomas's wealth back in America and, in turn, he seemed to believe that this would somehow be a good arrangement for both me *and* my father.

I was so anxious to leave my father and the hotel that I, too, pinned my hopes on Tomas the American, and so I agreed to the marriage. Of course none of this makes sense because in the end, we were simply staying at the hotel after we married. But only for the time being, I hoped.

I tried to be hopeful as my father's wife made wedding arrangements, and my father trained Tomas to work at the hotel over the next few weeks, and I continued cleaning rooms. And then one day, about four weeks after I agreed to marry Tomas, Nery returned from the farm camp, surprising me at the hotel, and setting everything else that happened into motion.

☺

"Nery!"

I greeted Nery in the back of my father's hotel where he had arrived and where I was putting out the garbage. I smoothed down my dirty clothes wishing I looked more presentable.

"Mari!" Nery wrapped me in a big hug.

"How did you know to come here?" I asked.

"I've been to the House of Mercies. Sister Magdalena told me where you were. Reluctantly, though." Nery looked sheepish.

I looked over my shoulder and said, "Come on."

We grabbed one of the hotel buggies and I drove us to the waterfall. I told Nery about the events of the last four weeks. Of my engagement. Of this man who was probably not worthy of me. I tried to make it sound less dire than it was, but it was no use. In turn, Nery told me of the last year—of the sights and sounds of the insurgency. He, too, tried to make it sound less dire than it was, but it was no use.

We sat there on the bank by the waterfall, side by side, like no time had passed since we last saw each other, until the clouds opened with the afternoon rainfall. When the rain started, Nery took my hand and led me deeper into the forest. We took cover under a huge *ceiba* tree, which actually seemed to shield us a bit from the pelting rain, and he pulled me close to him as if he held the only umbrella in the forest. I inhaled deeply, leaning into him and then grew self-conscious and pulled away. Nery smelled like mud and rain, and I realized I must smell the same, but mixed in with the hotel's smells. A masculine scent. I pulled further away—I didn't want Nery to smell that scent on me.

Nery held me away and I could see his eyes—thick with dripping rain—his face splattered with mud. "Do I look as filthy as you?" I laughed.

"You look beautiful, Mari. I'm going to paint you just like this when I get back to the camp." *Leaving.* Nery was always focused on leaving. "Covered in mud and moss and rain. You look like a forest nymph—like you grew straight up from the soil. Come closer. Let me stare at you so I'll remember."

"Oh Nery, you are hopeless."

"I can't take my eyes off you, Mari."

I buried my head back into his muddy, sopping wet shirt. It was better to smell him and have him smell me than stare at me, I concluded.

"Mari, wait for me. Please," Nery pleaded into my hair. "I'll marry you," he promised desperately.

"I don't believe in marriage, Nery. You know that. I've told you that many times."

"Then why are you marrying him?"

"That fact alone should tell you how much I do not believe in marriage."

"I love you, Mari."

"Marriage and love are unrelated, Nery. Marriage has nothing to do with love. It is a contract with only one way out—" I clamped my hand over my mouth, appalled at all I had said. Afraid of what more I might say out loud.

"Death." Nery said it for me. "You believe death is the only way out of marriage. Of *this* marriage."

"Nery, I need to leave this place. I want to get to America. This may be my one way out. I need to take it." I pushed my nose deeper into Nery's shirt. I inhaled the waterfall and the mist, the musky scent of soap, the greasy scent of oil paints, and something that might have been laundry detergent. For a moment, I drifted away from the Guatemalan rainforest to America, and imagined myself standing over a washing machine with Nery's shirts, scrubbing mud and dirt and paint from his clothes. I imagined him coming in at night from a day at work. (Where would he work in America? Who would buy his paintings?)

I imagined myself cutting vegetables and beef and making soup for him and serving it to him in an American kitchen where all the appliances were new and in working order, and had been gifts. Upon the occasion of our marriage. Mine and Nery's marriage.

"Our marriage will be different, Mari. Our marriage will be sacred." I shook my head, remembering my father shushing my brave mother all of those years. Before she disappeared mysteriously. What would my father say if I told him I was marrying a farmhand orphan rebel? What would he *do*?

I shuddered at the thought. "My father, Nery. He would never allow it."

My strong and rebellious Nery nodded a concession to me, even while he pulled me tighter and tighter. "We could have children, Mari—" I wanted to stay in the daydream with him. The one that could never last. But I wondered: *Could I ever raise a proper child? How would I know how to do that? Who would tell me what to do? How to carry my children? What to feed them? How to love them?*

I wondered aloud: "What if I did wait for you, Nery? What would happen?"

"This." Nery's whispered response unlocked my resolve. Permission and release swirled in my brain. I was crying, now, but the rain was coming down so thick all around us, Nery couldn't see my tears from rain. Nery bent his head to me and asked, "Mari, if you won't wait for me, then what are we doing here?"

"Nery. I love you. That's a bigger promise than marriage. I'll love you forever. Until the day I die."

"Well then, it's a lot like marriage isn't it?" Nery started to push me away angrily.

"No. You didn't let me finish. I'll love you until the day I die. And then beyond."

I reached up and pulled his muddy, rainy head to me and kissed him so hard I felt his knees buckle against mine. I let him pull me down into the mud where the tears and the rain and dirt and confusion and pain and lust all joined us together.

"Mari, please. I don't want to lose you. Ever."

And at the moment we conceived our son, I told him: "You will never lose me, Nery. We are only one person. I will never love anyone the way I love you."

In other words, I lied to him.

Nearly a month after the plane crash, I was pouring coffee for my Sunday regulars—largely island residents avoiding church or family or killing time until the bars opened—when I was greeted unfamiliarly.

"Lu Roselli? You look like you could use a shot of that coffee yourself—you look so tired!"

I splashed some coffee out on the saucer under the cup I was pouring it in and blinked hard at the bright blue unlined eyes looking up at me accusatorily. It took a few minutes for me to recognize the eyes. "Bridget. What on earth are you doing here?"

Besides Seamus, Bridget Riordan had been one of my only friends in high school, but we lost touch shortly after graduation when she headed west to study art. Last I heard she was working at a prestigious art gallery in California.

Five of my and Seamus's parochial school classmates—along with Mrs. Bouther, and including Rae—had died on 9/11, and we felt their absence every day of the remaining school days as seventh grade and eighth grade dragged on mournfully. At the end of eighth grade, when the rest of my class was making plans to attend the various local parochial high schools, I begged Mari to send me to the local public school, and not just because Seamus had applied to and gotten into a local boys-only Catholic high school. I needed a fresh start. I needed to be in class next to people who didn't know my story the minute they saw my face. I needed to be around people who hadn't necessarily known Rae.

So when I met Bridget on the first day of AP English at the local public school, she and I struck up the kind of friendship I imagined was as normal a friendship as I was going to have in high school. Sleepovers—mostly at Bridget's house—football games and post-game pizza parties. Group movie dates, sneaking each other into the mega-Cineplex in nearby Sheepshead Bay and bonfires on the beach in Rock Harbor. Seamus went along with my insistence that we remain boyfriend and girlfriend during high school, and Bridget and Seamus got along well enough. So did Seamus and Bridget's string of mostly handsome basketball-center boyfriends.

Bridget was never going to stay in Rock Harbor. I had pretty much triaged that prognosis from the first day of high school. Maybe that's why she had seemed such an easy choice for friend. The pressure of forever was lessened. And maybe that's why we clicked easily and completely for those four years. When she left for California to study art history, I hugged her tightly but finally, without promises to visit or write weekly. Seeing her in Rock Harbor more than five years older was mildly shocking.

"I'm back, Lu. I saw a posting for an art teacher back in my hometown. I applied. And I got it. Imagine that." Bridget tapped the chair next to her. I sat down in it with only a quick backward glance over my shoulder at Mr. Sheehan who gave me a look that I ignored.

"That's wonderful. You'll be a great teacher," I said truthfully. "I'm on my way to becoming a licensed social worker myself, if you can believe it. Just got my degree this past spring. As you can see, I'm using it well." I chuckled without humor and then conceded: "I'm pouring coffee here until I can, well, settle up some things at home."

"How's your mom?" Bridget asked without fanfare. I remembered then that Bridget had always been what I'd called an "over-sharer." She had no qualms about letting those in her inner circle know what she was thinking when she was thinking. I hadn't always been able to reciprocate the trust, but I had done my best. Letting her in on bits and pieces of Mari's unavailability—if only as a means of explaining why I often wanted to "just have the sleepover at your house tonight, Bridget, ok?"

"Not good, I'm afraid. She was ... one of the ground victims of the plane crash. She's in a coma at City Hospital. It's pretty bleak actually."

And then I blurted out the rest before I had time to change my mind. "And it turns out she is pregnant on top of everything. The doctors are keeping her alive until the baby can be delivered safely, and we are trying to find a good family to adopt the baby. To give the baby a real chance, you know?"

"Oh, Lu." Bridget covered my hand like no time had lapsed in the phase of our friendship that would have allowed for such intimacies. "Seamus still around?"

I snorted a small laugh. "No. I think things are finally over between us. Since the summer, actually."

Bridget nodded like she expected that. And approved. "Well, I'm really glad to run into you. I hope we'll be seeing a lot more of each other."

"Me, too." I said, meaning it and headed back to pouring coffee and serving omelets. As I refilled an empty creamer server, I felt a little pang as I checked the expiration date on the carton, letting my mind wander for a moment back to the first day of summer vacation before Seamus and I broke up for good.

⑨

"Seriously, Lu. This refrigerator is like a biohazard." Seamus had his head in the refrigerator and I giggled at the far away echo his words made.

I had been so busy with school; I hadn't had time to clean out the refrigerator in weeks. Half empty cartons of milk and half and half were still showing month-old expiration dates. A bowl of leftover soup had turned into a petri dish. Old Styrofoam takeout containers made a pyramid shoved way in the back behind newer containers creating such a confusion of food that I couldn't rely on eating any of it. I just kept phoning in new takeout orders and creating a bigger mess.

Finals would be over in a week and I'd officially have my social work degree. That fact terrified me. More so than the finals looming over my head—I dreaded being done with school and expected to actually work in the field full-time. I hadn't applied for a single position or even finalized my resume. I was paralyzed by the terror I was feeling and had called Seamus over to talk me out of it, or distract me from it with a study break. He was home for summer break, and when he walked into my apartment after his morning run, he had an air of carelessness surrounding him that I wanted to cover myself in. I was just about to launch into an exposition about my fears and insecurities when he reached in my refrigerator, apparently expecting something other than a hazmat scene.

"Just grab a beer. Nothing else is good in there. I mean you can try checking the dates—but—I doubt it—"

Seamus grabbed a Corona and a bottle opener that he had left on the counter last time he came home a month prior. I hadn't bothered to put it back in the drawer it belonged in because—wait for it—yes—he left it right in that same place again after popping off the bottle cap in his hand. He twisted the spiky cap around in his hand as he leaned against my refrigerator and drained his beer slowly. I watched him from my place at the kitchen table where I was surrounded by notes and textbooks and my laptop, stopping my slow tapping on the keys to watch him. He raised his eyebrows over the bottle at me and I could see the sides of his mouth turn up in a sexy smile around the neck of the beer bottle. I should have been drawn in. I should have walked over and put my arms around him. Let him put his arms around me and distract me from my finals for a few moments. An hour even. But I couldn't stop my eyes from drifting to the cap he twisted around and around in his hand, until finally I couldn't take it anymore.

"Seamus! Stop it!"

His raised brows furrowed in confusion. I walked across the room and grabbed the cap out of his hand and tossed it into the garbage. "Jesus. You'll slice your hand open."

I took my seat at the table again and felt the spell broken. There'd be no study break. Seamus put his running shoes back on and headed out the door with a quick kiss on my head and his prophetic advice.

"Good luck, bookworm. And when you're done with finals—clean out that frig already. Enough keeping everything around long after its expiration date."

⑨

After my shift at the café the morning I ran into Bridget, I was walking home alone when I heard it not too far behind me. It was only 11 am on a Sunday so most of the Mom and Pop shops were closed and there weren't usually people out on the commercial street at this hour on a Sunday. I told myself that I was just imagining things but I continued to hear them. Soft footsteps behind me, matching mine stride for stride. I felt my heart in my throat as I walked, pulling my purse full of cash tips close to my side and standing up as straight as I could, trying to remember all the self-defense tips I had ever seen on Oprah.

Don't let him take you to a second location.
Bite.
Scream.
Claw.

I stopped to pretend to window shop at a closed boutique. I hoped whoever was following me would pass me by and I'd stay in my spot until it was safe to move. But the footsteps. They stopped as I stopped. I tried to see in the reflection of the window but I couldn't see my stalker. I was going to have to turn around. I was going to have to confront him. I took a deep breath and still clutching my bag, turned on my heel dramatically and confidently. "Stop following me!"

I found myself face to face with a cleaned up version of Freda Cross, my first real social work client from the year before. I had not seen her since, but had wondered on more than one occasion what had happened to her. I hardly saw Lynn Cooper anymore since I had graduated. I spent most of my time at the café, working up the motivation to prepare my resume and application for a full-time social work job.

The first thing I noticed about Freda was that she was dressed. And not just in a barely-covering-her tee shirt. She was wearing black pants and a blue polo shirt embroidered with the name of a convenience store a few blocks away on the island. Her eyes were not glassy, although they were decidedly tired. Her dark hair peppered with a little gray was pulled back in a ponytail and she carried a purse and a plastic bag bearing the name of the same convenience store as her polo shirt.

"Freda." I exhaled loudly.

Her posture relaxed with relief—possibly that I had recognized her.

"I'm sorry I yelled at you, Freda—I thought—I was afraid..."

Her quick nod reminded me that fear was not an unfamiliar emotion for this struggling woman.

"You look wonderful, Freda. Tell me how you are doing. Can I buy you a cup of coffee?"

Freda nodded again, and I turned and walked with her back the few blocks to the coffee shop. "Back again?" Mr. Sheehan asked as I walked in. "You know me. I can never stay away." I smiled, as I led Freda to the back of the café to an empty table.

"I didn't mean to scare you." Freda finally broke her silence. Her voice was neither as hoarse or as scratchy as I remembered it from our last meeting. I saw you coming out of this place on my own way home from work, and I just—"

I interrupted her to order us two cups of coffee. "Some breakfast, Freda?"

"No. Just coffee, thank you." She held up the convenience store bags and said, "I have cereal for me and my son here. I'm going to have lunch with him at his foster home this morning. I'm due there in about an hour."

"Oh, that's great. How is Roberto?"

"He's really good. He's getting all As in school, except one B still in spelling, but the teacher says not to get all bothered about spelling, because he's a smart boy and can learn how to use 'spell-check.'" She smiled brightly with that story and I laughed along with her. "And I get to see him three days a week now at his foster home—only—with them keeping a close eye on both of us—but soon, I hope, I'm going be able to take him out to the playground, and then eventually, you know—" Her tired eyes lit up from within as she pointed to her overstuffed convenience store bag.

I gave her my warmest smile. *Yes, I knew.*

"I'm clean now. For three months."

I reached over and patted her hand like I had that first day months ago in her filthy kitchen. "That's good, Freda. You didn't give up. That's good."

"No, I didn't. It's hard. But—"

"All the best stuff—the stuff worth doing—is hard, Freda. Good for you."

"Oh, that's pretty—the stuff worth doing is hard. I'm going to remember that." She looked down at my hand covering hers with a look of recognition. I was surprised she remembered anything from that first day we met—she'd been so glassy eyed and I assumed high, that day.

"I remember what you said that day. About your own mama. At first when you came in my door, I thought you were like all the others. Like you thought you were better than me. But you didn't. You were nice to me. And you told me about your own mama giving up on you and your sister and that your sister was dead because of it, and that stayed with me." I didn't correct her cause and effect assumption about Mari's giving up and Rae's death.

"I got a job and I've been sober for three months now," she repeated, "And I ain't giving up on Roberto. This time, it's going to take, I know it."

I paid for our coffees and when we stood to say goodbye, as Freda headed off for her supervised visit with Roberto, I fought off the sadness that was crawling over my shoulders. I shook off the whisper in my brain that said this was the same song of a thousand addicts before Freda Cross, and of a thousand addicts after her. I defied the doubt trying to creep into my response, saying instead, "Freda, I believe you will make it. I do."

She thanked me hungrily, enveloping my hand in hers one more time before we headed in opposite directions on the quiet street, each of us walking clear-eyed into the hard stuff of our lives.

MARI

For weeks after he returned, and as my wedding date neared, Nery came back and forth from the House of Mercies to Semuc Champey. He did odd jobs in both San Marcos and Lanquin to make money to take back to camp. When he was near Lanquin, he came to see me as often as he could. We would sneak away to the waterfalls together or into town, hiding from Tomas and my father as best we could. And after six weeks, Nery announced that he would be leaving again in the morning. Six weeks.

By then, it had been long enough for me to know.

On the night before he left, I snuck away from my work at the hotel at dusk, and made my way down to the waterfalls. I kicked off my sandals and crawled out of my loose pants and tee shirt and left everything in a pile on a rocky bank. As I stared hard at the rocks to pick out a smooth barefooted path toward the top of the waterfall, the ground came into focus like an abstract painting. The smallest rocks were moving—small crabs in tiny conch shells ducking in and out of the uneven rock formations, alternately greeting and hiding from intruders. It was *almost* perfectly pristine, but not quite. A few pieces of litter floated in the stream leading away from the waterfall—a crushed beer can, a metal can top, a discarded asthma inhaler. (I focused for a while on the inhaler, imagining its owner rendered literally breathless by the view, before taking a few medicinal hits and continuing on his/her hike.)

I crawled up alongside the waterfall on a ladder of mossy rocks, and then scooted along the slippery rocks feeling for footholds until I was fully within the mist of the waterfall that started high above me. I stood up into the waterfall and jumped to the pool below. The water was cool—such a relief on that hot muggy night when my discomfort could be traced to so much more than heat and humidity. I floated on my back in the pool below and let the waterfall spray take over my senses. It was all I could hear. It was all I could see through my closed eyes. It was all I could feel.

I did not think beyond that moment. I did not think about Tomas who would soon stand before me tall and regal in his wedding suit. I did not think about Nery who would be quite gone by the morning. I simply felt the water all around me, especially on my still flat belly which I caressed protectively as I floated.

I knew that Tomas seemed to sense—or maybe had seen—the time I was spending with Nery. And he was becoming increasingly difficult. He was threatening to call off the wedding. Threatening to take all he had learned and open another hotel to compete with my father in Semuc Champey. I knew he had access to hotel bank accounts. I figured I would have to come clean and sever the relationship between my father and Tomas once and for all before Tomas stole enough money from my father to make those threats a reality.

I decided as I left the falls that night that I would have to protect my father from Tomas at any cost. So the day after Nery left, I told my father and stepmother the news.

My father's wife was crossing herself repeatedly, and my father was pacing the way he did when he made important business decisions. I had started out with courage. Enough courage to tell them that I was pregnant. Not enough to tell them that I knew the baby to be Nery's. Not yet at least. I was summoning that courage as I continued to speak. "I want to call off the wedding. I want to—"

"Call off the wedding?" My stepmother looked stricken.

"Are you loco?" My father shouted. "We will move *up* the wedding, and we will ignore the whispers. And you will keep your nose out of trouble. For real this time. Or that baby of yours will end up at the House of Mercies with Mother Magdalena, and you will work in my hotel as a hired employee and not the owner's daughter—I promise you that."

I reeled from my father's words. From his wrath. His eyes looked black as he issued his warning—sizing up my reaction.

I lost my nerve. I lost all will.

"Call off the wedding? *Dios Mio*—why would you even suggest such a thing?" My stepmother looked me in the eye. My father continued pacing as my stepmother held me still with her gaze that wavered and then locked on mine in recognition. She had seen me too often with the rebel boy.

Her hand flew to her mouth. Her shoulders and back crumpled for a moment. But only for a moment before she straightened and brushed her pristine and clean hands off on her pants. My stepmother leaned in and whispered to me: "Mari. Can Tomas say that it would be impossible for this to be his child? Have you been innocent with Tomas?" I knew the timing would be murky, but I knew if I wanted to, I could make Tomas believe this was his child, conceived on our one mossy night together—six weeks or so before the baby was actually conceived. I shook my head at my stepmother, realizing that I was confessing to so many sins.

Through still clenched teeth, she hissed. "You and Tomas *will* marry. And raise this baby together. And I will deal with your father. And we will never again talk about calling off the wedding, or possible reasons to do so, or I *will* sell that illegitimate baby to the army. You understand?"

I nodded, sickened.

Out loud, my stepmother announced, "Mari and Tomas will get married next week. I will handle everything. Right, Mari?"

"Yes." My own shoulders and back crumpled with the concession.

My stepmother and I looked across the room at my

father who had stopped pacing and seemed to think that everything was resolved and closed, instead of a wide open gaping chasm. And even with the new baby growing inside me, all I could really feel was the beginning of a very wide empty loss.

According to flyers that papered the front window of the café, Rock Harbor was preparing a memorial service at the beach on November 11 for its five residents and the passengers on the plane who had died tragically a month earlier. American and Guatemalan flags and photographs of the deceased now decorated the plywood walls erected by town officials to cordon off the crash site right outside Mari's house. I walked by the makeshift memorial every day on my way to the café.

The memorial flyers reminded me that the tragedy from the prior month had befallen our entire island, and not just me. I was so wrapped up in Mari and her unborn baby, I had all but forgotten that others were in mourning on the island as well.

It was true that five of our neighbors had been confirmed dead. And while my general reclusive status on the island meant that none of the victims probably knew me, I knew *them*. A mother, a teacher, a doctor, a retired firefighter, and a mail carrier had all lost their lives in the plane crash, doing nothing but living and working on the island they loved that morning. When I saw the pictures on the memorial flyers, I recognized each as having been in the café at one time or another. I took a look around the café and acknowledged that yes, there were people *missing* from all of our lives.

It was the same feeling I remembered having after September 11.

At first I was not sure I would go to the memorial on the

beach. It was to remember "all the victims of Flight 555." I studied these words on the printed flyer with curiosity. Was Mari a victim of Flight 555? And if so, would it be strange to memorialize her when she was still alive—albeit kept that way by expensive machines and a fully committed medical team?

Was *I* a victim of Flight 555? I pondered this thought while I refilled coffee mugs at the café on the eve of the memorial service. The café had become a second home to me in the last few years, having spent so much time there and having been happy to have a place to go after school that wasn't Mari's house or the old garage apartment. But much like my first home, I wasn't that comfortable here either. The entire place had something of a forced feel to it. The bench cushions matched the window treatments matched the framed prints on the wall. Dark rustic and exposed brick lined the east side of the café, instead of windows that would face the beach and in turn the morning sunrise. I often marveled that people would tear themselves away from the scene just a block away from the café to come inside and eat egg white omelets.

While I was thinking about the upcoming memorial and whether it should include me—and Mari—I noticed that a frazzled-looking mother juggling an antsy preschooler and an often rebooting laptop kept calling me over to refill her cup. She had a look in her eyes and a shake to her hands that I attributed to over-caffeinating. I thought briefly about cutting her off like I was a bartender dispensing booze, but I didn't.

I circled past her table four times, refilling her mug and picking up crayons under her preschooler, whose art had drifted more than a few times from the back of the placemat to the distressed wooden table below.

I ignored the woman's frazzle through the morning commuter crowd until she signaled me to take her uneaten egg white omelet without looking up from the computer.

"Are you sure?" I asked her as I cleared her plate.

She looked up suddenly from her laptop and caught my eye directly. And began crying. "Oh miss. I'm so—"

I fumbled with her plate and then placed it down and looked over at her preschooler with a silent plea for her not to start crying next to her mother. No need. The little girl with blonde ringlets just reached down to slurp the end of her chocolate milk loudly and said, "Mommy, are you crying about Grandma again?"

The woman dabbed at her eyes and said, "I'm so sorry. I'm just—it's ok, sweetie, remember Mommy told you that I would be feeling a little sad this week. I'm fine."

"Grandma went to heaven last month." The little girl went back to coloring as if her work here was finished.

"My mother. Maybe you knew her? Mary O'Shannon? She was a teacher here in town. She died in the—" she stole a glance at the occupied little girl, "you know, event here last month." She recoiled as she whispered and glanced over her shoulder as if speaking even these coded words aloud with shrouded gestures was more than she could bear.

Mrs. O'Shannon. She was an art teacher at the local high school. Apparently—according to a news report I read in spite of myself one long day by Mari's bedside—she wasn't feeling well and had called in sick on the day of the plane crash which was why she was home and not safely tucked away at school a few blocks from the crash site at the time of impact.

I suddenly connected the dots realizing that Mrs. O'Shannon's was the art teacher job that needed to be filled. And that Bridget Riordan had moved back to town to fill.

Life goes on.

I had seen Mrs. O'Shannon around our small town, although I didn't really know her. She had apparently gone back to teaching about eight years ago after a long hiatus raising children and caring for a sick husband. I gleaned that information also from the news report. I vaguely remembered reference in the article to one surviving child and her family, now located out of town. I realized I was standing face to face with that surviving child and her family now.

"It's just—you can't understand until this happens to you. You expect you will have all this time to fix the past. Fix what's broken, and then—no. You don't."

I thought about correcting this mistaken woman. To let her know that I was more than familiar with this premise. But instead I stood silently with my coffee pot in one hand and my heart in the other.

The floodgates appeared to be open. I didn't even have to prompt her to continue. "I'm trying to write something meaningful and important to say tomorrow at the memorial service. I'm a writer for god's sake. I should be able to write a eulogy for my mother. And yet, all I have left are the regrets. I don't want to say those. You know, out loud."

"No. I can certainly understand that you wouldn't want to do that. But maybe—" The woman looked at me hopefully. "Maybe you can talk about what your mother was to people other than you. I didn't really know your mother, but she was an art teacher—that's a pretty generous vocation—no? And I remember her coming here, into the café, a few times a month. She was always cheerful and never came alone. She had friends and a busy life. I don't know, isn't there something about all that you can say?"

Mrs. O'Shannon's daughter looked at me like she was sizing me up and down. She said finally, "Yes. That's exactly what I will do. Thank you." And then she looked back down at her laptop and I felt a bit dismissed so I cleared the uneaten egg white omelet and, noticing that my shift had officially ended, I clocked out and headed home to change for the hospital.

The next morning, the café was closed down, as were most of the local businesses on Rock Harbor in honor of the memorial. Despite all of my ambivalence about actually attending, I found myself walking down to the beach without much of an attempt of talking myself out of it.

It was unseasonably warm and the sky was bright blue with thick cumulus clouds, but I wondered what the backup plan was in case of inclement November weather. Rock Harbor residents tended to be hopeful and optimistic. They must have assumed that Mother Nature would cooperate with their plans for a beautiful beachside memorial. Wooden chairs had been set up for the length of an entire beach block on the sand. A white canopy had been staked at the front of the chairs with seats for distinguished speakers who I recognized as including the mayor of Rock Harbor and the head of the community group that had been established shortly after 9/11 when memorial services like this one were all too common. Rae and my dad were two of over 70 residents of the town that died in the Towers—largely emergency personnel and first responders.

The plywood wall from the crash site had been moved to a place of honor under the white canopy—apparently during the night, as I remembered having seen it just outside Mari's home the day before. Flowers and small plush animals and photographs and handwritten notes littered the wall and the ground below it. I tried not to look too hard.

I stood deliberately behind the rows of chairs where my view was somewhat obscured. I noticed Rebecca close to the front. She looked over her shoulder scanning the crowd. I wondered if she was looking for me, and I ducked behind a taller gentleman nearby so she wouldn't see me. I wanted to stay where I was and I knew if Rebecca saw me and summoned me, I wouldn't have much strength to turn her down.

There were several officiants of the service who read Biblical verses and poems. Several speakers elevated on tripods around the beach vibrated with the lyrics of "For Good" from the *Wicked* soundtrack. While I had never seen the play on Broadway, I knew the score well, having played it over and over again after Seamus brought me the CD a few years ago.

He'd been to see it with his parents. "You would love this play, Lu. It completely changes *Wizard of Oz* for you. Like *completely* changes it."

That sounded horrible to me, as I had vibrant memories of *Wizard of Oz* coming on television once a year when Rae and I were young. We would stay up late to watch it, half scared out of our minds by the flying monkeys, but loving every last minute of the story. I didn't really want *Wizard of Oz*—like everything else in my life—to be changed forever.

Still. I played the soundtrack gift that Seamus brought me—and especially "For Good"—on a loop. After all, I couldn't deny that a song about people coming into your life and leaving after too short of a time could very well have been a song written just for me.

As the memorial continued on, names of the passengers, flight crew, and victims on the ground were read aloud, slowly and officiously by the mayor. The victims from the plane itself were eulogized en masse by the community head. I wondered briefly how many of those families were actually here as this seemed to be a largely local crowd. I hoped not too many of the plane victims' family members *were* here, as this seemed a rather impersonal way to memorialize a large group of victims. The focus was definitely on the five Rock Harbor resident victims.

Our own lost.

This was how the community representative referred to them as he handed the podium over to five speakers who spoke briefly about their respective loved ones who died the month before.

When Mrs. O'Shannon's daughter took the podium last, she was stoic and solemn. She spoke briefly of her mother's devotion to her family—foregoing her more lucrative career as a children's book illustrator to raise her family, and later, care for her sick husband in his final days, before returning to her first love: teaching. I noticed her glance toward one side of the crowd and I followed her gaze to see a familiar tow-headed girl in the arms of a tanned man I assigned the status of Mrs. O'Shannon's surviving son-in-law.

"My mother leaves a legacy of creativity. I see her in my young daughter's artwork, and passion for color and beauty. This town has lost a true gift. A resident, a teacher, a devotee to Rock Harbor history and beauty. I hope you will always remember my mother in terms of the little kindnesses and expressions of friendship she extended to you when she was alive."

The crowd wiped their tears and applauded as Mrs. O'Shannon's daughter took her seat next to her husband and daughter who both joined in hugging her. I wondered if anyone other than myself noticed that she had said absolutely nothing about her own relationship with her mother in life. Or in death.

I walked back home to Mari's house, fed Catt, and took a shower, attempting to wash off the memorial and all the bad and familiar feelings that came with it. I was in my bathrobe when the doorbell rang.

I sat very still thinking maybe it was a delivery person or a wrong number. *Can you have a wrong number at your door,* I wondered. And then I laughed, realizing what a funny notion that was. Something Mari might confuse with her sometimes language barrier. But now it was stuck in my head, and I couldn't get rid of it and I also couldn't stop laughing.

I figured whoever had knocked probably heard me laughing, too, so I decided I would have to open the door. I walked quickly across the room as if I might avoid talking myself out of hiding again. As I paced the length of the floor, thoughts sped through my brain in rapid fire—it could be a bill collector, a serial murderer. I could do something foolish. I could invite the stranger in. I could tell all my secrets to him or to her. I arrived at the door and threw it open with all the appearance of confidence. "Helloo!" I bellowed.

I was still laughing a bit. I felt a little hysterical. Actually a lot hysterical. And then I did what I truly had feared I'd do all along. I began crying uncontrollably.

It was Bridget, my over-sharing friend who was at the door—with her arms as open as her expression. "Come here, Lu," she said, even as it was she who came to me. "I saw you standing near the back at the memorial, and I was thinking you might need a friend this afternoon."

"Yes," I said in between sniffs.

"So," Bridget continued, eyeing my frayed terry cloth bathrobe: "How about if you get changed, and show me around Rock Harbor. I haven't been home in years, and I could use a good tour."

Hours after the beachfront Memorial Service, Rock Harbor was beginning to open up again for the afternoon. I showed Bridget where the new butcher shop was, and which market, pizzeria, and sandwich shops I thought were the best these days. I even introduced her to the Russian woman at the salon around the corner where I had my hair cut every 12 or 13 weeks or so, the same woman who was always insisting on plucking my thick eyebrows, even though I never let her. As we stopped outside the salon, Natalie waved me in. "Let me do those eyebrows, Lu. In America, all the girls keep little eyebrows, now. Just look at your friend's eyebrows," she sang out in her old familiar way.

I studied Bridget's tiny plucked eyebrows—which were just a shade or two darker than the golden brown of her hair—and then I shrugged and headed inside the salon and deeper still inside the room Natalie called the "waxing room." Turns out there was no plucking at all as I had believed, but rather boiling hot wax that was poured on my eyebrows and then ripped off violently—making my eyes sting and my lips pucker with each pull. When I came out of the waxing room to meet Bridget, with my thin American eyebrows, Bridget laughed mockingly, and then said, "Well at least they'll grow back. I like *your* eyebrows better on *you*, Lu."

While I had been inside being pruned by Natalie, Bridget had made herself comfortable at a pedicure bath inside the salon. I decided to join her and rolled up my pants legs and climbed into the seat next to her. "I'll have a pedicure, also," I announced to Natalie who nodded at a slender girl flipping through a magazine. The slender girl came over and started my pedicure bath next to Bridget. There was an initial moment when I realized I hadn't shaved my legs that morning, or regularly at all now that Seamus wasn't stopping by unexpectedly anymore, and I reached down self-consciously to rub my shins.

Not too bad. Considering.

I congratulated myself silently on having been unprepared. I seemed to have let my guard down on being prepared for every eventuality in the last few weeks, which I actually saw as a positive development. Rubbing my prickly shins, my confidence metered up a bit higher than usual, and I launched into conversation with Bridget.

"So, Bridget. Tell me. How are you ever going to get used to living back here in our small town after you've been living in LA all this time? How soon til you get bored? From what I remember, you were never going to be that girl who came back to her hometown, married the former basketball star, had lots of babies, and lived happily ever after."

Bridget laughed. "No, you're right. And I wouldn't go and marry me off just yet. But, I have to tell you, when I saw that art teacher job open up ... something in me just ... clicked. Here's the truth, Lu. I missed the energy of Rock Harbor. That's something you just can't get in LA."

"Energy?" I had never left, and yet I didn't feel very energetic. What was this energy she was talking about and where could I find some?

"This town. You know we're not so hidden as we used to pretend." Bridget waved out the window in front of the pedicure chairs. "People know about Rock Harbor out there in the world. They've heard of us. Did you know that this town lost more people in 9/11 than any other town in America?"

I shook my head. We had lost so many. Firefighters. First responders. Seventh graders. Rae. Dad. But I assumed we were like many small towns in the area.

Bridget continued somewhat evangelically. "After 9/11, life went on. The shops reopened. The beach continued to fill with sun bathers and children. We never stopped mourning. But we never stopped living either."

"I guess that's true. I never really thought about it that way. I was too busy, you know, surviving."

"Yes. Exactly, Lu. This is a whole town of survivors. Resilience in large measures. Just look at how this town has rebounded from the plane crash. A horrific tragedy occurred right outside these doors only a month ago, and yet the town is mourning its dead and celebrating its living all at the same time. We went to a beautiful, solemn beachside memorial this morning, mourning our lost, and yet, here we are getting pedicures. The shops are reopening for business. The business of living. It's beautiful. I'm telling you—it's not like that out there. In LA, people act like the living is the real tragedy. Everything is so hard and so stressful and so difficult … about *living* for heaven's sake. It grew exhausting long ago, and when I saw the art teacher posting, I just knew. It was time to come home."

I liked Bridget's version of Rock Harbor, but I wasn't quite sure I fit into her resilient survivor theory. Nor did Mari. "But what about those who aren't quite as resilient as everyone else? What do you think happens to *those* Rock Harbor residents?"

Bridget waved these people away as if they were fictional. "They don't exist. Not here anyway. This is a very special place." She turned to me and looked me in the eye. "With very special people, Lu." She clapped her hands on her legs loudly. I jumped. "And now you're a social worker. I mean, it's absolutely perfect. That's exactly what I'm talking about. Taking all the bad that's happened and channeling it for good. You, my friend, are the precise embodiment of the Rock Harbor energy I came back home for.

"You and your mother, and I'm sure this new baby, too, are very special people, Lu. Survivors and resilient. Don't ever downplay that."

Was I really so special just because I survived? I wasn't sure I shared Bridget's certainty on that issue.

⑨

Last summer, I asked Mari about something she never really spoke about—to Rae and me, at least. I asked her about her life in Guatemala—before us. It didn't go all that well, actually.

Other than naming me after her mother, Mari spoke very rarely about her childhood, or her mother, or her life back in Guatemala. Sometimes while we cooked, and every year when we made the Day of the Dead *fiambre* she'd sing out, "This was my mother's recipe!" But if we pressed her for any more, she'd clam up.

But last summer, when I asked Mari about her parents, she had sighed. Twice in succession. The kind of deep, deep sighs that for me, signaled the fact that she would answer my questions. We continued cutting vegetables in silence for about three minutes. Which is longer than you might think, and then she said:

"Mama was gentle and sweet and perfect. But it was my father that I always took after. He had sharp edges. Many sharp edges. Yes, I take after *him*. I am sorry about that, Niña."

The sadness in her eyes when she talked of sharp edges made me think of something I hadn't thought about in a while.

The squirrel.

⑨

When we were about nine or ten years old, Seamus

announced that he was bored with our usual summertime games of tag and hide and seek, and he started patrolling the street for some trouble to get into. It didn't take too long before he found it.

Seamus had been shooting at some cans with a BB gun in a neighbor boy's backyard. After the boy promised him 20 minutes for $5.00, Seamus managed to negotiate 15 minutes for $4.65. He was furious with Rae and me because we would not "loan" him the extra 35 cents. We were furious with him for wanting to shoot a gun. He lined up metal cans in a pyramid and we held our hands over our ears while pellets ricocheted off the aluminum, and while the neighbor yelled, "That's enough, that's enough, you're using up all my ammo!"

I had my eyes closed tightly waiting for the eternity that was 15 minutes of clamor and shooting to end. It ended abruptly just after a weird squeaking noise, and I opened my eyes and looked around frantically for Seamus, certain that he was dead. I was so relieved when I saw him alive, but he was flushed red, standing over a squirrel that had run into his path accidentally. "Oh god, oh god, oh god," he was muttering, hardly audible. I let out a shriek so horrifying, it sounded foreign to my own ears. Rae stood speechless, which seemed louder for a moment than all the muttering and shrieking.

Mari came running out from a few doors down then, with her apron, and a cutting knife, smelling of tomatoes and onions and cilantro. "What is it?" For a moment, she seemed too busy counting human heads to look down at the body of the apparently still alive squirrel. She exhaled visibly after accounting for all of the humans, and when her shoulders sagged in relief, her head moved down with it. To the squirrel. "*Dios Mio!* Who? What?" She looked squarely at Seamus, and the horror on her face caused some sort of physical reaction in Seamus that led him to drop the gun on the ground and topple over next to it himself.

Mari looked at her own hand, at the knife that she had seemingly forgotten was there and then reached down as if to plunge the knife into the squirrel. I closed my eyes instinctively when I saw her knife moving toward the squirrel, and remember only the strange sound I thought was the ripping of squirrel hide. After a few moments when the noise did not subside, I opened my eyes, and it turned out to be Mari's retching in a nearby bush, the squirrel safely put out of its misery. Mari turned on her heel and left us there, with the squirrel carcass.

I said to Seamus, "My poor mother. I can't believe she had to do that. All because of what you did." And Seamus looked at me coldly from his spot on the ground and said "Your poor mother? Did you see what she did?"

I hadn't of course. I had closed my eyes when I saw her reach down toward the squirrel. I closed my eyes again instinctively at the memory when Mari spoke of her sharp edges.

And I wondered if maybe there were some things Mari would rather not discuss with me—but only with her dolls.

MARI

After Tomas and I married, I realized I was tied to him and to Nery by an unborn baby. I started to panic.

I hitched a day's ride to the House of Mercies and I asked Sister Magdalena to take a walk by Lake Atitlan with me, and then I asked the question I had been asking the dolls over and over again at night. Every night. "Should I have this baby, do you think?"

"You are asking me such a question? But you know what I must say."

"I know what you feel you should say. But what is the right answer? What do you really believe I should do?"

"I had a baby," she responded silently.

"Had? Did something happen to her?"

Sister Magdalena's hand reached up to her throat. "How did you—how did you know it was a baby girl?"

"Oh!" Now it was my turn to be alarmed. "I have no idea. Did you not say it was a girl?"

"I did not."

Sister Magdalena kicked off her sensible shoes and socks, folded the latter neatly in her black shoes and held up her long skirt as we walked along the edge of the water line. We walked along in silence for a long time. I wondered if Sister Magdalena was praying or if I should try to fill the silence in some way. I was still wondering when Sister Magdalena broke the silence dramatically. "My daughter would be 16 this year. June 26. I like to imagine that someone will throw her a beautiful party. I like to think she loves the water as much I do—no matter where she lives."

I silently did the math. Sister Magdalena would have

been little more than 16 herself when she gave birth. "Did you give her a name?"

"I called her June. I have no idea what she is called now, or where she is. It's lonely not to know June. Not to be part of her life. No one else can possibly understand how I feel. I've never told anyone before, because there's no point in trying to explain."

"You're explaining it pretty well to me, Sister Magdalena."

"Ah," she sighed as if caught.

"What about the father?" I asked suddenly—before I could rethink asking the question.

Sister Magdalena shook her head violently. "He never even knew she existed. It's for the best for everyone. And it will get better with time. That's what we say. It hurts to have to give that advice to the young girls I see leaving their babies with us." Sister Magdalena released her skirt into the water where it deposited sediment on the lightweight fabric.

"Then why do you?"

"It's the kindest lie I can possibly tell. Because it serves as an anesthetic at a time that the pain is potentially its sharpest—its most paralyzing. The pain that could kill someone if I didn't dull it with my lies. The excruciating pain at the very moment of the goodbye."

She turned to me: "I think you should have this baby, Mari. Did you really need to hear me say it aloud?"

"But then what? Should I keep this baby, Sister Magdalena?"

"You know that I cannot advise you on this."

"I'm begging you. Please don't tell me to follow my heart."

"I'm not. I would never insult you like that. It's not your heart you need to follow. That's the advice I should really be giving these girls. Not 'it's for the best for everyone.'"

"Whose, then? Whose heart should I be following?"

Sister Magdalena looked fleetingly at my belly, and I followed her gaze, but she said nothing more.

LU

The doctors kept saying that everything was progressing "as expected." Despite Mari's "advanced gestational age" (*yes, I know she's 44!*) and her continued "medical status" (*just say it! She's in a coma!*), they still planned to deliver a healthy baby. They hoped to wait until the early February due date to deliver the baby—but they were prepared to do so in January if necessary, late-December at the absolute earliest.

The social worker helped me prepare the temporary guardianship papers so I could make custody decisions for the baby when he or she arrived. The court approved me as temporary guardian of Mari's unborn baby in mid-November, according to a very official piece of paper that arrived by certified mail. As I stood in the doorway holding the paper that declared "Luna Roselli, Legal Guardian of Unborn Child Roselli, contingent upon Unborn Child Roselli being born alive," I involuntarily registered an old memory. I had missed *Dia de los Muertos*.

I decided to make a belated *fiambre*. It was what Mari would have insisted upon doing, I told myself, and I needed a distraction. This could well be Mari's last *Dia de los Muertos* on this side. I tried not to let my brain go to that place, but it went there anyway. *And I should recognize it properly.*

I stopped at the market on the way home from the café and bought as much produce and deli meat and cheese as I could carry. I made a large platter of salad and meats and cheeses and sliced cucumber, carrots, and beets. I tried to remember what other ingredients Mari used to add to our *fiambre*.

I drove slowly into the city with the platter sliding and

rocking on the passenger seat next to me. Every once in a while, I would whip my arm over to protect it, remembering when I was a teenager in the passenger seat of Mari's car and she used to whip her arm across to protect me at every stop sign and stop light in Rock Harbor. When I arrived at the hospital parking garage, I parked and then I carried the platter awkwardly into the nurse's station on Mari's floor. Anita was getting ready to leave. I didn't waste time with greetings—I felt too rushed and out of breath. I simply greeted her efficiently with: "I made a dish of food."

"Oh, sweetheart, I was just leaving. I brought a ham and cheese sandwich from the cafeteria that I was going to eat on the train on the way home. Thanks anyway."

I felt my whole body slump. I was even holding the platter lower at my hips at her words. I tried again. "It's meant to eat with family. A holiday dish of sorts in Guatemala. Actually, everyone is supposed to add something to the *fiambre* salad. We never really did that when Mari was, well, but—"

Anita looked me in the eye, and took her arm back out of the jacket she was just sliding into. "I can stay for a little while." Then she took her uneaten sandwich out of her bag, and cut the ham, cheese, and roll into little pieces with a blunt white plastic cafeteria knife, and sprinkled her contribution around the salad. We spooned some onto paper plates she grabbed from the nurse's station and we ate in silence in my mother's room, with the guardianship papers lurking nearby in my purse, while Anita murmured, "It's very good, Lu. Thank you for sharing with me. What do you call it again?"

"*Fiambre.*"

"*Fiambre.* Well, then, I'll always remember that."

⑨

It was about a week after the guardianship appointment arrived when the social worker came to Mari's room with more paperwork for me.

The first was for a year-long paid internship program—

social work at the City Hospital. "In case you're interested," she said. In truth, the days had begun to drag. I knew I needed to start thinking about long term. Needed to start looking for jobs in my new field of social work. Although social work had always felt like an antidote to the chaos of my own life, I now felt ill-equipped to help anyone else with my own life in such a shambles.

Another was a file on the family that wanted to foster Mari's baby with the intent to adopt. Paternity was still an issue, of course. As well as another nagging thought I couldn't relinquish, not even then, more than a month after Mari's initial dire prognosis had been delivered to me.

I thumbed through the papers as I asked anew, "Is there no chance? Is there really no chance Mari could wake up? Could survive all this?"

The social worker simply pushed the paperwork closer to me, and said, "You need to assume that when this is all done, it will just be you ... and a baby who needs a home."

MARI

When I said goodbye to my father for the last time as I left Guatemala, I turned back around and hugged him one last time. He seemed surprised that I would do that. Frankly, I surprised myself.

I wanted to hate him. I wanted to hold him responsible for all that had happened. Starting with my mother's disappearance and continuing forward. But I couldn't. His eyes looked so very sad. And while my stepmother held back, my father hugged me and he whispered again and again, "I did what I had to do to protect you, Niña. And the business. For your future, Mari. I wanted to give you a real future. It was only for you, Mari."

And as I looked at his sadness and slumped shoulders, I could feel only his defeat and sadness, and it was hard to hate a man for those things. By then I was a mother myself. And I understood on some level what a parent will do for their child. I understood, too, the mistakes—the very grave mistakes that could be made in the name of a parent's love. I forgave my father in that moment.

But I couldn't forgive myself.

After Catt's cancer diagnosis, sleeplessness became more and more of an issue. I thought about breaking into Mari's Ambien supply, but decided against it, as Catt was having restless nights and usually needed to be taken out in the middle of the night.

One night after tossing and turning for a particularly long time, I got up, crossed the room, took my old worry dolls out of my hope chest and put them under my pillow. But I didn't know what to tell them. I didn't really know what I was most worried about. After a few more long hours of involuntary wakefulness, one thought went through my mind repeatedly.

Mama.

I got out of bed and walked to the window in my garage bedroom. Many nights like this one, I would walk to the window and look across the yard. Now Mari's house was dark as it had been for the last month, but I thought back on a sleepless night like this one many months ago.

How many months ago? I tried to remember, as the timing now seemed terribly important.

After a restless half night trying to sleep, I had gotten up and walked to this very window and noticed that Mari's kitchen light was on across the yard. For a moment I thought I needed her. I thought I'd walk across the cool grass in my bare feet, put my head on her chest, feel the weight of her arms around me, and that I'd feel better.

I need you, Mama. I said out loud.

I had even put my hand on the apartment door's heavy lock ready to turn it, when suddenly, through the window, I saw the door open across the yard and a stranger kissed Mari's head and walked out, his face turned down to the sidewalk as if he believed that would prevent him from being seen. Mari was standing in the doorway with a cocktail glass and a barely closed robe, but even across the yard in the semi-darkness I could see her sadness.

I could *feel* her sadness.

On that night, like this one, I had returned to my room and reached under the pillow for my under-used trinkets.

I knew what I was worried about. What I was always worried about.

Mama.

ⓢ

When I was about 15 years old and my father and Rae had been dead for over two years, my mother said she was going out and then seemed to be taking a very long time to get ready. She put makeup on and lipstick and puttered around the kitchen for an extraordinarily long time. I wondered where she was going without asking aloud. I did wonder however if she was puttering around waiting for me to offer to go with her so I finally asked: "Do you want me to go with you, Mama?"

"No," she had answered quickly, and then seemed to move about more energetically after my question and her hurried response.

She looks pretty, I remember thinking. Prettier than I had seen her in a while, and I had this thought that she was going to meet a secret boyfriend. I liked this thought and I smiled and hummed to myself as I watched her stuff her makeup and her wallet into her bag. I wanted her to stay out with him without worrying about me. So I said, "I'll be fine, Mama. I'll feed Catt and make myself some dinner. Don't worry about us." I wanted her to order dessert and an extra glass of wine at dinner without worrying about rushing home to her daughter and her crazy dog. I wanted her to enjoy herself and maybe even get better. So I said it again. "I'll be fine, Mama."

She looked at me then—with such clear eyes I was certain I'd said the right thing—and she hugged me warmly as she left through the kitchen door, with her purse and her makeup and her pretty flowered dress.

Her favorite dress.

Later it was stained with blood, when Mari returned hours later from her secret rendezvous, having run her car into a concrete divider on the bridge on her way off the island.

Lucky to be alive.

She had repeated the EMS words.

The car was totaled and her favorite dress was ruined. "But I'm lucky to be alive. That's what they said to me at the hospital." She had repeated the words so sadly as she dialed the insurance company to make a claim.

⊚

Soon after I made the *fiambre* for Nurse Anita and me, I decided to stay in the main house with Catt instead of the garage apartment as an experiment to try to alleviate both mine and Catt's insomnia. I sat on the edge of Mari's bed and looked at her littered nightstand. The room was still in disarray from the day of the plane crash, as I had very deliberately stayed out of this room since then, but certain items that had been knocked over by the crash had been replaced and uprighted after having been photographed and investigated by gloved inspectors. The only thing I had done was to wash the bed linens and re-cover and make the bed, and prop the fallen painting up against the wall next to the bed.

A wine glass and a bottle of sleeping pills with a pile of scattered worry dolls next to my mother's bed was not an unusual sight, but I did have a sinking feeling in my stomach as I reached over for the bottle and found it empty. How many had been there? How many had she taken? Did she know about the pregnancy? And if so, what was her goal after receiving the pregnancy news? A good night's sleep or something worse?

I rolled the empty bottle of sleeping pills around and around in my hand like it was one of my or Mari's worry dolls, talking to it like it was one as well: *Mama, what did you do? This time, what did you do?*

I slept on the sofa in the living room, but I shot up in the middle of the night after dreaming about storms and plane crashes and flowered dresses.

I headed back into Mari's room and started intuitively fumbling around the drawers looking for something else. Something I had been avoiding looking for ever since I found out that Mari was in a coma.

I started looking for a suicide note.

MARI

Ever since Joe died, his friends and colleagues have continued to check on me occasionally. In more recent years, some of them have even asked me to dinner. A few have asked for more.

I've never been offended, and in fact, I've always been grateful for the company—for the occasional distractions from sadness. But the only true companionship I've found since Joe's death has come from one man.

Nick.

I wonder how long I've been here. It feels like hours—some very restful hours if you must know—but something in Lu's concerned whispers at my bedside recently makes me feel like it's been longer.

Where is Nick? Does he know I'm here? He will worry when he hasn't seen Catt or me for a while.

When Catt first bounded away from me on the beach and up the steps of Nick's beach home, I was mortified. But later, after a gradual friendship that started on paper and ended in person, when I learned more intimately just how reclusive he was, I was so grateful to Catt for bringing us together.

I had known Nick from the butcher shop of course, but still, I knew so little about him until we met through Catt. It was then that I learned how he had remained in a kind of isolation in his home after his wife—an accountant who worked at the Towers—was killed on September 11. He and his wife were childless. After having tried for so many years to have a child, they had grown more and more devoted to each other. Her death was a tremendous blow to him, and he had closed his butcher shop down after 9/11 to mourn, but never was able to *stop* mourning. I could certainly understand.

We gave each other so much comfort. He shared with me his grief, and I shared mine with him. He knew my whole story—all of it. Probably the only one who truly did in this lifetime.

More so even than Joe, because I had told Nick about *this* pregnancy.

"I know now," I told him. "I know now that no living child can replace a dead one. That is not what is happening here. This is no accident. This is no mistake. This is simply part of my story which is not yet finished. There very well may be another page to start anew. Like the Mayan calendar."

When I found out I was pregnant, I thought about how my mother had survived great tragedies and had never given up on me—how she had stayed hopeful and joyful right up until her disappearance. I told all of this to Nick and he put his hand on mine so lovingly and nodded when I said, "And you know, Nick, I think I'm just going to go ahead and have this baby."

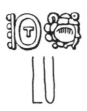

LU

I found the letters in the first drawer of her nightstand. Which I only checked—surprisingly—after rooting around other drawers in the room for about 15 minutes. I pulled out the pile of notes held together by a single black binder clip. Gingerly, I released the clip and spread the letters in front of me on the deep red down comforter covering Mari's bed, looking for dates to help place them in chronological order.

There were no dates. But I read and reread—hoping to make sense of them beyond only their words.

The first:
Mari,
I hope you are well. Your latest letter sounded cheerful, but of course it is always hard to tell when you haven't seen someone in a long time.

I do have information about Nery Santiago, which I am wary about sharing with you. But I know you have had a difficult time. And I send it after prayerful consideration and with the hope that you will use this information only to find peace.

The letter was somewhat faded, and undated, and it was missing an envelope or any attachments. But it bore the seal of the House of Mercies and was signed by Sister Magdalena.

And then, underneath the letter from Sister Magdalena was a series of letters on pale gray stationery:

Dear Mari,
Thank you for your note.

You will have to forgive me for sending this note in such an impersonal way as I do not leave my house.

Ever.

I will pay the paper girl $5 to hand-deliver this to your address and hope it makes its way to you.

If you are not Mari Guarez, please stop reading now.

I—[*some unintelligible crossed out words*]

On second thought, I will wait and make sure this makes its way to you before writing any more thoughts on paper.

—Nick

PS—if this is truly Mari, you will know what song was playing through the window when you arrived on my porch to recover your dog.

Dear Mari,

Thank you for dropping off the note and for recognizing "Madame Butterfly."

Yes, I agree tragic love story is indeed redundant, and I don't know why people always describe this opera that way.

Thank you for understanding how private I can be. When I saw you on the beach that morning, I was utterly captivated by you. That night I dreamed that I left my home and walked down the beach—something I haven't done in over 10 years. A few well-meaning friends ask why I do not give up the home if it reminds me of so much sadness, but I keep trying to explain to them that it doesn't remind me of sadness, it shields me from it.

I feel quite safe here. The very thought of leaving fills me with such panic that I am certain I will never leave.

—Nick

Mari,

You asked what I am afraid of?

But you did not tell me to stop being afraid, nor did any part of your letter seem to say that I was wrong to be afraid.

This comforted me greatly, so I will tell you what I am afraid of.

Not everything. Which is what my friends would tell you glibly if you asked them.

This is not a vague unknowing fear. It's very specific my fear. It's a fear of walking out into the world and being swallowed up by fire and finding out that nothing remains.

Nothing.

That is what I am afraid of.

Not everything.

But nothing.

—Nick

PS—please Mari. Tell me more about you and where you are from.

Mari,

I hope you are not put off by the fact that I am sending this to you so quickly.

The paper girl arrived at my home within five minutes of my finishing your letter, and I asked her to run an errand for $20. In return, I asked her to sit on my porch so I could finish this letter first. I am rushing with all I have to say and the little amount of time I have to say it. After all, how long will she sit there, really?

Well, you will know for sure when you see how quickly this letter makes its way to you.

As a side note, isn't it crazy how the paper girls are still called girls? With all this women's movement and such, you'd think they'd have come up with something more glamorous—no, not glamorous—something more powerful— than paper girls.

Oh. She says she has to leave now. I'll write more later.

—Nick

Dear Mari,

Thank you for your invitation. I would love to come to

your home, which I am sure is as beautiful and welcoming and warm as you are, for lunch or coffee.

Forgive me for saying, I need some more time to actually accept your invitation. To leave my home, and journey those blocks, which I know seem short to you, but feel like an entire universe away to me.

Something about you makes me feel like I could make that journey, though.

I beg for your patience.

In the meantime, I have my groceries delivered every Wednesday, and Wednesday night, there is usually plenty of fresh meat and vegetables for grilling and for having company.

Would you join me this Wednesday for dinner?

—Nick

I laid down on Mari's bed and tucked the letters under the pillow. By their crinkled states, I could tell my mother had probably done the same a time or two. I looked over on the nightstand where my mother's worry dolls lay.

I wondered—not for the first time— how Nick—and Nery Santiago for that matter—connected to my mother—and to the unborn baby I was going to have to find a home for. Sometime very soon.

I left the letters next to the dolls on the nightstand and headed back to my perch on the couch where I tossed and turned for a bit. I heard my mother's voice again the night we had our end of the world discussion—*you'll go to Sister Magdalena—she'll tell you everything.*

The night before the plane crash—I'd gone to Mari to say goodbye and while standing at her door, I instantly realized the insanity of my spontaneous decision to book this trip. "Do you want to go with me, Mari?" Even though the question— on the eve of my flight—was impractical and so not really sincere, my mother treated it as a real request, answering: "No, No, Niña. I think this trip is best for you to take alone."

I remember she was holding the goblet of pinot grigio that seemed to be sitting next to her bedside after all this time. As I recall, she put her goblet down on the coffee table at that point. Or maybe I'm just remembering all of this more dramatically than it went down.

Because as I remember it—my last words to her came as I left that night. My mother hugged me tightly and then as she let go, she exhaled deeply—so deeply, I was actually afraid she would forget to inhale. I slipped out of my recent insistence in only referring to her by her first name, and said: "Mama."

"Yes, Niña?"

"Nothing. I just wanted you to remember to breathe."

MARI

Lu would never stop hugging you first. You'd hug her and she'd wrap you up and you'd feel like you might be devoured. It was wonderful and comfortable at first, but then you'd have to let go. It was too intense. You might actually *be* devoured. You'd stop hugging first.

Everyone always stopped hugging Lulu first. Well, I guess I can't really know that.

The only thing I can really be sure of is that—I always stopped hugging Lu first. Except that last night. I hated letting go of her that night before she was leaving for Guatemala. Because I knew. I knew that she would soon know the truth. And while I was ready—was indeed sending her to Magdalena myself—still I was nervous. Panicked even.

That's why I gave in to the wine and the sleeping pills that I had sworn off months earlier. I gave in just that one night, and that turned out to make all the difference.

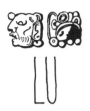

LU

"I'm feeling—I think, regretful, I didn't go to Guatemala after all."

I was sitting with Bridget over coffee, trying to explain the letters I'd found and sorting through what they might mean.

"Mari had a lot of unfinished business, let's face it." Bridget observed.

"Who was this Nery Santiago and how long was she looking for him? What was Sister Magdalena going to tell me, exactly?"

Bridget pressed on with the other elephant in the room. "And exactly what was her relationship with Nick the butcher?"

We both sat silently for a while and then I asked, "Do you remember that play from ninth grade?"

Bridget nodded, "Sort of. Weren't you a tree?"

"No," I chuckled. "I was not a tree. I was a narrator for the first half of the play. A main role in the whole thing." I sighed with exaggerated exasperation, and Bridget laughed. "I know. I was just kidding. I remember. Mari didn't make it in time to see you."

"Right. At intermission, I came out and found Mari outside the theatre waiting for my whole class to walk by so she could wish me luck in person, but we never came and she waited and waited, not realizing the play had already started, and that we had an actual backstage where we came onto the stage, and that she had missed half the show. The half I was in."

Bridget laughed again and put her face in her hands. "Oh, poor Mari. Poor you."

"I know. I mean—she really tried. She did. She missed the most important half of the show, smelled like pinot grigio and had hazy half-lidded eyes for the rest of the show—but she had tried. Most times, she just ... did her best, you know."

Bridget shrugged. "Yeah."

"I think Mari was sending me to Guatemala to find out something. Something she either couldn't or wouldn't tell me. But still wanted me to know."

I rubbed my temples.

"Maybe I'll go to Guatemala and look up Sister Magdalena after—you know—after everything is resolved around here."

"Well, that's one way to put it, Lu."

I met Bridget's eyes and raised my no longer waxed eyebrows, prompting her to keep going. "I just think—you should maybe think about, you know, bumping up that trip a bit."

We both sat silently, apparently thinking the same thing. *When the baby arrives, Mari will be gone.*

In my mind, I added: *And maybe then it will be too late.*

☺

It was an insurance guy who gave me the final push I needed. Funny but true. A pencil-pushing, numbers-crunching, claims adjuster who showed up at the house about a week after I found the letters in Mari's nightstand.

He had brought a roofing contractor to assess the damage done to the roof of the house and garage as he continued assessing whether our claim was going to max out Mari's policy limits or not. The roofing contractor spent about 25 minutes or so on the roof while I stood on the ground looking up with the claims agent, shielding my eyes from the late November sun. "Are you sure you don't want anything to drink?" I asked a few times to break up the awkward silence.

The claims adjuster just kept shaking his head no, and jotting down notes and numbers on a yellow pad of paper.

When the roofing guy came down finally, he looked at us both with his hands on hips and said simply, "Roof needs to be replaced in its entirety right away. As in yesterday."

The claims adjuster kept writing things down with his pencil, and nodding, without looking up, asked bluntly: "You got anywhere to go, Miss Roselli?"

"Excuse me?"

"We'll be happy to get you settled into a hotel tonight, but if you'd be more comfortable with family or friends, I can get you approved for a check for out-of-pocket expenses right away."

"Why can't I just keep staying here?"

The roof guy took over. "The house is practically uninhabitable, Miss Roselli. It's not safe for anyone to be living here. I'm going to clear my schedule to get started on this roof next week."

"Well, I've been staying in the garage apartment. I can just stay there for now, right?"

"Miss Roselli, both roofs are scorched beyond repair. I know you can't see it from here, but I wouldn't recommend anyone stay in either of these homes much longer."

For a moment, I thought, *oh who cares? I've survived worse than scorched roofs.* But then I thought about Mari's baby, and a vague idea that had been taking shape in my brain started to take an even bigger shape. Maybe I could bring Mari's baby back to *this* home for a short time. Before I decided exactly what to do next. And if I were to do that, we—the baby and I—would need a new roof.

I turned to the claims adjuster and announced, "I think I'll just go ahead and stay in a hotel."

"Sure, where will you be?"

"Um, Guatemala, actually." For the first time, the claims adjuster's pencil stopped ticking rapidly on his yellow pad, but I ignored his surprised look as I headed inside to make my reservations.

I booked myself on a flight just a few days away. And this

time I would not miss the plane, skip the flight, or talk myself out of it. It was time to finish the trip I started nearly two months before.

⑨

I told Bridget where I was going, and she offered to take me to the airport, but I told her it was a trip I really needed to take alone. I thanked her and promised to call upon my return, and then I packed for a two-week journey.

Before I left, I paid a visit to Rebecca. Seamus was home from school which was fortuitous because I wanted to say goodbye to him, too. For real this time.

Rebecca hugged me hard—it was the first time I ever remember being hugged by Rebecca so hard it hurt. There was a finality to her embrace. I wondered if leaving for a sojourn to Guatemala would finally sever the tie between her and me.

Seamus came in then and Rebecca left us alone. "So you're off, hunh?" he said with his usual eloquence.

"Yeah." I said with mine.

"How's your mom?"

I wanted to punch him—hard—because it was a stupid question, of course, but what else could he say?

I'm sorry your mom's dying.

I'm sorry you're in this shitty situation.

I'm sorry you're all alone.

I ran through the options and none of them sounded any better than "How's your mom?" So I forgave him the transgression.

"The same," I said. And then because I really didn't want there to be any confusion this time about whether I was coming back to him or not, I said, "I won't be kissing you goodbye today. You don't have to be confused about me anymore. Or rather I don't have to be confused about you."

He looked confused anyway.

"And I'm sorry I said I regret spending all my memories on you. That's not true. I don't regret that at all."

Then I said what I always tried hard not to say. Deliberately. "I know you miss Rae, too." At Rae's name, he looked a bit deflated. "So I'm sorry about that, too."

I sighed loudly and then: "I wish you all the best in Los Angeles, Seamus. I really do. I want amazing things to happen for you there and I will enjoy hearing about them from Rebecca and I will send you only happy good mojo from here on out," I lied. "We ok?"

"Yeah, we're ok," Seamus lied right back in return.

And then I headed toward the beach to see Nick, the butcher. I brought Catt and a bag of kibble with me. Nick invited us both in. Catt bounded right in, and I stood at the door instead. "I'm wondering. I need to go away for a couple of weeks." I tripped a bit on my words.

Nick smiled softly at me. "I would be happy to take Catt."

"It's going to be at least two weeks, I think."

"It's ok."

"You see; I don't really know how much longer she has." He nodded, sadly seeming to understand that I was not just talking about Catt here. "And I'd like to think that Catt was with someone who really knew her."

We stared at each other for a few moments, and I put off asking the questions I'd been wanting to ask. About my mother and the paternity of her unborn baby. Questions that would have to wait until I came back.

"My mother wanted me to go back to Guatemala—to hear her story from a woman she believed best able to tell it to me."

"Yes, Lu—she did. You're doing the right thing. You really are." He put his hand on mine paternalistically and I felt grateful and relieved and hopeful and confused and sad.

Which is kind of the story of my life.

Nick soundlessly took Catt's leash and her bag of kibble from me and all the awkward goodbyes were foregone as I left Catt with Nick and headed home to finish packing for a trip to Guatemala to find out what big secrets my mother had been hiding all those years.

PART III

I arrived in a touristy town on the banks of Lake Atitlan, somewhat by accident.

My Spanish is atrocious and immediately upon arriving in the airport, I realized how ill prepared I was for this trip. I wanted to go to the House of Mercies—but I was suddenly paralyzed with fear, and not ready to continue on the trip that I had come to make.

I asked the taxi driver who picked me up at the airport for the nearest town to House of Mercies and whether there was a hostel there, and he drove me the four hours to San Marcos. He pulled up to a modest-looking home, and I asked the woman at the door—who told me her name was Elena—if she had room for me. She did, and my gut told me to trust her, so I let the taxi driver leave, forgoing a ride away and a nightly deposit on the American chain hotel I had previously reserved closer to the airport.

I changed out of my travel clothes, spritzed some perfume on instead of showering in the communal bathroom, and headed down the road, where I suddenly found myself at a local café and bar. I sidled up to the bar like this was just the sort of thing I was used to doing.

The bar was open to the crisp air outside, with thick wooden beams framing its floor-to-ceiling window openings and the bar. Through the window behind the bar, I could see a long wooden dock in the lake with a volcano piercing the sky on the opposite side of the lake. There were no pre-framed matching prints hanging on the walls like there were in the coffee shop I worked in back home in Rock Harbor.

I saw a gentleman loading supplies into the back of the bar from a boat at the long dock. Beautiful, colorful birds flew in and out of the open windows. The apparently hand-made barstools (each one's wooden material and design was slightly different) scratched at the stone slab floor as cus-tomers—who appeared to be a mix of locals and tourists—ar-rived and left the busy bar. I suddenly felt at home here, in a way I hadn't felt in my real home, or my second home—the Rock Harbor café—in quite some time. Maybe ever.

The bartender was moving back and forth helping un-load the dock goods and catering to some tourists at the other end of the bar, so I had time to look around before the bartender arrived in front of me and asked for my order in English. Unclear just *what* to order, and embarrassed to re-sort to asking for a rum and coke, I saw a man down the bar holding a shot of something dark, and I pointed and said, "I'll have that."

The bartender smirked at me a bit, but reached under the bar for an unmarked glass bottle. I became a little bit flustered realizing that he looked like an actor from a movie Seamus had taken me to see at the end of the summer called *The Bourne Legacy*. "Matt Damon's not in this one. But Oscar Isaac's in it—he's from Guatemala. Have you ever heard of him?" Seamus had asked when he picked me up. "Seriously, Seamus. I don't know every Guatemalan that now lives in America."

But I knew Oscar Isaac of course, and damn, was he cute. And now I felt like I was staring right at him, as if he had walked off the movie screen right into this pretty bar in a tourist town. Chiseled Mayan features, day-old scruff and thick, wavy black hair.

And because I was embarrassed (and frankly, a little annoyed) by the bartender's patronizing smirk, no matter how much he looked like Oscar Isaac, I took very little time before demanding: "Make it a double."

Maybe I sort of thought I had stepped off the screen myself, because I slammed my shot glass down on the bar in front of me like I had seen people do hundreds of times in old movies.

And it shattered in a hundred pieces.

The bartender stopped smirking and yelled something at me in his Mayan dialect that I was certain was not very nice. And the embarrassment I felt over breaking the shot glass was aggravated even more by the ruffling he had done of my feathers. *No need to be snippy with me, you very handsome, very tanned man I just met, who also happens to look exactly like Oscar Isaac.*

I only *thought* this to myself. What I stuttered aloud was simply: "I'm sorry. I—"

His expression softened as he glanced down at my hand. My eyes followed his and now I could see that I was bleeding all over his bar.

He wrapped an obviously filthy bar rag speckled with stains of gray, brown, and orange around my hand, and revulsion, gratitude, and attraction engaged in a fierce competition inside of me before gratitude won. I kept the stained rag wrapped firmly around my hand while Oscar Isaac's doppelganger cleaned up my mess, muttering in Spanish that I could not understand. When he finished, he filled a wine goblet with white-pink bubbling liquid, planted it in front of me and smiled warmly. "Drink this instead, Señorita. Something tells me you need a sweet wine—no?"

"I just thought, you know, if the world was ending, I should probably drink something a bit stronger."

"El mundo? It's ending?" I loved how he dipped back and forth from Spanish to English—it felt more sincere than committing to either one when speaking to me.

He nodded, as if something had occurred to him

suddenly. "Ah, because you are American, of course. Americans always believe the world is ending. But especially now—no? This month?"

I kept nodding and sipping. The new drink was delicious and was also going straight to my head. I decided I would not be slamming its glass down any time soon.

"Well," he continued, "even though the Americans say otherwise, the Mayans do *not* believe the world is ending next month. So this is a good place to be."

"No? What do *you* believe is going to happen on December 21?"

"Simplamente. It begins again, Señorita."

"Hmm. So, December 21 is just the end of the old calendar? Time for a fresh start? Tear off the page, and start anew? No end of the world?"

"Why are you Americans always so anxious to talk about the world ending—but never *living* like it is about to end?" The bartender turned away from me with evident exasperation.

On a whim, I decided to pretend to be writing a story for an American magazine. After all, this was a fact-finding trip and I wanted this bartender to keep talking with me, but I could think of no other way to engage him. While I knew about as little about magazine journalism as I did about Guatemala, I told myself this was a good idea.

This will work out well, I thought confidently with the bubbling liquid fueling my bravado, as I fumbled about with my injured hand inside my bag for a notebook and pen, yelling out after him across the bar: "Oh that's good. That's really good." I scribbled in my book, saying each word aloud to him so that he could confirm his quote right then and there, "Why. Are. Americans. Always. Talking. About. The World. Ending. But never LIVING. Like. It. Is." I looked up to see him smiling—laughing really. "Did I get that right? Is that your actual quote, Mr. _"

He didn't bite. He didn't fill in the blank I had left for his name. He just reached under the bar—took what appeared to be a fresh, clean bar rag and started wiping the bar down, refilling drinks, and chatting with customers in Spanish. That left me to my bogus notebook, doomsday predictions, and worry dolls—which I promptly brought out of their pocket in my purse, and rolled them over and over in my hand. And then, as the bartender escaped to the opposite side of the bar, I laid the worry dolls end to end next to my drink as if they and the sweet wine could cast a magical spell over this moment and this trip.

"Where did you get those?" The bartender had suddenly appeared in front of me again, startling me.

"Oh." I put my injured hand and stained rag in my lap, and tucked my hair behind my ears with my one free hand. "A woman I know. Back in America."

"May I?" His forwardness was disarming. I knew I'd say yes to the dolls. I also worried that I might say yes to all sorts of things.

"Sure. Ok."

He reached over and picked up the worry dolls one by one and examined them. Closely, carefully. More carefully than I had done since my mother had delivered them to Rae and me all those years ago. He asked for the box they came in, and when I handed it to him, he opened and looked inside the box lid—something I'd never once done in the nearly 20 years I'd owned those dolls. He closed the box and handed it back to me. I opened it myself and peered at initials written delicately on the inside of the box that I'd never noticed previously.

N. S.

"You're really a writer, then?" I flinched at his words, as if someone might hear them, and then come in and call me an impostor. But I managed a nod.

"Do people pay you for this sort of story?"

I laughed harder now. But nodded again fraudulently.

Of course not.

This story is just for me.

"Are you here for the American woman's writing retreat?"

My brow furrowed involuntarily. "American? Retreat?"

He looked at me carefully. "There is a famous American writer who comes here to give seminars. Joyce Maynard?"

I racked my brain ... she sounded familiar, certainly. But this charade was going to give way soon.

"You'd know about Joyce Maynard if you were really a writer. She wrote Labor Day?"

"Oh. Wait. Labor Day—that's right. Isn't Kate Winslet going to be in that movie? I think I read something about that."

He laughed, or rather, did something that sounded like a very loud breath through his nose, and shook his head. "So not really a writer. Why are you here then?"

"To find out someone's story—but no. Not to write it." I conceded.

"Well, ok, then," he said, satisfied finally. I sat silently, waiting rapt for his next words which came after a few silent moments: "Hey. How'd you like to go on a hike around Lake Atitlan?"

⑤

The bartender's name was Alex and it turned out that he was recruiting me for a Lake Atitlan tour that was leaving from the tour office next door to the bar. A young man with a tee shirt emblazoned with the name of the tour office came into the bar to announce that his name was Marco and that the next tour was getting ready to leave; the announcement caused several couples to stand up from the bar and follow behind Marco.

I remained seated as the couples filed out, until Alex walked over and untied his bar apron, handing it to another bartender who had just arrived at the far end of the bar.

He appeared in front of me again: "Come on. I thought you were going to go on a Lake tour with me."

"You were serious about that?"

"Sí. I help my amigo out with this tour. It gets pretty crowded. And I can't exactly leave you behind while you're still bleeding." He nodded at my clumsily bandaged hand, and I blushed.

"Come on," he said again.

Next door, at the tour office, Alex waved to Marco who was handing out some sort of preprinted waivers to the assembled tourists; following a quick "add two more to this tour, Marco," he summoned me back behind the register where there was a small first aid kit.

"Should we be filling one of those out?" I pointed to the waivers.

Alex shook his head. "No."

"But, should I be reading it, at least?"

Alex laughed as he pulled bandages and gauze out of the first aid kit. "Ah, feeling cautious all of sudden, are you?"

I looked down at the blood-stained and filthy rag sheepishly. Alex took my hand brusquely and deposited the rag in the nearby garbage, and then washed and rubbed some ointment into my lacerated palm, before bandaging my hand expertly while I sat still. Allowing him.

"Thank you," I said after he wrapped my hand cleanly, meaning it. "So, tell me, Alex. Are you a part-time doctor in addition to part-time bartender and tour guide?" I laughed as I asked the question.

He smiled and patted my shoulder as he walked over to the group of earnest tourists assembled in the middle of the tour office, where Marco promptly introduced him as "my good friend, Dr. Alex Sanchez, who will be accompanying us on this tour. So don't worry too much about these waivers you just signed, everyone. Dr. Alex will make sure we stay safe as we head out to Lake Atitlan." Alex looked over the groups' collective heads and smiled at me, obviously quite pleased with the crimson blush that had spread all the way to my earlobes by this point.

MARI

In the end, I went through with the wedding to Tomas: not to save my father's business or reputation, but to save my baby. Tomas took the pregnancy news lightly, and agreed to go through with the wedding, assuring my father that he had all of the best intentions for both me and the hotel.

But, as I suspected he would, after the wedding, Tomas started to grab more and more power over the hotel. And he didn't come anywhere near me, staying out late with the pretty American tourists that came to the hotel, coming to bed late smelling of perfume and smoke, or not coming to bed at all.

I tried to warn my father, but by then he was quite enamored by Tomas. In the meantime, Tomas started asking more questions about my still flat belly. "I know when this baby was conceived. Why aren't you showing yet?

"Are you even pregnant? If I find out you tricked me into marrying you, I swear you will be sorry."

As my belly finally began to grow, he circled the date nine months out on the calendar from when he believed the baby would arrive, and I grew sick and nervous knowing the baby would never be here by then. I knew that the baby would in fact come weeks later than Tomas' circled date, and I started to prepare Tomas for that inevitability by saying, "My mother had me very late. Almost a month late. I don't think you should plan on the baby arriving on time. No baby does."

Tomas simply looked at me suspiciously and went back to work.

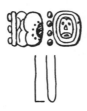

As we hiked around Lake Atitlan with the volcanoes looming large in the distance, Alex walked sideways in front of me taking long strides that I fought to keep up with. Marco had stayed behind at the office to recruit more tours, and I was learning that Alex was there as an assistant guide, doctor, and also translator for our almost entirely Spanish-speaking guide.

Our guide– via Alex—pointed out the multi-colored toucans in tree branches and passed around a pair of binoculars so we could all make out a family of three-toed sloths as we hiked.

At one point, when our guide stopped short, I almost ran right into Alex. As I stumbled, I reached my hands down into the dirt to steady myself. The guide was pointing and speaking Spanish to Alex. I thought I heard him say rain.

And venom.

I put my hand up to my throat, afraid to look down. Afraid to see if there was a venomous snake at my feet. I looked down anyway, cautiously craning my neck around my hand that was still lodged at my throat. Alex laughed at me. "What are you looking for?"

"A snake? Didn't the guide just say something about a venomous snake?"

"Not a snake. A frog. *Ranas venenosas*. Poison dart frogs."

He pointed to the colorful little creatures perched in the small crevices of the embankment near where I had just put my hands to steady myself. Red and blue and yellow and green. The most brilliant colors. I jerked away from the embankment, but the path was so narrow, a wave of nausea overtook me as I found myself too close to the cliff that marked the opposite side.

Will I be poisoned or fall to my death?

Decisions. Decisions.

Alex laughed again as I stumbled, but reached out to steady me. "They're not dangerous to you."

"No es verdad." The guide shook his head violently and whispered some Spanish cautions to Alex.

"Oh. My bad. He says they could be poisonous after all. So don't touch them." I let Alex take my injured hand in his. With the other hand, I reached inside the pocket of my parka and rolled one of my worry dolls around and around.

Ranas venenosas. I hummed the words quietly to myself. Beautiful and yet deadly.

☺

After our hiking tour, Alex and I found ourselves back in San Marcos. It was a small artisan village, filled with beautiful shops surrounding the café I had first found Alex in. We took seats in the courtyard outside the café, and without warning Alex asked me: "So, tell me. What's your story?"

"My story? I'm hoping that it's still being written, to tell the truth."

"Well, hurry up, you don't have all day, you know." He laughed and closed his eyes facing upward. I looked around at the beautiful countryside. I imagined my mother hiking the banks of Lake Atitlan and wandering lost in San Marcos many years ago. I can understand how this place continued to haunt her. It was already seeping under my skin less than 24 hours after my arrival.

Lost in the daydream, I told Alex about my mother—how she lived here and how something happened to her—"Something I believe the nuns at the House of Mercies will know. I'm heading there tomorrow."

"Did your mother give you those worry dolls?" Alex asked pointedly.

"Yes. She got them at the House of Mercies many years

ago. She lived there apparently for a short time—after her own mother died. Her father sent her to live and work there. I don't know what happened after that.

"Until she ended up in America, of course, apparently sent away to study at a convent there, and she met my father, and the rest is, you know, as they say, history."

"Who says that?"

"Oh. It's just one of those things—those American sayings," I said, embarrassed that I'd lapsed into American slang with this guy.

He laughed, though. "I was just teasing you. I learned my English from American tourists at the bar—I know more of your American sayings than I care to."

"Ah," I laid back facing up into the sun.

The day felt so lazy, but I was suddenly conscious of how little time I had there in Guatemala—how little time I had anywhere. "The days are long, but the years are short. An American writer said that. I read that recently." I opened my eyes and turned to Alex trying to impress him.

His brow furrowed. "What did you just say?" And so I repeated it word for word. Alex laughed one of his little choking-through-the-nose laughs that made me nervous about what would come next. "I don't know your American writer who said that, but Pope Paul VI said it about 30 years ago. "In youth the days are short and the years are long. In old age the years are short and days long."

I sat back deflated, realizing that this man would not be easily thrown ... or easily impressed. "I guess that is how it is going to be with us."

"Ah—will there be an us, then?" He reached out tenderly and moved a lock of hair out of my face.

I blushed, and flustered, asked: "So, do you know where the House of Mercies is?"

"Yes. Actually I lived there myself for a year or two after my parents died. I recognized your worry dolls as coming from there. I have some myself."

I did not know his story yet, but I wanted to. "When did your parents die?"

"My parents died in the village of Panabaj in the 2005 mudslides."

"Mudslides? That's terrible. Where were you?"

"Here. Working." He gestured vaguely behind him to the café. Where according to my calculations he had been working since he was teenager, maybe longer. "The nuns at the House of Mercies took me in while I continued working here at the café. The café owners were sort of surrogate parents to me. Helped me get my medical degree. And I happily stay on here when they need me. Working off a debt I can never repay. Marco is their biological son and a brother of sorts to me."

"So you help him, too." I connected the dots, although as I caressed my foolishly injured and bandaged hand, I was starting to feel like this man would help people for reasons much less compelling than familial ties. "The town where I live—Rock Harbor—it's suffered its own share of mudslides over the years. Not literally, but it seems to be a town constantly under attack by forces out of its control."

I told him about the impact of 9/11 on the generations of firefighters and first responders. And then the plane crash. "It is known as a resilient town. Constantly battling back. It's frustrating to live there if you don't feel very resilient yourself."

Alex said, "This land and its people are also known as being very resilient. That's one of the reasons I love it so much."

I had already shared so much with this stranger, so I was not surprised when I heard myself brazenly ask: "Would you want to come with me?"

"Where?"

"To make the trip to the House of Mercies tomorrow? I could use a tour guide."

"Oh, I was already planning on joining you."

"You were?"

"Yes. You couldn't find your way there, and even if y[...]
did, you'd need a little protection. From yourself."

He nodded patronizingly at my injured hand, and I bi[...]
my tongue to keep all the snarky comments from finding
their way out—replying dryly, with great effort, "Thank you."

MARI

Nery's baby arrived early. Very early. Which was a godsend of course, as Tomas seemed to believe that he had been wrong. That this was in fact his baby. When only I knew the truth.

When the baby arrived, Tomas held him first.

Even before me.

He held the baby up on his shoulder where the baby's thick head of dark hair scattered and the baby sucked loudly on his finger. I heard the baby's frustrated suck, and my breasts filled quickly with milk until they hurt, but still I waited. I did not reach for the baby. I did not cut their meeting short. I let Tomas hold that baby for as long as he wanted, because I needed him to bond with this baby instantly. I needed him to love this baby as his own so that I could keep him. And I would indeed be keeping him.

I knew that from the instant I realized I was pregnant with Nery's baby. I didn't need Sister Magdalena's advice, or my stepmother's admonitions. I knew right away I would do whatever it took to keep my son. Even if that was not what was truly best for him. In the end, for right or for wrong, I followed only my own heart.

I agreed to name the baby Tomas, and I loved him. For the fourteen months I got to be his mother, I loved him with a ferociousness that nearly killed me.

LU

When I first arrived at the House of Mercies, a small black-haired girl with curls caught my eye—or more accurately—my ear.

It sounded as if she was calling my name. "Lu lu lu lu." She was singing or clucking and I doubled back to stare at her. "Did you hear that? I asked the young girl named Maria who had greeted Alex and me at the door and who was escorting us to our destination, but she looked confused. Either she didn't hear it or I didn't hear it. Either answer was disconcerting.

I touched Maria's arm and pointed at the little singing girl standing in a nearby crib, asking: "Who is she?"

Maria didn't answer. Instead she said: "Her parents died. In the flood after Tropical Storm Agatha."

"Agatha?" I thought I vaguely remembered that storm. The girl with the dark curls was about two. She plucked at something on the crib, and when I realized it was peeling paint, I walked over to her.

"No." I wrapped my fingers around the toddler's fingers, and shook my head. "No."

"There." Maria pointed across the room at a woman's back, an overdue response to our announcement that we had come to meet with Sister Magdalena.

I stopped peeling the little girl's fingers off the crib paint and stepped away from her. I was anxious to meet finally with Sister Magdalena. But the real reason I took my hands off her was because I worried that this—*this*—would be *her*— first memory. And I wondered what Dr. Vell would say about a first memory that included only one word repeated

229

over and over again.

No.

⊚

Alex and I approached the identified woman slowly, as her head was cocked oddly to the side, and I had the unmistakable dread as we approached that we might well find her dead.

When we arrived in front of her, her half closed eyes flew open and she locked on us with her eyes holding us in our spots. The creases in her face—particularly in her weathered brow made her look fierce and strict, but there was an openness to her face—to her expression—that drew me in. I understood at once how such a woman could have convinced my mother to try out the convent—could have coerced Mari into leaving this place for a new country.

Sister Magdalena wasn't wearing a nun's habit, just a plain brown dress and her short gray hair was combed neatly in waves. We had been told when we arrived that Sister Magdalena was recovering from a bout of pneumonia and was napping—that she should not be disturbed for long. It didn't occur to me to turn and leave, letting Sister Magdalena convalesce. I had come much too far for second thoughts now. She was seated in a rocking chair with a red and blue checkered blanket across her lap, and she looked at me and said softly, "Mari. You've come back."

I shivered with the mention of my mother's name. I had to keep from turning around to see if she had followed me all this way. To see if my mother or Rae or my father's ghosts were behind me. Perhaps Sister Magdalena could see them even if I could not.

"No Sister. I am Lu. I am Mari's daughter. I've come to hear."

Sister Magdalena nodded, "She sent you."

"Yes. I want you to tell me her story."

Sister Magdalena's face opened wider then as if she had been waiting for this moment for some time. She gestured for Alex and me to sit, and we took up chairs near the fire beside her. "Did you know your mother had a son?"

I shook my head as tears pooled in my eyes. I thought of the crumpled letter in my mother's nightstand, and the Starry Night painting that my mother couldn't bear to leave on her wall after I noticed it. "Was he Nery Santiago's baby?"

"Yes."

I looked behind me, toward the room of orphan's cribs. "Did she keep the baby?"

"Yes, but—"

I wasn't sure I was ready, but I steeled myself for what would come next.

"It was Mari's stepmother who set everything in motion. While Mari always felt so guilty, it was the stepmother who set off the chain reaction. At the time Mari revealed she was pregnant, Mari was meant to marry an American man—a boy really—who would help run Mari's father's hotel—would keep her family business afloat. When the stepmother figured out whose baby it really was—the child of a militant in the insurgency—she threatened to sell Mari's baby to the Guatemalan government in order to protect the family business—to protect her own life, really."

I gasped, and Sister Magdalena brushed away my shock. "This was not unusual at the time. The country was at war. It was a very different time. It is estimated that up to 200,000 people died or went missing during the war, including 40,000 to 50,000 people who "disappeared." The government—they were running several of the orphanages at that time. And there were rumors. Terrible rumors that the Army was killing parents and stealing babies to make a profit to finance the civil war.

Sister Magdalena sighed. "Perhaps it wasn't right, but we helped silence those rumors as they threatened to jeopardize our entire mission. I don't know what other orphanages did or knew, but *our babies*?—they came to us from poverty, destitution. They had no parents, or parents who could no longer care for them. We did not know how or why—but we knew they came to us for a reason. And we cared for them, and loved them, and found homes for them.

"Mari was supposed to marry the man her father was grooming to take over his business. The money, the fortune, all of it would stay in the control of Mari's father and his much younger wife. A baby—a child of the insurgency—would ruin everything. And so her stepmother threatened to sell Mari's baby if anyone found out he was illegitimate."

"Did she end up marrying the American?"

"Yes. Mari suspected that Tomas had figured out what was going on, but he agreed to wed Mari in return for a 51% stake in the company. Her father went along with it all to protect the business and his future."

"And the baby's father?"

"Mari said that she never told Nery that he was the true father. And even though the stepmother seemed to guess, Mari never truly admitted it to her either. She confessed only to me. The secret would have died with me, I suppose. Mari feared greatly for Nery's life, but truly for the life of her baby. Remember, she was just barely 18 years old."

I thought about Mari—18 and pregnant. In the middle of a civil war with no one to guide her—with the people who were supposed to protect her failing miserably to do so. I knew that less than three years later, Mari would find herself in the convent, where she'd meet my father, and soon find herself pregnant again with twin girls. What had happened in the interim?

"So if it was fixed, Sister Magdalena, if all was arranged, what happened?"

MARI

Baby Tomas was barely fourteen months old when Tomas finally confronted me. He had figured out the baby who arrived "early" with the soft and dark Mayan features— a broad nose, curly hair, large cacao-colored and shaped eyes—was not his, but we seemed to be operating in a world where we'd both ignore that fact.

He had too much at stake in this marriage. And I had a baby to protect.

But when he confronted me, finally, I think I felt a kind of a relief. A gladness that the pretending might finally come to an end. That *we* might finally come to an end.

It happened after he arrived home early and I was just checking on the baby who was down for a nap shortly before dinnertime. The baby was in a deep sleep, his curls pasted to his forehead in sleepy sweat under a light blanket in the corner of our living room just off the kitchen. Tomas Sr. came in barking and I jumped knowing he'd wake the baby in no time at all.

"Your father is infuriating me, Mari. It's time he sign over more shares of the hotel to me. I am doing all the work now at the hotel. The hotel would not be open and running if not for me. And if I wasn't connected to him via flesh and blood, I would not have been so patient with him up until now."

"We are not flesh and blood, Tomas," I said too quickly. In one fatal moment, I had completely forgotten about the on-going charade of pretending our baby was his biological son.

And Tomas seemed to have been baiting me because he did not waste a moment in responding. "So it's true then. What do you think people will say when they find out you're a whore?"

"A what?"

"You heard me."

"Well, whores are paid for sex, and he had no money. So. I'm not a whore then, am I?"

Tomas looked shocked and stood still, and for a moment, I thought perhaps I would walk out of the room into the kitchen and put Tomas' dinner on like nothing had ever happened.

The briefest moment.

Tomas flew across the room at me and clutched my throat in one hand. I pummeled his head with one hand and scratched at the hand gripping my throat, but he was possessed. His grip grew stronger. I reached around frantically for something to hit him with, but he was gradually lifting me off the floor.

"Mama!"

I rejoiced in the momentary distraction which allowed me to escape Tomas's grip, but realized quickly how dangerous it was for my toddler to have woken from his nap at that moment. He stood up on his blanket in the corner of the room we were all standing in.

Tomas's steel gaze hardened on the boy he had always known was not his own flesh and blood.

"Tomas! No!" I screamed and ran across the room to physically block Tomas from lunging at the boy.

But Tomas reached behind me and grabbed our toddler.

I remember, though, there was something still there behind the hatred in his eyes. Something that was still Tomas. Something that reminded me of—of my son, strangely enough. *He wouldn't hurt him,* I hoped. *Only me.*

"It's all a lie." Tomas was clutching the boy at this point.

"When did I ever lie to you?"

"You pretended he was my son."

"Tomas. He *is* your son. You love him. He is yours. Stop pretending otherwise. It is the boy's father, I lied to. It is he who should hate me. Not you."

"You are crazy. You are a crazy, lying woman and I have let you live in this house for far too long." Tomas moved toward the door.

"Are you kicking me out?" I steadied my breathing to keep from breaking into hysterical laughter. *Did he think that was the worst thing he could do to me?*

"Are you kicking me out, Tomas? Tell me."

"Of course not."

He reached above the doorframe and pulled down a gun and pointed it at me. "I'm going to kill *you*. And then I'm going to sell your bastard son to the army for cash. For more money than you're worth—that's for certain. And he will never even know the whore and the traitor that conceived him. I'll be doing him a favor."

I can remember the taste of bile rising in my throat, and my vision was becoming tunneled—speckled with black and green dots—as if I might faint. I was determined not to faint. Surely, if I did, Tomas would cut me into pieces and feed me to the *coati*. And what would he do with the baby he was holding? The baby whose cries were turning the night into shards of glass as Tomas held him inches away from the barrel of a gun. I clutched the sofa harder.

"Tomas. He's. Your. Son."

"No. He is no one's son, Mari. No one's."

With an adrenaline surge, I lunged at him, grabbing wildly for the gun. Afterward, I could never be sure whether I actually took possession of it or whether he was still holding it when it fired.

But after the crashing sound of the gun exploded, I backed up unsteadily to the couch, where I clutched hard to one arm of the sofa while the black and green dots danced in front of my eyes, and began blocking out the view of

Tomas in his bloodstained shirt now lying on the ground. Tomas's eyes were frozen open staring at the ceiling, while a pool of dark brown blood pooled under his head, wider and wider, spreading underneath the baby as well. The baby was in his arms on the ground, and he was no longer crying. The baby was silent now. Silent and still. And while I continued my hold on the sofa's arm, the black and green dots kept circling, finding each other, connecting, patching themselves together.

Until there was nothing at all left but the blackness.

LU

I sat in shock, staring at Sister Magdalena. Trying to wrap my head around what she was saying.

"It wasn't until a few months later ... that Mari came back to tell me. I thought that she was coming for help with the baby ... but it turned out, the baby was ... gone."

Sister Magdalena spoke of the boy's death with the weariness of someone who had seen far too many babies die in her care. On her watch.

She continued on about Mari. "Her father sold off most of the remaining hotel shares to pay off some government officials. He bought paperwork and financed her exodus to America. It was his attempt at redemption for all that had happened. In his own way, he was sorry, truly sorry. When Mari came to me, I helped her to move. I called in a favor to a young, wealthy American couple who had recently adopted from the orphanage. They agreed without question to help arrange Mari's move to America. They wanted so much to give something back to the House of Mercies.

"She left for the convent but soon enough ended up in Rock Harbor with your father. What a precious name and a beautiful island. Mari sent me postcards from there every few months. With small notes. I kept them and saved them all. She told me in her letters about you and your sister. She told me the sadness of your father dying while saving your sister."

I winced.

"I haven't heard from your mother in months," Sister Magdalena said tentatively, and then: "Is she unwell?"

We nodded together.

I told Sister Magdalena then about the plane crash in

America and my mother's coma. I took a deep breath at the end of the story and revealed: "And she's pregnant as it turns out."

Sister Magdalena simply nodded again—a woman who had known a great deal of life and who was surprised by little.

"Did my mother even want to join the convent, Sister Magdalena?"

"I think so. She saw no other way at that point. She needed to get away. She had no family left in Guatemala, other than her father—but that relationship was severed irreparably by all that had happened. I think it all made sense at the time."

I sat quietly for a moment with Sister Magdalena as we both reflected on my mother in our own way. "And then she met my father."

"Yes, and then she met your father. Before she took her final vows. And she said that she just knew. That everything—getting pregnant and married and losing her son—all of it—had led her to this man. This one man. Your father. She was so very grateful to him."

"Then why couldn't she just be happy? Just be happy with him. And us?"

"She wanted to. She did. But a lost child is a difficult hurdle for a mother." Sister Magdalena looked past me like she was remembering something very personal before continuing on. "Your mother had such a terrible time and was so sorry that she wasn't able to save baby Tomas. That she had married the wrong man. Your mother—she just felt everything so clearly. I think she had a lot of guilt. Tomas's death. Leaving the convent. Loving your father so much. It was always a lot for her. She loved big. And she grieved big. It's just who she is. You shouldn't regret anything of her or wish it away."

"What happened to Nery Santiago?"

"Ah, yes. He stayed a part of our lives over the years,

coming back occasionally to check on us."

"Is he still alive?"

"No, he died. In 2005, we believe. In the Panabaj mudslides."

"Oh, that's terrible." I found myself looking over at Alex. He'd been such a silent observer up until this point. But with the mention of the same disaster that had killed his family, he shuddered noticeably.

Sister Magdalena then got up, and folded the blanket that had laid across her lap, and brushed her hands off on her pants. I hadn't noticed that her hands had anything on them, and so I knew that consciously or subconsciously, she was signaling that the conversation and these intrusions were over for now.

"If you ever need anything—anything at all—please get in touch with me," I held both of Sister Magdalena's cool hands in my own as I said it and Alex and I started to leave.

Alex also took her hands in his own. "Yes, Sister. Anything."

Sister Magdalena looked at us both back and forth, back and forth, and then exclaimed suddenly: "Yes!"

And with that simple word, we—Alex and I—had taken on a job painting the exterior of the entire building known as the House of Mercies.

The entire.

Exterior.

"What on earth?" We had been mixing paint remnants from the storage shed at the House of Mercies to create a musky gray color. The sky was so blue, and the landscape so lushly green, the color was actually pretty against the stone walls, but after a full day of painting, we had turned the corner to find a collage of oranges and reds and purples in an explosive mess near the bottom of a far wall of the building.

"How are we ever going to cover *that*?"

"Maybe we shouldn't," Alex suggested.

I rolled my paint roller around and around the colors creating a gray border that dripped into but didn't cover the emotional colorburst on the wall. There was something familiar about the shapes—I thought I might have remembered seeing a similar colorful mess among Mari's more pristine landscape paintings over the years. I had almost talked myself out of the similarity until I saw Sister Magdalena come out into the yard with bowls of supper for us, signaling the end of our "work day."

"Sister. When was the last time this building was painted?"

"Hmm. Probably before you were born." She looked squarely at the colorful half wall I had not bothered to paint over and answered my unspoken question. "Your mother and Nery were likely the last ones who painted this area of the building. You know, I had almost forgotten about that."

For a week, Alex and I went every day to paint. Sometimes I went ahead of him while he took a shift at the café or completed a house call. Marco gave him a short reprieve from tours for the week because he was so busy now painting, and collapsing with exhaustion each night with me in the grass outside the House of Mercies.

Sister Magdalena seemed to have recovered from her bout with pneumonia and brought us a heaping dish of rice and beans each night, when she stood and admired our day's work and reliably, every night, she repeated, "What beautiful work. I can't wait to see how much *more* painting you get done tomorrow."

Alex and I laughed each night at her back-handed compliment and yelled, "We'll take it!" as we devoured our rice and beans gratefully.

"My mother is a great cook. I miss her cooking," I said as we ate. This is how we spent our nights. Exhausted from hard work, with all of our defenses down, we shared our lives and families with each other. Alex told me about his hard-working father and his beautiful if just a bit lazy mother, both of whom he missed equally. "I talk to them sometimes still in my dreams. So real I know they are not dreams at all."

I felt a pang of jealousy at his revelation. It had happened to me, too, but only once.

"I saw Rae once long ago. After she died." He nodded in response, so I told him.

⑤

Rae and I had never been allowed to go to the beach alone. Ever.

My parents gave us strict instructions with all sorts of terrible scare tactics.

The beach is not safe.

Don't be fooled by the ocean. Riptides are invisible.

You could be abducted.

And my personal favorite that came exclusively from Mari: *I don't trust that water—it's the wrong color.*

For good measure, Mari would throw that one into the litany of warnings and it would usually get a funny smirk and shaking head from my father, and one good solid all-the-way-around eye roll from Rae and me.

Nonetheless, they were our parents, and while we secretly thought they were crazy as we plotted almost daily to go to the beach alone, we never went through with it.

They made it clear we had to wait for them and wait we did. All summer long, on Dad's days off from the firehouse, we'd help them lug beach chairs and a cooler and a blanket the two blocks up the road to the sand. Then we'd quickly throw everything down near the lifeguard at a spot on our block that was usually reserved in an unspoken way for our family.

We'd jump into the waves and climb on and off boogie boards and wrestle each other in the ocean. My father would sometimes come into the water and sometimes sit on the sand in a chair. Mari would sit in her chair with a wide-brimmed hat and a modest black bathing suit that still made her look elegant and exotic like a rare bird. She could usually be seen with a scowl on her face and her eyes only partly in one of her Spanish magazines while occasionally asking my father, "Please, Joe. Tell them to come in where the water isn't so deep."

If Seamus was free, we'd dodge waves with him, too, or the three of us would walk along the water line ("but not too close, girls!") and plan out the very detailed rules for a later game of flashlight tag or hide and seek in our backyards. When we'd worn ourselves out, we'd lie in the sand on our threadbare towels used well during those summer months and plead with our parents, "When will we be able to come here alone?" They never answered us, but one day during the summer after sixth grade, our father waved our question away with one word: "13."

"What does that mean?" we both wondered aloud.

"Thirteen. When you're 13, we'll let you come here alone." Mari looked like she might protest, but my father tapped his hand on the air near her as if boxing up some of her worries in a little container similar to the one that housed her worry dolls.

"Really?" I leaned up on one elbow excitedly.

"But that's not til next summer, Dad!" Rae didn't share my elation, clearly.

"Well, we'll see how we all feel then. Next summer, we might let you come here alone." Dad equivocated a bit.

Rae and I both collapsed back on our towels weighing the news, trying to decide how willing we both were to be patient.

"Next summer, then." Rae confirmed for both of us.

"Yes, next summer, then," my dad said.

The next summer, after Mari and I came home from the *E.T.* movie birthday outing, I fell asleep soundly and dreamed that I walked to the beach at sunrise. When I arrived at our usual spot, near the lifeguard chair, there was Rae. It was the first time I'd seen her since the morning of 9/11 and I wasn't surprised or scared or relieved. I had been expecting to see her, somehow. Seeing her there felt like the most natural thing.

"Well," she greeted me with her half smile. "What took you so long? I thought you'd never get here."

"Happy belated birthday to you, too, Rae."

We walked along the water line, but not too close, and later, when I woke, I felt calm and unstartled by the dream. Even when I noticed that my sneakers on the floor by my bed had fresh sand on them.

☺

"I'm not sure if I really saw Rae that morning or if it haunted me that she never got to be anything more than a 12-year-old girl."

Alex reached over and lifted my chin up to look at him. "But *you* did. It's not Mari's story or even Rae's story you are writing the end to, Lu, it's yours."

His words stabbed at my heart. But they made sense, too. "I've never told anyone that I saw Rae that morning." I looked down and kept digging into my rice and beans as I made this confession out loud. "Not even Seamus," I said before I could stop myself.

"Who is Seamus?"

"Great question. No good answer. We all grew up together. To a point. And then he and I kept pretending we were more grown up than we were. Or maybe I just grew up more than he did and realized we shouldn't be together."

Alex just nodded into his rice and beans, so I volunteered the rest. "We aren't seeing each other anymore. He's off to the other side of America and I've come to my senses."

"Fair enough." Short pause. "So what about your father? Tell me more about him." Alex asked.

I was able to tell him about my old boyfriend, and that I had seen my dead sister on the beach back home in Rock Harbor. And yet, for some reason, when Alex asked finally about my father, I clammed up. Not because I didn't want to tell him. But rather, because I desperately wanted to tell someone what I had found out about my father, something I had never told anyone. Not Rebecca or Seamus, and especially not Mari. I wanted someone else to know what I knew, and perhaps share a little of the pain of this secret with me.

At some point during the week, working side by side with Alex, I had decided that I wanted it to be him, but now that the moment was here, I was stuck.

"Come on. Tell me about your father," Alex repeated over hungry spoonfuls of rice and beans.

And so I told him. "The thing is. My father didn't die the way everyone thinks. Saving Rae and a floor full of Wall Street bankers."

"Are you sure, Lu? How do you know?"

◎

There was a photographer. He took a picture of my father and Rae that day. I saw it in the paper that was dropped at our front door by the paper girl on September 12. A photo of a tall, muscular firefighter in full gear, smeared with grease and dirt, with my father's fire house number on the helmet, carrying a young girl away from the building, both of them completely recognizable and identifiable to me, although the photo's caption read: "Unidentified firefighter carries unknown injured woman."

I cut the picture and its caption out of the paper so Mari wouldn't see it and I hid it in my top dresser drawer. Occasionally, I would take it out of the drawer and stare at it for a few moments, but it was like looking into the sun. I could never look at it for too long. The photo had a photographer's credit listed, but I never had the guts to look up the photographer until a few years ago.

I emailed the photographer who apparently still worked for the paper and kept the same email address. I described the picture in my email and told the photographer that it was my father and sister in the photo. I invited him to coffee at the Rock Harbor café on my day off, and he showed up.

We sat facing the exposed brick covering the sunrise, and he told me he had taken a lot of pictures that day. He had gotten his photos into several papers and national magazines, and even won some awards. His hands shook as he held onto his coffee cup. He told me: "The photograph of the firefighter carrying the girl always got to me."

He knew the girl was already dead and that she was clearly a girl, although the paper insisted on running the photo with the caption "unknown injured woman."

"The firefighter looked so despondent, his face was absolutely distorted with grief. We were all of us that day grieving. When I looked at him, I thought his grief should have seemed relatable, and yet it didn't. It seemed far removed from anything I was feeling—could be feeling. His grief seemed different than all of ours. It seemed very, very personal.

"After I took that picture, he went back for his daughter," the photographer told me.

I brought out the picture of my father carrying Rae like a doll, then, and I placed it on the table between the photographer and me. I reverently traced Rae's lifeless body the way I did each time I got that picture out.

"But, he had already gotten her out. This *is* his daughter," I corrected the photographer.

"I know that. By the way, I tried to have the paper print a retraction—that the injured girl had actually passed away. I wanted to print her name and identity to pay respects—but without the proper clearances they wouldn't do it.

"Anyway, I knew because shortly after this picture was taken, the firefighter placed her in the arms of a chaplain. He said, 'Please minister to my daughter, Sir.'"

"He knew she was already dead?"

"I think so. He gave her to the Chaplain—walked right by medical personnel and some triage stations at the site. And then he walked back into the building—actually ran in—and

I jogged up to him before he hit the entrance way and I said 'Excuse me, what are you doing? Why are you going back in?' And he said without any fanfare, 'My company's in there. And so is my other daughter.'"

I heard a ringing in my ears that drowned out the din in the coffee shop but I strained through it to hear the rest of his story. My memory crowded with the realization that my father had signed permission slips for both of his daughters to be in the Tower that morning. He had no idea that only one daughter had actually gone through with it. Only one pair of linen pants with a cardigan twinset had traveled into the city that morning.

"A few minutes later, I heard a noise, and those of us on the ground ran for it—scattered in different directions. I ran off toward uptown and made it to a coffee shop by noon where I emailed in my story and my pictures. It was a chaotic day, and I blame myself for the misprint and the callous photo printing and wrong caption. I always wondered what happened to that firefighter. And his other daughter. I prayed he was able to somehow save her even though that seemed like a far-fetched dream given what I'd seen that day."

He reached right across the table then and placed his shaky hands on my own. "I'm so relieved to meet you."

"Relieved?"

"Well, you're her, right? You're the daughter he saved."

I didn't have the courage to do anything but nod.

The photographer smiled and put his shaky hands back onto his coffee cup, as he exhaled with many years of stored grief in an act of release I couldn't share in. "That's good," he said. "That's a really good ending to that one story, at least."

◎

"Except it wasn't the end," Alex said simply at the conclusion of my confession. "It was only the beginning of *your* story. And you are still writing it, as they say."

I nodded at Alex's words, wishing I could exhale properly, something I hadn't done since I met the photographer who last saw my father alive.

MARI

I should never have kept the baby. I should not have followed my own heart. I should have listened better to what Sister Magdalena tried to tell me when she revealed her own story about June to me. I should have given my baby a better chance.

But once I made the decision to keep the baby ... well, then I should have let Tomas kill me, of course. That's what I *should* have done.

I saw his eyes that day. Saw deep within them. He was angry and frustrated and embarrassed with the realization that I had married him and put him in a position of loving a child that was not his. But he wasn't a monster.

He wouldn't have killed that baby he held at the moment of his birth. The same baby whose curls had scattered across his shoulder the first minutes on this earth. No. Even standing there armed with his doorframe rifle, he would only have killed me and not my son, and *that* has been the impossible thing to live with all of these years.

After that night, I went through the motions necessary to leave. Tomas had no family that I knew of, having been allegedly estranged from them since before he arrived in Guatemala. He became yet another statistic—another of the lost. Like my mother, and Nery, and so many others.

I was lost, too. From that moment on. I felt then that my life had absolutely no value.

This is what I believed always, with certainty.

Until I met Joe, and gave birth to his children, and then everything was uncertain again.

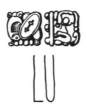

LU

The week Alex and I painted the orphanage, Guatemala was having unseasonably warm days reaching into low 80s. We walked down to the Lake and swam in our clothes after dinner each night washing off the day and the paint and the aches and pains of hard work.

Alex told me that Lake Atitlan is often called "el ombligo del mundo"—literally translated as the umbilical cord of the world—although the Spanish version sounds more poetic. "It is thought to anchor, feed, and nourish those who come to it like a mother and her unborn baby," he explained with his best tour guide voice.

So as I dove into its waters, I couldn't help but think of Mari—who was anchored to her own baby—feeding and nourishing even though Mari herself was being kept alive by hospitals and doctors and machines. Deep inside her womb Mari was connected to and serenely keeping her baby alive—through *el ombligo*.

I sank deeper into the Lake each night with the volcanoes rising high around me on all sides—large and majestic but viewed only from the water's surface. I hid under water, and closed my eyes—drowning out the sounds and smells and the sights of the Lake and the volcanoes and the surrounding areas until I was one with the water.

It was on one of those days that I emerged from deep within the water, turned to Alex while treading in the lake, and said: "I feel silly."

"Well, you have a big patch of gray paint on your nose, and I've been trying not to laugh at you for hours. Is that what you mean?"

"What?" I dove under the water and scrubbed my nose wildly.

"Still there," Alex said smugly when I came to the surface.

"Argh. I'm not talking about gray paint. I'm talking about all this time that I've been wasting. Ever since my father and sister died, I've been feeling guilty. For surviving 9/11 in America. For surviving the plane crash that has all but killed my mother.

"All this guilt has been making me lazy. I forgot what it was to work hard. Like we're doing this week. And I've forgotten how to feel grateful. Like I have this week."

"There is no substitute for hard work."

"Is that another Pope Paul VI quote?" I smile.

"No—that's one of your Americans. Thomas Edison, I believe."

"Well, whoever said it was right. And you *really* inspire me. Here you are dropping everything to help Sister Magdalena and the House of Mercies. Seriously, Alex, you might be the least selfish person I've ever met. I could really learn a thing or two from you." I treaded close to the lake bank where I could stand.

Alex swam over to where I was standing and rubbed at the gray paint on my nose, while he said, "Stop. You have this all wrong."

More rubbing—now on my forehead, too. I stood very still, reminding myself to breathe.

"Let's get something straight here. I have purely selfish motives. Don't make me into some kind of false hero."

"Selfish? What are you talking about?"

Alex stopped rubbing my face and stood back to admire his work. "There. Now the paint's finally gone. I mean that the only reason I paint that orphanage all day until my back is about to break is because I keep hoping that you might just get a little paint on your face and I'll need to help you get it off."

On the day we finished painting, Sister Magdalena sent us on our way with a warm embrace, a thank you, and a packed lunch for the road, with fruit and bread and more rice and beans. We took her generous picnic, borrowed a boat from one of the fishermen who docked at the café in town, and headed to a neighboring town nearer to a volcano, where we devoured our food in a clearing.

"Now what?" Alex said.

I looked in the basket for more food, but came up empty.

"That's it. We've eaten everything."

"No. Now what are you going to do? When do you go home?"

It was a question that I had been asking myself continuously the last few days. The insurance adjuster had told me to stay away until at least December 21, and that's when my return flight was booked—a red-eye traveling through the night. The roofer was going to be working against cold temperatures and was trying to beat a mid-December snow forecast when I left. He hoped to have the roof completed by no later than December 21. An ominous date to be sure.

But the day Alex asked, "Now what?" it was only December 15, and I didn't have a real plan for how to spend the remainder of my days in Guatemala. Nonetheless, I blurted out: "I'd love to see where my mother grew up—Semuc Champey."

Alex did not pause for long before saying, "Well, it's a day's trip from here—but if you're up for an adventure—I'll take you there tomorrow." It was settled in that moment. I was definitely up for an adventure.

The next day, we left at dawn and took two buses to Lanquin, the nearest town to the waterfalls at Semuc Champey, where my mother's family's hotel had once been nestled. The second bus on the way to Lanquin was a chicken bus whose rank smell smacked me as I climbed aboard for the last leg of the trip. But as we traveled through the lush countryside, and as Alex pointed out and named the pastel-colored villages with rows of hanging meats outside narrow roadside porches, I forgot about the smell of the bus, or maybe I simply started not to mind it.

We arrived at Lanquin shortly before sunset, so Alex suggested we head right to a hostel and journey to the waterfalls in the morning. I agreed but with one condition. I wanted to try to find the hotel my mother's family had owned. I understood from Sister Magdalena that it was long since closed and vacated, my mother's father and step-mother having died years ago with no one to take over running the place.

Alex made some inquiries at the open air market in Lanquin near our hostel. Eventually we took yet another chicken bus a few miles away, and asked the farmer to wait for us as we'd only be a few moments.

We walked around the main building, reverently. It was a sprawling wooden building, dark with moss and rain and years and overgrown with weeds—its windows largely broken, and caving in on more than one side.

Alex followed behind me as I grasped at thick roots in the soil and crawled up a hill outside the dilapidated hotel to get a better view. I closed my eyes and imagined the hotel well-preserved, regal and beautiful rising from the hilly soil, the sound of howler monkeys staking out their nighttime perches rising above me, the faint sound of waterfalls competing with the monkey's calls.

I opened my eyes to the caving walls and broken windows. "This. This is where I lost my mother. Long before I knew her."

Alex sighed deeply next to me and put his arm around my shoulders, pulling me close enough to lean my head on his shoulder, changing my view. High up one wall, a row of golden orchids climbed the weeds and splintered wood like a ladder.

As I stared at the soil-less flowers, I thought about my

motherless mother trying to thrive here and again in New York after every tragedy that had befallen her. I imagined her rooting around for soil in a New York beach town, and coming up empty-handed again and again. A long-ago memory came to me of a history class counting the lost Guatemalans from the Civil War. "There is no accurate count of those who were truly lost," my teacher had said solemnly.

"I'm sorry for you, Mama. I really am," I whispered into the night as the sunset painted the dark gray blue sky with a familiar colorburst of oranges and reds and purples.

Early the next morning, we headed for the waterfalls at Semuc Champey. I stood on the bank breathless when we arrived. The churning, frothing water next to still pools of water a turquoise blue color I was certain I had never before seen outside of paintings. My mother's paintings, I realized.

My mind played tricks on me, conjuring up the scent of my mother's oil paints and turpentine in the Rock Harbor garage studio before it became my home. But after I exhaled deeply, I filled my lungs with the clean fertile scent of the mossy rocks and the cool water mist, imagining my mother swimming in these very waters as a girl.

Alex jumped into a still turquoise pool below, and immediately jumped back out, sunning himself on a large gray-green rock. Eventually I jumped in myself, and I looked up at him sunning while I swam, and wondered if I had met him in Rock Harbor, whether I could ever impress a man like this. I was sure I would have annoyed him—eaten the wrong food, said the wrong things. He'd become charmed by me, and then learn to love me and hate me before the day was even done.

Like Seamus.

Actually, he's not LIKE Seamus at all, I quickly reminded myself.

I was thinking of all of this as I felt Alex reach for me through the cool water.

He had jumped back in without me hearing him.

"I'm so cold," I said stupidly.

Goosebumps lined my arms and legs and I thought it important that he know they weren't from him. Even if they were. He said nothing before he kissed me.

Fiercely.

I didn't kiss him back because I didn't really have time—he pulled away quickly while my head was still trying to catch up with what had happened. He swam away from me—long strong strokes to the nearest rocks at the water's edge. I watched him pull himself up on the rocks, where he pulled a towel from his backpack and wrapped it loosely around his shoulders while he began fishing in the backpack for what was left over from our food rations from the day's trip. I swam over to him clumsily. He had towel-dried his dark hair and I saw goosebumps on his chest and his arms under the draped towel. I treaded water and rubbed my own arms under the water, before reaching up for him—"Come back in. It's warmer in the water."

Alex jumped back into the cold, clear water and reached for me again. That time, I reminded myself to kiss him back. And when he pulled away, he said simply: "So. Want to go steal some orchids?"

MARI

I have always kept orchids in my kitchen in Rock Harbor. And I feel guilty not knowing exactly how those orchids arrive in the United States. Illegal poaching? Perfectly legal channels? You can't know where they were first grown, when you buy orchids from the corner market in Rock Harbor.

But the orchids remind me of home and connect me to a place and a time when I was stronger. My mother and I tended to an orchid garden behind my father's hotel. No one had planted them. No one had started the garden. They just grew wild back there. The tourists would wander through the garden and my mother would follow behind silently clucking if someone tried to cut one or steal one. "No, no, must stay." She'd say in her limited English. And they would listen to her. Purples and pinks and whites and yellows and blends of all of those colors would dance in the yard. They needed very little care. They grew in rocks, their long winding roots circling around and around anchoring them to the rocky hillside.

"They remind me of you, Niña," my mother would say as we walked through the orchids after a long day of cleaning and cooking and caring for Americans. Sometimes, if it had been dry, we sprinkled the roots in the garden with ice cubes that provided the slow trickle of water that was all those sturdy winding roots needed. "Look how they grow in no soil. But still these flowers draw everyone out to see them. They are beautiful and strong." She would hug me then and I would let her, smelling the orchid scent and the earthy soil remnants on her dress. Later, one glance at the orchids I kept on my windowsills in Rock Harbor could conjure up those memories. I would close my eyes and hear my mother's voice again.

You are strong, Niña.

I hate that no one would describe me as strong anymore. I'm so disappointed in myself—people just meeting me now would describe me as frail—I'm sure of it. And I wouldn't be arrogant enough to disagree with them. They would be right. But my question is: When did I become frail? When did I stop being an orchid—beautiful and hearty and rare?

When was that moment?

Alex and I were crouched down low behind a bush across the street from a roadside stand in Lanquin. We had traveled there by foot through a forest that bordered the falls, with me like a petulant child asking the entire time: "Are we there yet? Where are we going?"

And once—very embarrassingly—I had said, "Wait up. I need to go."

"Go where?"

Shivering and damp, I had apparently left modesty at the lake. "You know—*go.*"

"Oh!" Alex smirked a bit, and pointed me to a cluster of trees that looked a bit too see-through so I headed deeper into the forest until I couldn't see him any longer.

And then we resumed our stealth trip.

When we arrived at the apparent intended location, Alex kept shushing me, finger to mouth, and I kept questioning what we were doing. "Why are we stealing orchids? Isn't that illegal?"

"Yes!" He had yelped too quickly. "It's absolutely illegal—that's why we're doing it."

"Oh good. I was afraid you were starting to make sense," I sighed as I glimpsed at our apparent target—a woman manning a roadside stand across the street from the forest. Cars—looking like rental cars with tourists crammed in—lined the street next to her stand. They stopped along the side of the road allowing the occupants to eye her merchandise—potted plants—mostly orchids of purples and whites.

"Cattleya," I recognized.

Alex shushed me, but I kept talking nervously, still not

exactly sure what we were doing there. And why we were stealing orchids. "My mom's dog. She's named after those orchids. We call her Catt. Get it?"

Alex put his finger up to quiet me again, and then did a double take with the realization and language recognition setting in.

"You named your dog, Catt?"

I nodded, smiling. And he let out a little snort. "That's funny."

Then he turned to the roadside vendor, shed his sense of humor, and pointed to her while he silenced me with one finger again.

She had a long red braid and a dark gray skirt and lighter gray tunic top embroidered with a purple design that matched the color of some of the orchids closest to her on the stand. Her red hair reminded me strangely of the waitress in Serendipity from all those years ago who had made Rae and me laugh as she called our father Prince Charming. I kept staring at the red-headed orchid vendor until I reassured myself that the waitress had, in fact, *not* followed me all the way to Guatemala.

"Who is she?"

"An American woman. She arrived last year and she steals those flowers from the banks of the waterfalls. It's illegal—orchid poaching—which is why she sells them here, out of the way, to tourists who won't report her."

"So you're going to report her?"

"No. I'm going to steal her orchids. I've been coming here every month or so to steal her inventory. I'm figuring within the next month or two she'll be so fed up, she'll find something new to steal or do."

I eyed him curiously. The woman seemed harmless enough and this Robin Hood orchid mission also seemed relatively harmless. The red-haired entrepreneur didn't look homeless or starving and I doubted orchids were providing her sole livelihood. I also doubted that closing down her roadside stand would wipe out the widespread problem of orchid poaching across the country, but for a brief moment I admired Alex's idealism and tenacity and it was all the moment I needed to follow after him as he yelled, "Now!"

With the red-haired woman helping some tourists place purple and white bespackled flowers in the trunk of their rental car, we jumped out from our hiding place and snatched up as many pots as we could—sending a few errant pots crashing to the roadside as we headed back into the forest with our contraband. The red-headed lady stood quietly on the roadside as I imagined her feeling too sheepish to yell out "stop thieves!" when she herself had been the thief.

Nonetheless Alex yelled over his shoulder, "We will report you for poaching—stay away from the orchids!" To drive his point home as he ran off with as many orchids as he could cradle and I followed clumsily behind him—with the pots falling to the ground while the flowers and their thick roots stayed behind in my hands.

We ran for about 15 minutes, looking over our shoulders periodically, until we reached the area where we had previously been swimming and kissing not 60 minutes earlier. The trip to the roadside stand had seemed to take so much longer than the trip back. I stopped on the side of the water, panting and bent over, with him laughing and mocking me for stopping.

"Come on, we're not there yet."

I followed him up a rocky hill with my flowers crushed into my now filthy sundress and my flimsy sneakers giving way with every step.

"Ouch." I followed behind Alex slowly, picking my steps carefully and painfully, nursing sore feet and aching, winded lungs.

But when we reached the crest I forgot all about the pain.

A field of orchids, as far as the eye could see, grew out of the rocky soil on the steepest side of the hill we had just climbed. "Oh Alex! This is amazing."

In answer to the question I had not yet asked, he dropped his harvest of orchids, picked up a loose rock from the side of the hill and began piercing a small hole with it near his hands. He made a pile of rubble and placed the orchid inside the new hole he had created—replacing the rubble around its thick roots to anchor it in place.

I watched him repeat the process several times, moving precariously around the steep incline, while I held onto my spot.

"You did all this?"

"I've been bringing the stolen orchids here and trying to replant them. I'm not sure it will work—but it seems to be working so far. She will never climb up here—it's treacherous as you can see." He pointed at my sneakers riddled with holes and my skinned knees which I wiped with the hem of my impractical sundress, now embarrassed about an outfit that had seemed so adorable this morning as we left the hostel.

"There is something special about this flower," he said as he smoothed the rich purple flower of one of the orchids nearest to both of us in the palm of his hand. "It's almost mystical, don't you think?"

I closed my eyes and then reopened them several times, and each time, I experienced anew the magic he had created on the rocky hillside. The scent and sight of orchids on the rocky incline was overpowering. But I resisted being pulled into this still-sort-of-a-stranger's euphoria.

If this was a line, I wouldn't fall for it. "It's a flower. It's not a magic potion." I dismissed him without meaning my words. I found myself staring at his palm and the orchid bud hypnotically, until he broke the spell. "You're right, Lu. It's just a flower."

Alex grabbed my hand and pulled me back down the hillside on the opposite side from the makeshift orchid garden. When we got to the bottom, he suddenly caught up with my fatigue and laid down in the cool wet soil with eyes closed. I had a chance to study him and my surroundings without self-consciousness as I dipped my legs and feet in the spring to clean my dirty bloody legs and feet.

As I glanced up and in the trees, I saw more purple flowers, sensual and beautiful, clinging to the uppermost branches over us.

"Are those orchids, also?" I asked Alex.

He opened his eyes, and followed my pointing finger. "Un hunh."

"I didn't know they grew on trees and alongside buildings like the golden flowers we saw at the old hotel last night."

Alex laughed at my ignorance. "They can grow anywhere. On volcano tops and by the rivers. They don't grow on trees but they wrap themselves around the trees nonetheless."

"Then why are they nearly extinct? Why are you stealing them and replanting them? Why are you so worried about them if they grow everywhere?"

Alex shook his head at me for a moment. And seemed to be grappling a bit with the language, whispering phrases to himself until he felt confident enough to make his point: "Lu, I didn't say they *do* grow anywhere—I said they *can*."

He closed his eyes and lay back down, having had the definitive last word on this subject. I interrupted his solitude with, "So, tell me, Dr. Alex, what's *your* story?"

He opened up his eyes and sat up on one elbow. "Still being written, too, I hope."

"Touché. Well, this is some life, I can tell you." I lay back on the bank, disrupting the moment because I was unsure what I wanted to happen next.

"Yes, true. It's been a pretty ok life up until now."

"Up until now?"

"Sure. It's actually been better than ok lately."

"How lately?" I asked, knowing the answer, but wanting to hear it anyway.

He lay back down and faced the sky with eyes closed again.

I thought for a moment that I wasn't going to get the answer I was hoping for but then he smiled—eyes closed—"Ever since a pretty American girl walked into my bar with her worry dolls."

⊚

The next day, I woke at the hostel in Lanquin with one thought: *if I never see another orchid, it would be too soon.*

And then: *What is wrong with me?*

My feet and back were sore from the long ride from Lake Atitlan and the orchid mission. My skinned and scabbed knees were so tender and my lacerated hand was throbbing—the palm I injured on the broken shot glass that first day having been cut open again on the mission.

The weight of the sheets was killing me, and I was thinking a little too much about kissing Alex at Semuc Champey. I didn't like how my heart was rolling over and over in my chest. I was starting to miss him even though I hadn't even left him yet. I turned over in my bed and hugged my arms around my sides tightly, willing myself to sleep.

MARI

Oh!

Along with the vanilla scent, the soft sheets and the melodic voices in the room, there is a brand new sensory experience overtaking me lately.

Kicking.

You are making yourself known, little one.

LU

After we returned to San Marcos, I began packing up my meager belongings, sore and tired, but oddly refreshed.

And then on the last full day before I left, I found myself dreaming of plane crashes. Or one plane crashing over and over.

My mind was filled with orange-red flames tinged with the most beautiful shade of yellow—so beautiful in fact that I was distracted from being afraid—and so my subconscious kept replaying an image of an airliner exploding again and again accompanied by a roaring noise that became greater and louder—and not dimmer—as I emerged from the dream.

My tense body began to relax with the realization that the images were conjured by my brain and not reality. But the roar. It was still there. I continued trying to catch up with my subconscious.

There's no airliner.

There's no crash.

But still there is that sound.

A terrible roaring sound that was growing louder and louder and seemed to be next to me rather than above me. I threw my hands up over my head in my bed to shield myself from crashing planes and deafening roars.

I lay there in bed for what seemed too long a time to still be alive and then my ears began to discern yet another sound in the noisy din—voices—yells—in Spanish—and I strained to remember—both where I was—and what they were saying.

"Come!"

"Go!"

Two different commands being yelled alternately and simultaneously and the confusion over the language barrier and the juxtaposed commands and the noise that is not—cannot!—be a crash paralyzed me, pinned me to the bed.

I tried to think about orchids instead.

I closed my eyes, but voices began overtaking the roar, and I could not keep rolling back and forth hugging myself trying to imagine orchids when voices were commanding me in opposite directions.

"Come!"

"Go!"

I moved gingerly from my bed to the doorway and then down the hall to a window where I saw the flurry of activity outside.

"Lu!" Alex called out to me as he bounded up the steps of the hostel, and I walked slowly to him—much too slowly because his face was frustrated and yet I felt like I was in a dream unable to move my limbs any faster than they were going.

"Lu! It's a landslide! We have to go."

Alex woke me suddenly out of my stupor—out of my dream that was not a dream. He grabbed my hand and we ran down the path and away from town—away from Lake Atitlan and away from the volcano that could be seen across the lake from the café open air windows, the same one dumping land and mud. We could not see any of this—we could only hear it. And the locals who have lived in harmony with this land knew what the sounds mean even if they could not see it—and they crossed themselves as they ran. As they gathered up their sparse belongings—as each of them grabbed a potted orchid among their possessions and art and ran away from the noise.

We arrived an hour later at what Alex called a "safe" place. The roaring noise had either subsided or we were far enough not to hear it anymore. I asked Alex how often these landslides occur. "Often. Too often."

"Then how can you live here?" I was a bit out of breath and I had to ask the question twice before he understood me.

At which point he answered simply: "How can I not?" He told me then about the terrible landslide of 2005. When a volcano dumped mud and debris on a small town named Panabaj—his own hometown. "I was here in the café and couldn't get back to check on my family. The roads were closed even to rescue personnel for two more days. After four days, our Mayor announced simply: "'We are tired. And we don't know where to dig any longer.' 250 of the residents were never found, never accounted for. My parents among them."

I thought about our talk with Sister Magdalena. That Nery Santiago might well have been among the victims of that same landslide. The father of Mari's first child. Did she know? Because none of this made any sort of headlines in the US. "You've taught me quite a bit in the last few weeks, Dr. Alex."

"About painting?" He chuckled.

"Well, yes, you make hard work look impressive. No doubt about that. And you make surviving look good. No doubt about that either."

"Surviving? Is that what you think I'm doing?" Alex looked disappointed, and I worried that I had inadvertently insulted him. I started fumbling over words.

"Well, it's just that your parents—and you weren't there—and now you help everyone—the café, and Marco, and the orphanage, and ... me. You helped me so much."

Alex reached up and rubbed some dirt from my forehead, and said: "First of all. I never feel guilty about not dying in the landslide that killed my parents. That would just dishonor their memory. I spend my time living. Not surviving. And I don't help everyone. Just people who happen to need me at a time I can help them."

"I'm going to spend some time living, too." I reached up

and rubbed some imaginary dirt off his forehead, and then I leaned in to his goodbye kiss followed by a long hug that had no finality attached to it at all.

"I'll be back," I said.

"I know," he smirked at me the way he did that first day when I smashed a shot glass all over his bar.

"I just don't know when."

"I know that, too." His expression turned as tender as when he had wrapped my hand bloodied by shards of glass.

And when I headed to the airport the next day, and for a long time afterward, I rolled Alex's farewell instructions around and around in my mind like my mother used to roll worry dolls around in her fingers.

"Lu, don't just survive. There are others who haven't been as lucky as you and me—don't dishonor their memory by forgetting that. And remember, Lu. It's *your* story you are here to write now. No one else's."

MARI

That last time I was in Guatemala, when the girls were 10 and I left Joe for a week after a terrible fight, and before I returned home to him for good—there was a mudslide. Maybe I mentioned that already? Not such an uncommon occurrence in the area, truth be told.

I'd be lying if I called the trip an awakening of sorts. If I called my experience some sort of epiphany there on the banks of Lake Atitlan with the roaring and seeping of land and mud. A realization that I needed to get home to my children. That I needed to be their mother.

My time left is too short to lie to anyone, particularly myself. Because of course, that is not what happened at all.

Sister Magdalena had—yes reluctantly—told me how to find Nery in her letter. And when I arrived in Guatemala, with his contact information in hand, I found Nery easily. He had been working odd jobs in San Marcos, including helping out around the House of Mercies.

That's where I first found him. Outside the House of Mercies. I hopped out of a smelly bus I'd taken from the airport, and I saw him out back hammering loose boards behind the building.

Yes. Long before I had shopped the marketplace and told the old woman I hadn't yet found what I was looking for, I had, in fact, *found Nery*. We looked up and we saw each other and said hello, like no time had passed at all.

And when I saw him, I saw his son. I saw baby Tomas. And I wanted to tell him. I did.

No, that's not true at all. I did *not* want to tell him. Because my brain fast forwarded with a landslide of information, of facts, of truths that would result from his knowing.

He will be grateful that he did not know. And sad. And he will need me to reconcile these emotions for him that he did not have a moment ago. He may even blame me. More than I already blame myself. And then I will resent ... Nery ... of all people. I will hate Nery.

I went there. To this ultimate place of me loving and hating and resenting Nery in a split second. My heart filled with so much emotion, it came out in choking sobs that I could not control. And Nery took me and held me and put everything out of my head that was not the pressure of his arms around me like a warm den. I put it all out of my head to deal with another day. And I let him hold me and hold me and I was so grateful he did not pull away first.

As he murmured "Mari" into my hair, I felt in that moment that I could not pull away. Ever. Not for Joe. Not for the girls.

He continued to hug me and hold me and we cried for joy. It was the most cleansing cry I had had in years. I felt like the tears could heal me. I felt the closest thing to whole that I had felt since I left this place. And the sense of relief was overwhelming. I almost could feel the ground give out below me. My knees buckled, and I sat down on the ground.

Nery sat down next to me. "You came back to me," he said. And I pulled out one of the dolls and he gasped aloud.

"They brought you back to me. I always hoped they would."

"Yes. They did." Nery reached for the doll in my hand, but I shut my hand quickly. Too quickly. He looked puzzled and the spell—the beautiful spell we were under was broken.

I clutched the doll tighter and tighter, until my nails dug into my palm, and some of her edges burned the skin inside my hand. But I did not let him hold that doll.

She holds far too many secrets.

She knows.

She knew about baby Tomas, but she also knew that I

had already decided never, ever, to tell Nery about his son.

And that—that moment sealed it for me. If I could not be completely honest with Nery, then I could not stay. If I could not reveal all the secrets in my heart to him, then this was not where I belonged.

I studied his face as if I was memorizing every feature. I knew at that moment we would never see each other again. It was as if he was dying.

Til death do us part.

And of all my life regrets, I have never regretted the decision not to tell Nery—or the decision to leave him behind after that trip.

When I learned later from Sister Magdalena that Nery died in the mudslides of 2005, I felt a different kind of sadness than I would have expected.

Because for me, Nery had been long gone. I paced the house for a little while with the news and then I decided to start a garden.

⑨

At first, I started an herb and vegetable garden. I was surprised to learn that not every plant was like the Guatemalan orchids I remembered from my childhood—hearty and able to grow in rocky soil. I took on the challenge of growing cabbages and red lettuce and rosemary plants in that beach soil.

I started the garden on nearly every side of the house accounting for sun and soil and making adjustments each year. And every year, my garden failed. Every year, until last year, that is.

In the Spring of 2011, I was walking around the neighborhood and I happened upon Joe's old house. The one he had grown up in and lived in with Carla and his father for his entire childhood.

Joe had pointed it out on occasion—the new owners took fastidious care of it. But Joe seemed to have no attachment to it since he had moved into his aunt's former bungalow when he turned 21, just a few years before meeting me, and the same year Carla had sold his childhood home and headed south to Boynton Beach.

It was a small A-frame clapboard home, white with black shutters. A beautiful stone path started at the street, and then journeyed toward the front door, although it never quite made it. I knew from Joe and Carla, that the stone work had been laid by Joe's dad, a firefighter by day—a stone mason by night. The path had been started a few years before he died, but because he was always helping neighbors and friends with their own stone work, the path to his own home remained unfinished when he died. His firefighter buddies had offered to finish it, but Carla had refused, saying only that it would be a "silly luxury to waste time on" now that she would be selling the home. She paid a concrete contractor to finish the path with white concrete—creating an odd and—it could be argued—ugly path on the eve of selling the place.

Joe once mused that, "Maybe my Mom didn't really want to sell the place," and had ruined the curb appeal on purpose; but that possibility seemed far-fetched given the speed with which Carla did sell the place and relocate. She had left only months after Joe's father died, apparently.

On that spring day when I happened upon Carla and Joe's former home, I realized for the first time that the entire west side of the house was covered with the most beautiful rose bushes—red and white and pink blooms competed with each other as they climbed over each other up a marching trellis, and eventually onto the side of the home itself. The west side of the home I had shared with Joe was the last place I had tried to grow a garden, fearing that the sunlight was not the best, and the sandy clay soil didn't seem very airy on that side.

Joe's childhood home had been sold at least one additional time since Carla lived in it, that I knew of, and I wasn't sure who had planted the roses, but suddenly I needed a little planting advice from the current owner. On an impulse,

I walked up the incomplete masonry path, landing on the white concrete patch as I rang the bell.

A pretty blonde woman with messy hair and tired eyes came to the door with a blonde toddler on her hip. The toddler was equally messy and tired looking, with pink overalls and a splash of red juice leading from her mouth up her cheek.

The woman gave me a kind smile that reached her tired eyes. "Hello."

"Hi, I'm sorry to bother you. It's just that—my husband used to live here. I live now just a few blocks down, and I know this is going to sound *loco*—" The woman dismissed my lack of confidence with a smile and a nod, so I continued on.

"I've been trying to start a garden at my home, and this is the first time I ever noticed the rose bushes here. Did you plant them?"

"Oh no. They've been here since we moved in. Since long before that, actually. The previous owner said the Roselli's had planted them. They require literally no care, thank goodness, or I would have killed them long ago. As you can see, I don't have much luck with live plants. She waved her hand around her front stoop, where a few dead potted plants took up residence next to the only plants that were thriving—silks.

I was surprised to hear that Carla had planted the roses, and also disappointed that her planting secrets had died with her. "Would you mind if I took a cutting with me? That means they're my mother-in-law's roses. She passed away a decade ago. It would be nice to have some of her roses at my home."

"Of course!" The woman headed inside and came out with some planting shears and I cut a little piece of the rose bush from the west side of the house, with plans to replant it on the west side of my own home.

And just like that, my garden grew. I had been about to give up, but by the spring of 2012, cabbages and herbs rose from the dust, and even a transplanted rosebush. The first thing I did when I saw sprouting vegetables was to run and tell Nick the good news.

In many ways—for me, at least—that new garden signaled a second awakening—a rebirth. Lu was finishing up her social work training and seemed finally ready to move on from Seamus. I watched her flounder a bit from afar as she decided what to do next. I had no wisdom to give her, but I noticed with joy over that year her budding independence. I realized with relief that Lu didn't need my wisdom. She only needed herself.

As I tended my roses and my garden, without any children who were dependent upon me, I started to think about things that I hadn't thought about in a long, long time.

Like the end of the Mayan calendar for example, and babies.

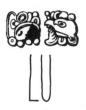

LU

Two weeks after first arriving in Guatemala and meeting Dr. Alex, I was back in the hospital room with my mother and the machines. The blanket stretched taut across her raised belly—which had grown in just two weeks—and I touched it gently, greeting both Mari and the new baby.

When Anita came in to fill out her papers, I hugged her tightly. "I'm sorry I was gone so long, Anita. I had so much to figure out. "

"And did you? Did you figure it all out?"

"No. Why would anyone ever think that was possible?" I laughed wryly, and then: "Did she have any visitors?" There was a guilt nagging at me for having left her for so long.

"One gentleman was here quite frequently."

"Oh?"

"A white-haired gentleman. He said he had been your dog sitter."

I flinched at the reference to Catt, but didn't explain why to Anita. I didn't want to burden her with the news that Catt had passed away while I was gone. Nick had left me a beautiful note in my mailbox in his now familiar script, which I found upon my return in the early morning hours. I read his note tearfully, and gratefully, knowing that Catt was well cared for in her final days. I hadn't called him to thank him, though. I had simply come to the hospital right away, eager to see Mari after such a long time away. Especially since I now knew why Mari had been both anxious and afraid for me to find out all I would find out from Sister Magdalena.

"Although, the way he sat so patiently and lovingly with

your mother, it's hard to believe that he was only the dog sitter."

I was starting to really love Anita. She was so warm. So sweet.

So nosy.

"Yes, Nick was a very good friend to my mother, I have learned. Maybe even a lover." Anita took the news in stride so I tried out something I had yet to say out loud to anyone yet.

"Honestly, I know it sounds a little nuts since he was considerably older than her, but I'm starting to wonder if he's the father."

"The father? Of your mother's baby?"

"Yes."

"Lu." Anita looked confused, concerned even. "But Lu—haven't the doctors talked to you? About the baby's paternity?"

"No. What? What do you know that I don't, Anita?"

Anita turned back to my mother instead of answering, and sighing, she wiped her face. "Oh, I hate when she does that. She's crying again."

MARI

I had never seen Joe like that. He came home in the middle of the day while the girls were in school, after a five-alarm fire.

He was distraught. Not even consolable. He went into the master bathroom and sobbed loudly. He turned on the shower and both of the sink faucets, and I could still hear him. I sat on the bed, waiting for him, but after a little while, I reached into my nightstand for earplugs, because while I wanted to be there when he came out, I really couldn't stand the sound of Joe crying.

It was heart-wrenching.

It was a long time before he came out again. Maybe an hour. Hard to know as time crawled by while I sat there deaf but in terror.

When Joe emerged, his hair was not wet, and I knew the shower and running water had only been meant to drown the sound of his tears. Literally. He came and sat next to me. I moved over on the bed, and guided his head into my lap.

"Joe."

He lay still for a long time and then his voice came out hoarsely. "Matthew died today."

Even though I knew that something terrible had happened. Even though I sat waiting for him all that time to begin a conversation that I knew had to include death. No matter. That it was true and that it was Matthew took my breath away. I rubbed Joe's head, and tried to find some words to say. I tried to push my own fear and crowded thoughts out of my head to make room for some compassion for Joe.

I stayed silent.

"He died, and I had to go to tell Tricia."

"Oh Joe."

"And do you know what she said?"

I could only shake my head.

"She said: 'I want to have Matthew's baby. I wish I had had his baby. I wish I had something more of him left on this planet.' She tore my heart out with those words."

I nodded above him, as I stroked his hair, but he couldn't see me, so he mistook my silence as the wrong answer.

"Listen to me, Mari. The girls and whatever children we have down the road—that's our legacy. It's everything to me."

"Down what road, Joe?" I felt sick to my stomach. "I can't have any more kids, Joe."

"What do you mean, you can't? Is something wrong, Mari?"

He sat up and his hoarse voice softened with concern.

"No, I mean—I can *have* more babies. I think I can. But I can't even imagine. I've been so terrible with the ones I have had. How could I bring any more into this world?"

"Mari—you are the sweetest, gentlest spirit I know. You're finding your way around motherhood in the same way I'm finding my way around fatherhood. You never had a chance before. Please stop being so hard on yourself."

He took both of my hands in his. "Please."

I shook my head, preferring his sorrow than this exaggerated concern. "Joe, let's not talk about babies today. Please. It's too much for me."

"Ok, ok," he conceded.

But a week later, he came home and gave me some paperwork. It was in a folder, marked with the name of a clinic.

"What's this?"

"We don't need to talk about it now. But I want you to have this. I donated ... you know, sperm. It's frozen in storage at the clinic. This clinic."

"Joe!" I threw the folder across the room at him. I even

crossed myself prudishly.

"Mari—I know you don't understand this, or like this, and that's fine. But if anything ever happened to me, I would want this. I would want you to have another baby. My baby."

"That's nothing I could ever do again, Joe. You know why."

"I know you think that today. But Mari, what if I was gone tomorrow—what would be my legacy? My children. That's what."

"Joe! Stop talking like that." I crossed myself again and then picked up the folder, storing it in the old secretary in the hallway, certain that I would never want to discuss this topic as long as he and I both lived.

And strangely, as I closed the folder into the secretary, I remember thinking ...*What if I was gone tomorrow? What an odd thing to say aloud.* And I looked at the calendar sitting inside the secretary and noticed the date for no other reason than superstition.

September 10, 2001.

LU

Anita had buzzed the doctor and ordered him, along with the social worker, to tell me the overdue discovery about paternity. That my mother's obstetrician had finally tracked my mother down here at the hospital while I was away in Guatemala.

When she hadn't showed up for her latest prenatal appointment, hadn't refilled her prescription for iron and folic acid, she became worried at the silence and started making phone calls. She tracked her down here and was now consulting with her medical team at City Hospital.

But for that night when my mother lapsed—sleeping pills and a single glass of white wine to help her sleep the night before I was leaving for Guatemala—about to find out all of her secrets finally and at once—my mother had been caring for the baby and giving the pregnancy her very best attention and effort. All up until that very last night.

My mother's obstetrician had filled in the missing pieces. And explained unequivocally that my father was this unborn baby's father as well.

"So. There is no longer any issue of paternity." The social worker said as she tapped on her foster family's file.

As they explained all of this to me, I smoothed Clinique Happy lotion into Mari's palms and hands and forearms as I wept. I wondered only briefly what my father would think of this news. He and my mother would certainly have discussed it before he died. Would have agreed upon it. I would never know all of the details and I would have to learn to live with that. No matter what I had learned about Mari, she would still be taking some secrets with her to her grave.

And the decision was not made in that instant. It had been in the making for over a decade. As I held Mari's hands in mine, I thought about the photographer who had seen my father run back inside the fire to save his only living child at the time, and I thought solemnly:

Now it is my turn.

I stopped rubbing lotion into Mari's arm and I whispered, still facing Mari, rather than the doctor and the social worker, "There will be no foster family. No other custodial arrangement. I am the legal guardian. I will take the baby home with me when it's time."

The social worker asked the question: "Do you think that's the best answer, here?"

I looked at Mari's serene face, no more tears flowing, as I responded, "I only know it's *my* answer."

☺

Anita seemed to be lingering longer than usual after her shift, but I didn't mind. I wasn't quite sure if I should leave. Nothing seemed particularly different today with my mother, but that wasn't necessarily a good thing.

Anita said softly as she cleaned up around me. "I never told you but I lost my mother, too, when I was young. It's never easy to lose a mother."

I thought of my mother carrying the burdens of a disappeared mother, a dead baby, a tragic marriage, a lost lover. She had come to a new country to escape and found a man whom she loved—seemed to truly, truly love—and who loved her so much in return, but whose love she never felt like she deserved. A man who died, leaving her alone to try to save her only remaining living child. An act she always felt she'd failed at, too.

"We never really had a chance—my mother and I. It wasn't my fault. It wasn't hers either." I thought about Rae and me counting in the closet all those years ago. "My mother and father did their best. And my mother did her best. And kept trying. That's all she knew how to do."

Exhaustion lowered my usual defenses. "I lost my mother so long ago, Anita. Losing her isn't the hard part. The hard part is knowing now why, and not being able to tell her I forgive her."

I braced myself for clichés or some half-hearted attempt to cheer me up. But Anita did not disappoint me. She just patted my shoulder, lingered some more and headed out. After about 15 more minutes of lingering myself, I patted my mother's hand, and walked out of the hospital quietly.

When I got home to Rock Harbor, I went to Mari's room. Before Guatemala, I had been sleeping in the garage apartment or on the couch in the main house—uncomfortable with the idea of sleeping in Mari's bedroom.

But exhaustion overtook me that night. I was so tired. To-my-bones tired, and I couldn't bear the thought of sleeping on something that wasn't a bed. There were still no linens in my old room, so I headed to the bed in Mari's room and settled under the covers. Sleep seemed to find me quickly, because I had none of my usual restless chaotic thoughts as a precursor to sleep that night.

I fell asleep before I heard the knock. The knock was soft but insistent. I didn't jump out of bed. I wasn't alarmed. I just headed quietly to the door, opened it up and greeted my mother at the bedroom door like it was the most natural thing either of us had ever done.

"I'm still sleeping, right?" I asked her.

She put her finger to her lips and took my hand. We headed out of the bedroom together. We headed out of the house. Outside the front door was not Rock Harbor, and it certainly wasn't December. It was lush and green and balmy. I was wearing the tee shirt and yoga pants I had climbed into bed in and Mari was wearing the white dress from the painting. Close up the dress was even more beautiful than in the painting. It had embroidered eyelet detail, and I even reached out to touch it. I was so grateful that she let me. She smiled beautifully as I studied her dress, and studied her.

She was so radiant, that I had to tell her.

"Mama, you look absolutely stunning."

Yes. I called her Mama, and not Mari.

"Thank you, Niña. Now come." She took my hand, and we picked our way along a beach that wasn't our Rock Harbor beach. Pebbles of alternating sizes littered the way, and I realized I was barefoot as I made my way clumsily behind my mother, still holding her hand. She was more graceful and I tried to keep up. She made her way with certainty until we reached a waterfall that I now recognized as Semuc Champey. Only then did she let go of my hand and swan dive into the turquoise waters below.

I followed her in without hesitation. The water was cool, refreshing, jarring. For a moment—underwater— I worried that the jolt of cool water would startle me awake, but when I emerged again, rubbed the water from my eyes—we were there together. Still in Semuc Champey.

"Why didn't you tell anyone about your son, Mama?"

She treaded water away from me. "It was my grief. It was mine, not yours. You couldn't have understood—not as a child—not back when it might have helped me to tell someone. It would have confused you. And I believed I could get past it.

"Your father knew," she revealed.

Ah. I wondered.

"I think he would have eventually helped me through it. I think he would have helped me accept love eventually. He was a wonderful, generous, patient man, your father. But when he left, we had so much work to do. So much was unfinished. *I* was still so unfinished. Losing your father and Rae that way—I couldn't wade through the grief. And I couldn't share it. And it ate me alive.

"I loved your father, Lu. I did.

"And God knows, I loved my son.

"And You. And Rae.

"And yet, all that I loved in this world was taken from

me. Violently. When your father and Rae left, I left you for good then, to try to trick God into thinking that I didn't love you enough. I thought maybe God would let you stay. And he did. But at the cost of us."

"Mama."

"I don't regret it, though. I saved you. I feel that. I saved you by pulling away. I would have destroyed you with my love. And my grief. I believe that."

We both kept swimming. I didn't know what to say. She said it for me.

"I wanted another chance. I wanted nothing more. For so long, that was what I truly wanted for you. For us. To start over."

I found the words then. "I forgive you, Mama."

My mother smiled and then climbed out of the water onto the bank. Her dress was almost immediately dry, and she smoothed it out around her. She was so very beautiful; I almost couldn't look at her—tears were stinging my eyes.

"Oh!" she squealed in delight. I was certain I had never heard her make such a sound. It filled me with joy. I immediately swam over to climb out and be next to her on the bank. I saw the cause for her squeal. White flowers decorated the base of the mountain she sat next to.

"Orchids, Niña. Aren't they beautiful?"

"Guatemalan orchids?" I asked although I knew.

"Yes. I haven't seen this kind since I was very small. The monja blanca. So rare. And it only blooms in December. Strange, no?"

I shook my head in response. Nothing was strange anymore.

"These flowers. So beautiful. Always in my heart and my mind, and I never painted them. Why is that?"

"I don't know, Mama."

"I don't think I could have done them justice. They are perfect. To be experienced live, only."

I remembered Alex's orchid forest on the rocky hillside

in Semuc Champey. How I had closed and reopened my eyes, over and over again, trying to reclaim the magic each time. The orchids were indeed powerful. I reached down to feel if my knees were scabbed over, knowing that they wouldn't be. I felt my palm for scabs from the broken glass. Nothing.

"Mama."

"Yes."

"I love you."

"Thank you, Niña. I love you, too. Always."

"Come." She stood up, and I stood to follow her.

But I realized immediately she wasn't talking to me. Catt bounded around the corner and my mother bent down to her and Catt set out to licking her face enthusiastically.

My mother walked away with Catt at her heels and I sat and watched them, unable to rise from my perch on the bank—able only to see the eyelet fade in the distance as my mother and Catt headed toward a young girl and a handsome man in the distance.

"Daddy!" I propelled from my seat on the bank and ran ahead of my mother and Catt to my father, jumping straight into his arms with abandon. "Daddy. I'm so sorry."

"Sorry—what for, munchkin?"

"I'm so sorry you went back for me."

"But Lu –don't you know the truth? I'm so very grateful that you weren't there. You have always been where you are supposed to be." He let me down and tousled Rae's hair and the two of them turned to join Mama. Mama had overtaken them and had a nice head start now and was—I could see faintly—now holding a squirming toddler as she walked away, Catt still right at her heels. Rae looked over her shoulder and motioned to me—something like blowing me a kiss and I exhaled fully for the first time in a long, long time.

"Good-bye," I called after them. Without longing or regret. Without sadness. Only a small twinge of jealousy that they were all together for now. *That Rae—she always won*, I thought, as I watched her walk away in my favorite navy linen pants and tan cardigan twinset.

Actually, you know what? To be honest, I'm not really sure whether Rae was blowing me a kiss or sticking her tongue out at me.

⑨

The phone ring cut the air. I had it in my hand before I was even fully awake, and I simply replied "ok" without startle or surprise when Anita said "Lu. It's time. Come now."

⑨

When I arrived at the hospital, it was just before midnight. As I navigated the maze of halls and elevator banks, I wondered what the baby's official date of birth would be?

December 21 or December 22?

I didn't have to wonder for long, as Anita greeted me in the room that used to be my mother's with a small creamy bundle wrapped in a hospital-issued blanket lined with pink and blue stripes. My mother was not there, and none of the machines that I had become accustomed to were there either.

"She's beautiful," Anita said as she placed my new sister in my arms.

A girl.

She was very tiny—but not dangerously so, Anita assured me, as I continued to stare at her—more stunned than anything—for a very long time before Anita asked gently: "What will you call her, Lu?"

I hesitated only a moment, before replying: "Blanca. It's an orchid. From Guatemala. Beautiful. And rare. And they only bloom in December."

Anita smiled solemnly, and wrote my sister's name on her birth certificate. Then she asked: "Are you ready now? To see your mother. To say goodbye?"

For the first time since I had left the hospital room yesterday afternoon, someone had said something to surprise me. "Say goodbye? To my mother?"

Anita examined me while I found the words, sorting through my memories, concluding with our moonlight swim. "There's no need. I already did, Anita."

Anita reached out and touched my hand that was caressing my new blanketed sister, before bending down to continue filling out her paperwork and readying us—Blanca and me—to go home.

FOUR YEARS AFTER THE END OF THE WORLD
12/21/16

"Blanca, careful!"

Blanca is reaching over to tuck my tray table into its upright position at the flight attendant's cautions, but I have the remnant of a Styrofoam coffee cup on it.

"We're almost there, right?" She's so excited she can't keep her voice to an inside whisper or her hands to herself. There is so much to love about four. There is so much not to love about four. I lean down and kiss her head. "Yes, sweetheart. We're almost there."

I look out the window at the lush paradise below and marvel anew as I have so often as we have prepared for this—Blanca's first trip to Guatemala—about the paradoxes of life. I am still amazed by the path that led us here. How I stayed *out* of the Towers on 9/11. How I stayed *off* that fateful plane on 10/11. How I got *on* that plane to Guatemala on the eve of the end of the Mayan calendar.

All so that I would eventually be on *this* plane with Blanca *today.*

You have always been where you are supposed to be. The full realization of my father's words have been coming to me slowly. Unfolding like a long-held secret made known for the first time.

"And will Dr. Alex be at the airport or will we meet him somewhere else?"

"He'll be at the airport, Blanca."

We've been over this a hundred times, but still she loves to hear it. Her favorite pen pal, Dr. Alex writes to Blanca almost weekly, and she writes back. Or rather she tells me what to write, and I write it for her. And usually I insert a note or two of my own.

Alex has been to Rock Harbor exactly seven times in the last four years. Each time he comes, we spend most of the visit painting and rebuilding the no longer scorched home Mari left to Blanca and me. I always apologize about how little we do other than construction jobs and insurance paperwork when he comes to visit. But Alex always waves off my apologies and tells me to "get back to painting, would you?"

Despite our geographic locations, Alex has become one of my dearest friends—perhaps more. We'll see. This is my first trip back to Guatemala since 2012, and we are staying for at least three months to introduce Blanca to her mother's homeland, and to try out the countryside for a little while as we rent out our home in Rock Harbor to a new family who is trying out Rock Harbor for size before they buy a home of their own. A young firefighter and his very pregnant wife. I can't help but think my father would love for them to have his inherited home someday.

For the last year, I have been doing the year-long social work internship at City Hospital. They have offered me a position to begin in three to four months, if I want it. Blanca has been in preschool while I completed the gig at City Hospital. Occasionally, I meet Nurse Anita for lunch. She still has the kind of maternal lap I want to crawl into. I keep her entertained with stories about Blanca, and she gives me good advice about raising a child on my own, as she fusses over my pictures with all the clucking of a real grandmother. I work flexible hours, and Rebecca helps care for Blanca after preschool before I get home.

I turned my old bedroom into a beautiful and bright room for Blanca. When I was cleaning out my room, I found the picture of Mari and the birdcage that Nery Santiago painted. It was hidden in the back of my old closet—but not too well—and so I took it out and hung it in Blanca's new room. I told her recently that it shows "Mama's beautiful spirit," remembering Anita's words all those years ago, and Blanca said, "you mean, because now Mama is a spirit-angel?" And all I could do was nod gratefully.

Seamus comes home every so often with his very pretty, very chatty aspiring actress girlfriend from LA. She is named Rachel, but I notice that Seamus calls her Rae now and then, and I have to bite my lip to refrain from telling Rachel that she is and ever will be just an understudy in Seamus's life play. I try not to feel smug about this fact.

I sometimes succeed.

Bridget Riordan—now Bridget Hall—and I have a comfortable friendship these days. She married a fellow teacher at the local high school (a former local high school basketball hero—go figure!) and had a baby last year, not necessarily in that order. Bridget is still a hopeless over-sharer (*My God—if he doesn't start taking one nighttime feeding of this baby, he can forget about ever having lunch hour sex again*), and I can't really return the favor. Nevertheless, I can't deny that it helps me in many ways to have a friend in town with a child as I muddle through the responsibility of raising Mari's daughter on my own.

Nick the butcher has reopened his shop on Rock Harbor. Blanca and I make a trip there almost weekly for fresh cuts of meat and heart-shaped burgers that Nick makes especially for Blanca. Nick always looks so happy to see us when I arrive with Blanca on my hip or holding my hand, and each time I see him, I try to make a mental note to visit him more often. He says I remind him of my mother, and I take that as a compliment coming from him—one of several men who loved her madly in life.

Sometimes Blanca and I dog-sit for Nick. I miss Catt like crazy, and while I feel too overwhelmed by work and raising

Blanca to take on a new puppy of our own, Nick has rescued a three-year-old Weimaraner named Blue (named he says after the beautiful color of the ocean outside his home). Blanca and I love to take her for overnight visits or for Saturday hikes now and again to give Nick a break, as Blue is adorable and high energy and just as anxious as I remember Catt being all those years.

Today on the plane, I feel a bit anxious myself. Actually, I feel all the same feelings I usually feel when I am about to see Alex. Nervousness, happiness, turmoil, peace.

The story of my life.

The lady to my right leans over me in that aggressive way strangers have with small children. I notice that now. I notice so much now that I never noticed before. Because of Blanca.

"Are you and your mommy going to do anything fun in Guatemala?"

Blanca blinks hard at the woman and then yells—"Oh! This isn't my mommy. My mommy is dead. She died when I was born."

The woman flinches and I put my hand on the stranger's arm the way I'm used to doing when Blanca delivers her matter-of-fact eulogy to her mother. To our mother.

"It's ok. She's my sister. And you didn't say anything wrong." I reassure the stranger.

There are too many secrets in life, Blanca and I have discovered together, and we don't keep any from each other. Pixie dust and fairies are probably not in this little girl's future. I don't really foresee secret tooth fairy visits, or hedging around the subject of where babies come from. When the time is right. Certainly, I never hid from Blanca the circumstances of her birth. Or her mother's death. It never felt right. And she accepted it as she accepts everything so far. With innocence and trust. And with love.

Our airplane neighbor nods too quickly and I see the woman's eyes pool with tears, and I know what will happen next, so I keep patting her arm in preparation and Blanca launches into her full-size eulogy of our mother. The one she created, and the one she tells all the strangers who have the misfortune (or great fortune, depending on your perspective) of asking this precocious little girl if I am her mother. Or where her mother is. You often get more than you expect with Blanca and me—that's just how it is.

"My mother was beautiful, you see. And so loving and wonderful. And she was from Guatemala. And she died. But not until I could be born. She waited until I was ready to be born. I'm Blanca. What's your name?"

And now the woman is crying a little, and so am I. Because I always cry at that part.

And Blanca pats my arm as she is apt to do. "Lu, why do you always cry when I say that?"

"Because it's true. That's all, Blanca. Because it's true."

And I feel somehow that eventually with the telling and re-telling of my mother's story through Blanca's eyes, and lips, that I will have something one day soon. Not peace or closure. No clichés. No easy shortcuts. But the real and true ability to see Mari Guarez Roselli the way Blanca does.

With all that innocence.

All that truth.

I kiss Blanca's head again and she—who only knows my mother in all of her original—and final—radiance—laughs loudly like I am the silliest creature she has ever met.

I think about all of the people I have lost.

Seamus.

Rae.

My father.

My mother.

All of those people I lost broke my heart anew.

But now my heart is taped back together by this little girl whose hand wraps around mine—her fingers barely covering my knuckles, and she points out the window at Lake Atitlan below us with zeal and squeals with delight the way her mother did once on the bank of that Semuc Champey waterfall four years ago, to the day. The last day of the Mayan calendar: 12/21/12. The day everything started anew.

As the flight attendant makes one more trip through the aisle, I throw away my Styrofoam cup, and Blanca excitedly succeeds at securing my tray table in its upright position, just before she points out the window to Lake Atitlan below—*el ombligo del mundo*— as she exclaims:

"We're here, Lu! We're finally here!"